79N

SEE HOW THE

"Give me a hand   n.
"I need you to lif
window."

He looked up at the window, and he looked at
me.

I pried my shoes off.

"Come on," I pleaded, "just a quick lift. I'm
lighter than I look. Honest."

He sighed, bent over, and laced his fingers into
a stirrup. I stepped into it and he hoisted me up.

A patch of sunlight cut through the darkened
room, and dust motes danced lazily in its
beam.

Mrs. Turner's bed had been torn apart, the
mattresses cast to the floor and slit. Drawers
hung from the dresser like protruding lips. The
closet door stood open. Clothes and hangers
were scattered on the floor. In some places, wallpaper hung from the wall in neat strips.

Mrs. Turner sat in an overstuffed chair. It had
been shoved into a corner facing the window.
She sat well back in the chair, her head leaning
to one side as if she were tired. The other side
of it was missing. I was screaming by the time I
hit the ground. . . .

SIGNET **ONYX**

MURDER MYSTERIES

☐ **POISONED PINS A Claire Malloy Mystery by Joan Hess.** When a sorority sister is killed, Claire refuses to believe it was a simple hit-and-run accident and decides to investigate herself. (403908—$3.99)

☐ **THE WOMAN WHO MARRIED A BEAR by John Straley.** A bitingly vivid and suspenseful journey that will take you from the gritty Alaskan urban lower depths to the dark heart of the northern wilderness, and from a sordid tangle of sex and greed to primitive myth and magic. (404211—$4.99)

☐ **SEARCHING FOR SARA, A Barrett Lake Mystery, by Shelley Singer.** A street-smart runaway puts teacher turned detective Barrett Lake to a deadly test in which she must uncover the secrets of the lost kids and discover who has crossed the line to the dark side where innocence dies and murder dwells. (179854—$4.50)

☐ **CARNAL HOURS by Max Allan Collins.** No sooner is Chicago detective Nathan Heller in the Bahamas when a billionaire turns up murdedred. With his client—and meal-ticket—suddenly gone up in smoke, Nate's left without a case. Until Sir Harry's beautiful daughter convinces him to take on her problem. Her husband has just been accused of murder. (179757—$5.99)

*Prices slightly higher in Canada

SOMEBODY ELSE'S CHILD

Terris McMahan Grimes

AN ONYX BOOK

ONYX
Published by the Penguin Group
Penguin Books USA Inc., 375 Hudson Street,
New York, New York 10014, U.S.A.
Penguin Books Ltd, 27 Wrights Lane,
London W8 5TZ, England
Penguin Books Australia Ltd, Ringwood,
Victoria, Australia
Penguin Books Canada Ltd, 10 Alcorn Avenue,
Toronto, Ontario, Canada M4V 3B2
Penguin Books (N.Z.) Ltd, 182–190 Wairau Road,
Auckland 10, New Zealand

Penguin Books Ltd, Registered Offices:
Harmondsworth, Middlesex, England

First published by Onyx, an imprint of Dutton Signet,
a division of Penguin Books USA Inc.

First Printing, March, 1996
10 9 8 7 6 5 4 3 2 1

To my mother, Elb McMahan Jaggears,
my champion and inspiration
and
my mother-in-law, Zella Mae Grimes,
who counted me as her own.

ACKNOWLEDGMENTS

To those who read and critiqued the manuscript, greeted each new chapter with enthusiasm, encouraged me to keep going, and provided those intangibles that meant so much to me, I thank you. I also thank Patricia Canterbury, my mentor and friend; Ethel Mack Ballard and the members of Zica Creative Arts and Literary Guild; Reona James, who was always there with literary insights and a pat on the back; Sergeant R. Cordell Ford of the Sacramento Police Department, who shared his extensive knowledge of firearms and police procedure with me (any errors are mine, not his); Maggie Anderson, Ceola Jackson, and Geri Hunter of the Sunday Writers Group; Henry Hawthorne; James Matthews; Curt Sproul; Gretchen and Adrian Easter; Donald E. Owen; the staff and management of the California State Department of Water Resources; and whoever came up with the concept of flex time.

My warmest thanks to my beleaguered and neglected family, Roy, Mariama, and Jared; my agent, Jacqueline Turner Banks, for believing in me; and my editor, Danielle Perez, for believing in my work.

Chapter 1

Mother has always been rather excitable. What can I say, she's my mother and I love her. But the truth of the matter is, she gets into other people's business and she gets carried away in the process. Now, I'm fully aware of Mother's excesses, and I try to stay clear when I sense she's getting ready to go off the deep end, but somehow I always manage to get sucked right in. My one New Year's resolution this year was not to get caught up in any more of Mother's messes. So when Mother called me about Mrs. Turner, I wasn't biting.

"Theresa, when the last time you seen Mrs. Turner?"

"I'm fine, Mother. How are you? It's been a while since I've seen Mrs. Turner. But enough about me, Mother. Why are you calling at three in the morning quizzing me about your neighbor?"

Mother doesn't start her phone conversations in a conventional manner. She doesn't say hello or even good-bye, for that matter. She simply starts talking when someone answers and stops talking when they hang up. Her conversations are a long series of uninterrupted non sequiturs. I just hate that.

"Her lights are on."

"Good. That means she paid her electricity bill."

"But it's three in the morning."

"Believe me, Mother, I am painfully aware of the time."

"Something's wrong."

"Call 911."

"It's not that kind of wrong, but I am tempted. That

girl LaTreace is over there with all those bad kids. Been staying there a couple of months, and I haven't seen Mrs. Turner for weeks now. People coming and going all hours of the night. You know Mrs. Turner doesn't run a house like that. Shh."

"Mother, what is it?"

"A car just drove up. Somebody's going to the door. The girl's leaving with somebody. She's gone. Left the lights on, doesn't look like she even bothered to lock the door. Still had on her house shoes. Theresa, we may be watching a crime being committed."

"Mother, I admit it is a bit on the tacky side, but it is no crime to leave home wearing house shoes. At least not in 'the community.' "

"You are not funny, miss. I'm talking about those babies she left there by themselves."

"A moment ago they were 'those bad kids' now they're 'the babies.' "

"That's all they are really, just babies. There's a set of twins about eighteen months old who don't even walk yet and a mannish little boy about seven."

"I'm sure Mrs. Turner will look after them."

"Where have you been, girl? I just told you Mrs. Turner's disappeared!"

"Mother, you're being melodramatic. You haven't seen Mrs. Turner for a few days . . ."

"Weeks."

"All right, a few weeks. But that doesn't mean she's disappeared."

"Shh!"

"Mother, stop shushing me."

"Somebody's coming."

"Who is it?"

"It's a different car. A man."

"Mother, what's that noise?"

"I'm going over there."

"Mother . . ."

"He's beating on the door. 'Bout to break it in. Those poor babies must be scared to death. I'm going over there."

"Mother, wait! Mother? Mother? I'm coming, Mother." Mother never says good-bye. She just hangs up.

I didn't take time to dress properly, but I made sure I put on street shoes—no house shoes for me. I grabbed the essentials, a coat, my purse, and the garage door opener.

Since we broke down and subscribed to cable TV, the sleeping habits of Temp, my husband, have changed drastically. Now he stays up late watching badly dubbed movies and falls into a stupor, clutching the remote, or "clicker" as he calls it, around one in the morning. After that, nothing rouses him for a good five hours. Our kids, Aisha and Shawn, though endowed with much of my grace and charm, take after their father's side when it comes to their ability to lapse quickly and completely into deep sleep.

I shook Temp. He only snuggled deeper into the sofa, his hands tucked between his knees. I gave up and went into the kitchen and got the pad of stickie notes. I wrote "I've gone to Mother's" and stuck it to the middle of the TV screen. Then I left, and nobody even stirred.

There's no quick and easy way to get from my house in Greenhaven to Mother's in Oak Park. The freeway takes you all the way downtown before doubling back and dumping you off on Oak Park's periphery. The streets are a direct route, but you move at a slower pace, it's a spookier trip at three in the morning, and it just seems to take forever.

I may appear to be the intrepid soul sister, but the truth of the matter is, I don't like being out after dark. I've become increasingly paranoid in my old age. Strange children in primary colors make me uneasy, particularly when they start doing peculiar hand signs. I am always on guard for potential muggers and rapists who, as a class, just happen to be partial to the dark. And, I must know the scene of every violent crime committed in Sacramento over the past two decades. I don't know why, but I read about a crime in the paper or I see one on the news, and I don't forget. It becomes a part of my psychic makeup. It's scary to think such hateful things are being done to people everyday. Sometimes it seems the hatefulness is getting closer to my own personal comfort zone. I just don't want it to get too close. Maybe that's why I keep track.

I decided to take Highway 5, since it's right there almost at my door, get off at the Sutterville Road exit, and take the streets from there. By the time I reached Sutterville Road, I had myself spooked. I headed east past Franklin, where there'd been a gang shooting just last night.

The speedometer began to creep up a little too much above the speed limit. I made a conscious effort to slow down. The last thing I needed was a ticket. Especially since the outstanding fix-it ticket I already had for a defective driver's side headlight had probably matured into a warrant. I'd had the darn light fixed, I just forgot to get it cleared. It's amazing how an outstanding warrant can improve your driving.

I was shaky but still functional when I turned onto Mother's street. No police cars were in sight. Mother's porch light wasn't on and neither was Mrs. Turner's. I parked in front of Mr. Aragon's semi-rig, wondering if I had beat the police, and got out of the car. Mrs. Perkins's dog, Parkay, started barking, setting off a call and response of other dogs up and down the street.

Making my way to Mother's house as quietly as possible, considering my arrival was already being announced by the hound heralds from hell, I opened the gate to her yard and closed and latched it carefully behind me. I stood where I was and surveyed the yard. I was a little uneasy about Mother's porch light not being on. I didn't want any surprises like some incompetent mugger leaping out of the shadows. Any mugger who attempted to rob me would have to be incompetent because I carry absolutely no cash. I live from payday to payday, and spend the intervening days darting from one brightly lit ATM machine to the next. Muggers are supposed to be able to tell these things, but I was taking no chances.

There aren't many hiding places in Mother's yard. She had the hedges that once lined the front of the house removed. "Too many hiding places for crooks," she said.

"It would have to be an awfully short crook," I'd said. She'd also had the fruitless mulberry unmercifully pruned all the way down to its knobby crown. No hiding places there either. The esthetics left a little something to be desired, but she felt safer.

The roof of the porch formed an arched enclosure around the front door. Inside it was pitch-black. I mounted the two steps leading to the door, took a deep breath, and stepped into the darkness.

Everything happened so fast I didn't have a chance to scream. A hand shot out of the darkness, fastened itself around my neck, and with one mighty jerk pulled me into the corner.

"For goodness sake, stop making so much racket, will you, girl?" hissed Mother.

"What the hell are you doing out here, lurking in the dark, like some goddamn, demented . . ." I stopped before I said "asshole," which was what I was thinking.

I could feel Mother freeze beside me. "I think you better watch your tongue, miss, and keep the damn racket down like I told you."

"What are you doing out here?" I hissed back. "Did you call the police?"

"Shh."

"Stop shushing me. Did you call the police?"

"No, I did not. Mrs. Turner doesn't run that kind of house. She would be heartbroken if she found out the police had been out to her house in the middle of the night like it was some common juke joint."

"Didn't you say someone was trying to break in on the kids?"

"Yes, that's why I'm out here. I was keeping an eye on them until you got here. Now you can go over and make sure everything is all right."

"Mother, are you crazy, I'm not going over . . . ouch! What was that?"

"The pruning shears. I needed something for protection."

"Please move them. You've got my left foot pinned to the porch."

"Shh."

"Mother, if you shush me again, I am going home."

"Someone's coming. I think it's LaTreace."

"That's her, all right, and she has on house shoes, too. I thought you said she left in a car."

"She did."

"Why is she walking?"

"I don't know, but now's your chance."

"My chance for what?"

"To go over there and make sure everything's all right . . ."

"I am not going over there! Stop pushing me!"

I tried to scramble back into the shadows of the porch, but Mother kept jabbing me with the pruning shears and hissing, "go on over there." The dogs started barking again, and a couple of lights came on down the street. I figured I'd better do something. So I went.

LaTreace had already gone in the house by the time I got there. The dogs' barking had died down to a few desultory yips.

I rang the bell. Nothing. I rang again. I didn't really know LaTreace that well; she wasn't in my age-group. In fact, I hadn't seen her since she was about three or four. I'd gone to school with her mother, Sharon, who I understood was doing time at the Women's Correctional Facility in Stockton. I didn't know what type of woman LaTreace was, but if she took after Sharon, I was in for some excitement. Way back in high school, Sharon had been one of the pretty girls. She had long hair, a cute shape, and a kind of full-lipped lazy smile. But even then she'd been sort of "out there" as we used to say. She ran with a rough crowd and wore flashy clothes, leaning toward streetwalker chic or *'ho couture,* as my college prep friends used to call it.

High school was twenty years and, for me, several dress sizes ago. I know I've changed since then, and I'd be the first one to admit it. Sometimes it seems like I settled for forty pounds and my very own house shoes instead of holding out for my forty acres and a mule. Even so, I wasn't prepared for what time and a few substances had done to Sharon's baby girl.

The door flew open just as I was getting ready to ring

the bell again. There stood LaTreace, a squeezed-looking little woman with bulging eyes. A few scraggly strands of hair dangled almost to her shoulders. The rest was matted and broken off in uneven patches. She wore a jogging suit jacked over a housedress, and on her feet were the ubiquitous house shoes. One thing was for sure, she didn't have her mother's sense of style. The most jarring thing about her, though, was her mouth. Several teeth were missing from the upper front, the others had shifted, giving the effect that she had one rather large tooth in the dead center of her mouth. One of her lower teeth was broken off, leaving a black stump. She had been such a pretty child. I guess that's what crack will do to you.

"Hi, LaTreace. Is your grandmother in?" I asked, trying not to sound too bright and chipper and in love with life. That's what one of my old boyfriends once accused me of being and somehow, after all of these years, it still rankled. I guess being chipper somehow just wasn't Black enough for him.

"What the fuck you mean coming 'round to people's houses, waking them up when they trying to sleep?" La-Treace's words were in the right order, but something was wrong with the inflection.

"I'm sorry if I woke you up, but I really need to see your grandmother. Can you tell her I'm here?"

"Mama never did like your ass, bitch. You always thought you was white. Why don't you get the fuck out of my face and go on back to Greenhaven where you belong?"

What can you say to accolades like that?

"Honey . . ." I began while frantically trying to think of something down and witty and, most of all, disarming to say to this chemically imbalanced child.

"Who's at the door LaTreace . . ."

"Mrs. Turnip, it's me, Neesa," I called out, lapsing into my old neighborhood's patois more successfully this time and using both the name we neighborhood kids had given Mrs. Turner a long time ago and my baby name.

"LaTreace, your grandmother wants to see me. I heard her calling."

LaTreace blocked the door. I debated putting my foot against the jamb to keep her from closing it, but I was wearing lightweight canvas shoes and I thought that might prove to be a losing proposition if she decided to slam it.

For the second time that night I was pushed from behind. I smashed into LaTreace. She stumbled backward, letting go of the door. It flew all the way open and slammed into the wall. Mother marched in carrying a large casserole dish in her hands; the pruning shears were tucked under her arm.

"Mrs. Turner, Mrs. Turner," she trilled as if this was a midday visit and not four in the morning. "Mrs. Turner, I cooked a lovely mess of greens, and I'd thought I'd bring you some."

Chapter 2

When Mrs. Turner answered again, she sounded fainter. Mother darted down the short hallway to her bedroom. LaTreace didn't try to stop her. I followed. The smell hit us about halfway there. It was a mean, evil, aggressive smell. A smell that said something is dead or dying and I don't care who knows. It was a smell that promised a fight.

Mother pushed open the door and whispered, "Lord have mercy." Then she said, "Sister Turner, I heard you weren't feeling so good, and I thought I'd come over and see if there was anything I could do."

"Thank you, Sister Barkley. I am a bit under the weather, and I appreciate your help. The children have been doing all they can, but they're just babies."

I had to strain to hear her. Mother very carefully did not allow her facial expression or voice to register her shock. She looked directly at Mrs. Turner as she spoke and did not let her eyes wander about the room. Mrs. Turner very carefully masked any feelings of shame or even relief she might have felt by having Mother find her like this. They greeted each other as they always had. They were two genteel colored ladies from the South; graciousness was a way of life for them, no matter how mean their circumstances.

The babies, Mrs. Turner's great-grandchildren, Sharon's grandchildren, and LaTreace's afterthought, huddled quietly in bed like shipwreck survivors. It was obvious from their quietness and the way their eyes followed us that they were scared. It was also obvious from the foul odor that the bed had been soiled and diapers needed changing.

Mrs. Turner sank back on the bed and closed her eyes. A partially eaten peanut butter sandwich lay on the nightstand next to her. It was old, the bread had dried out and curled back into a sneer.

"Sister Turner, I'm going to fix you something to eat, something light. When's the last time you ate, honey?"

"I couldn't keep anything in my stomach the last few days, and I had a touch of diarrhea, too. But don't worry about me. I'm more concerned about the babies. They've been eating whatever they could find. You know I always try to keep plenty of food. Sir has been doing a real good job taking care of all of us." Sir stared at us. "But he just a child." A spark of defiance flickered in his eyes. "You fix them something. I'll be all right."

"I tell you what, I'll have Theresa stick those greens I brought over in the microwave. They're frozen, so it may take a few minutes. In the meantime, why don't we get the kids cleaned up and get your bed changed?" Mother turned to me, "Theresa . . ."

"I know, I know. Heat up the greens." I retraced my steps to the front of the house. LaTreace had left. I checked the kitchen, bathroom, the other bedrooms, and the service porch just to make sure. But she was gone.

I found the microwave buried under a pile of kitchen debris on the counter by the refrigerator. I stuck the greens in and gave them ten minutes on high.

Dirty dishes littered the counters and the table. Two plates with bits of food still on them were on the floor under the table, others were stuck in the sink full of gray, scummy water. The custom, built-in double oven that had been Mrs. Turner's pride was encrusted with gunk; the doors looked stuck together. The floor was sticky, and the collection of potted plants in the window over the sink were wilted and dying. Some were already dead. Mrs. Turner was such a fastidious housekeeper, the condition of her kitchen would break her heart.

The dogs had stopped barking. I leaned forward to look out the window into the darkened backyard. Mrs. Turner usually kept a light on in the back, but it was out, too. I could just make out the outline of the old vine-covered toolshed in the northeast corner of the yard. I was trying to catch a glimpse of Mrs. Turner's dog, but it was too dark and I was unable to make it out. This had to be some dog considering, if my memory served me right, that Mrs. Turner did not like dogs. In fact, she absolutely hated them. When I was growing up in Oak Park, it had been somewhat of a neighborhood tradition to keep a dog, preferably of undetermined pedigree, feed it chicken bones and table scraps, keep it tied up all day, and let it bark at will during the night. "That's why they call them dogs," a young philosopher patronizingly explained to a lady, new to the neighborhood, who had suggested that chicken bones weren't very good for dogs and that there was some benefit to exercise and human companionship. Mrs. Turner never had a dog during all those years. I was surprised that she had one now.

On impulse, I opened the door of the freezer. It contained a few packages of frozen vegetables, some bagels, and an opened package of freezer-burned wieners. No ice cream. But what did I expect in a household where a seven-year-old was preparing the meals. It stood to reason that the ice cream, Ho Ho's and Chee•tos would be the first to go. This was going to be one of those days, and a nice prophylactic serving of ice cream would have done much to fortify me for what was to come.

I checked the kitchen window and the door leading from the service porch to the backyard. The window was securely locked, but the door was slightly ajar. It took me a couple of shoves to force it shut. Either the door or the frame was warped. A large lock swung from each of the cabinets on the service porch. Someone had securely, if inexpertly, installed them. They were a jarring, discordant note in a household that I remembered as open and gracious and sharing.

I made my way back down the hall to Mrs. Turner's room. Except for its need of a good cleaning, the house really hadn't changed much from when I was a child. There was the same fine furniture, the well-cut custom drapes, and the hardwood floors covered with colorful rag rugs. Mrs. Turner was shopping at Bruener's way back when most others in our neighborhood, my parents included, considered Big Al's "three rooms full for $99" to be the height of sophistication. The big-screen color TV was missing and so were the ginger jar lamps. There were no pictures on the walls. The house could have stood some cleaning, but it was still Mrs. Turner's house and it bore her indelible mark.

"Don't bother about me, Sister Barkley. You go on and take care of the children." Mrs. Turner sounded weaker.

"They're not used to me. And they're kinda scared. Let me help you up first, then I'll see if they'll let me help them."

Mother gently turned the covers back from Mrs. Turner and helped her stand.

"Girl, you're as weak as sweetened water. Do you think you can make it to the bathroom?"

"Just let me rest here in this chair for a while, and I'll be all right."

She sank into an armchair near the bed and closed her eyes. Mother leaned over and peered at her.

"She's too weak. We got to get her to the hospital quick. Theresa, help me get the kids up."

Sir stiffened.

"Don't worry, honey," I said. "Your grandmother's going to be all right soon as we get her to the hospital. But we need you to help us."

It wasn't until I pulled the covers back that I realized how frightened he was. That's when I saw the knife. It was a large butcher knife, and he clutched it with both hands. I locked my hand over both of his and drew him to me with my other arm.

"It's all right, honey. Nobody's going to hurt you. I won't let anybody hurt you. It's all right." I held him tightly and rocked him.

I pried his fingers off the knife, and his hands clenched into little fists as if they had memories of their own. I thought about my own children, and for some reason, I don't know why, I was nudged by a profound sense of sadness.

"It's all right, honey," I chanted. His hands were still clenched. His whole body was a tight little fist. The twins had burrowed deeper under the covers and were crying softly, making sad, little mewing sounds. Gradually some of the tension left Sir's body, and he began to cry, too. Tears fell, but his expression didn't change and he didn't make a sound. He cried silently as if he were practiced at this type of stealth.

"It's okay to cry, baby. You just go on and cry, it's okay."

If these were my children, I would buy them pretty clothes and comb their hair and put beads in it and let them eat Cap'n Crunch cereal and watch hours of cartoons on Saturdays and take them to church on Sundays and marvel at how much they've grown and put money under their pillows for missing teeth, I thought as I rocked Sir and fought back my own tears.

"Theresa, I'm worried about Sister Turner. I can't get her to wake up all the way. While you were getting the children up, I tried to find the phone to call emergency, and there isn't one. At least, I can't find one, just some empty jacks."

I looked over at Mrs. Turner. She was curled up in the chair. I was worried, too.

"We'd better do something quick," I said. "I don't like the way she looks either. Maybe I should run over to the house and call from there."

"I know where the phone is." Sir's voice was high and sweet.

"You do, honey?" I asked, looking down at him. He needed a haircut. The hair at the nape of his neck, the kitchens, had rolled up into soft little balls. Right in that little indentation where the head meets the neck had been one of my favorite places for kissing my son when he was Sir's age.

"Here's the key," he said, holding up a shiny key attached to a chain around his neck.

"I'm going to try to find the phone and get some help," I said to Mother. "Why don't you try to get Mrs. Turner to drink something? Don't worry about getting her dressed."

Sir had already gotten out of bed and gone toward the kitchen. By the time I got there, he was out on the service porch, kneeling on top of the dryer in front of an open cabinet, sorting through its contents.

"I think it's in this one. Here it is," he said, reaching in back and pulling out a pink princess phone with the cord wrapped around it.

I grabbed it from him, plugged it into the jack by the refrigerator, and dialed 911. It rang only a couple of times before there was an answer. I asked for an ambulance, spelled my name, verified the address, explained my relationship to Mrs. Turner, verified the address again, asked them to please hurry because she'd had another seizure, had lapsed into a coma, and was hemorrhaging. Then I hung up. If that didn't get them here quickly, nothing would.

I went back to the service porch, but Sir had abandoned his perch on the dryer and the cabinets were all locked. Mother had roused Mrs. Turner, and I could hear her talking to her in soothing, even tones as she tried to get her to drink a little water.

The back door stood ajar. This bothered me. I was certain I had closed it earlier. I peered into the darkness, but I couldn't make anything out, just shadows that bled into other shadows. Somewhere in the distance, I could hear the faint sound of two people conversing intimately, one speaking, the other moaning softly in response. Some neighbor's window must be open, I thought.

Suddenly I wanted to get the door shut very badly. I wanted it shut more than anything else in the world. I tried to force it, but the swollen wood resisted. I grabbed the knob with both hands and lifted the door to give it some clearance. Goose bumps as large as mosquito bites rose up on my arms. My bra felt too tight. I seemed to be moving in slow motion, but my mind was in fast-forward, that's why I saw it before it actually hit the door and was able to brace myself. It hit the door about shoulder height, a large black blur, rattling every window in the house. Then it slid to the porch clawing and scratching the length of its descent.

Whatever it was out there was making noises, a deep, low, rumbling growl. I turned my head and quickly looked over my shoulder. For a second it seemed as if the sound was coming from behind me. Something gave the door a shove, and I panicked, pushing desperately. Another inch and I would have had it closed.

"Hey, let me in." The high voice didn't go with the low, rumbling growl.

"Who's out there?"

"It's me, Sir."

"Who's out there with you?"

"Nobody just me and Tonton."

"Tonton? Who is Tonton?"

"He ain't nobody. He just a dog." Sir gave the word "dog" two syllables. I'm a sucker for a diphthong.

"Okay, Sir, tie the dog up, and I'll let you in."

"He doesn't like to be tied up. He won't bother you. I promise."

"Tie the beast up or you won't get in, and that's final."

Sir didn't respond directly to my ultimatum, but I heard him murmuring and the dog whining. They left the porch and Sir returned, still murmuring. I heard him say, "Stay, boy, stay," a couple of times.

I opened the door only half as wide as necessary for him to enter, and watched with a certain amount of sadistic glee as he squeezed one body part at a time through the small opening.

"What the hell were you doing out there?" I don't like to curse around children, but I was mad.

"Nothing."

"Nothing? Boy, are you crazy? Nothing. You expect me to believe that?

"I just wanted to make sure Tonton had enough to eat."

"At night, in the dark? How many meals a day does that beast eat?"

Poor Sir. He was just a little kid trying to take care of a sick grandmother and two little sisters and worrying about a drug addict mother and being scared stiff and trying to act tough. I'm also a sucker for scared little boys trying to be tough. I put my arm around him and drew him to me. He pulled away. I reached for him again, and he scrambled away and ran to the kitchen.

The sirens of the arriving ambulance diverted me from my nurturing activities.

I rushed down the hall to Mrs. Turner's room. Mother had wrapped a blanket around Mrs. Turner's shoulders. She'd found one of Sir's jackets for one twin. It hung down to her ankles. The other one wore a sweater that was too small. Mother had buttoned it up to her throat. The second button from the top was missing.

"Go open the door," Mother said over her shoulder.

Sir wasn't there, so I assumed she was talking to me.

Chapter 3

The good Sisters of Mercy were represented in the emergency room by an admitting nurse whose abundant and unruly hair was so red, he looked like the biblical burning bush. Apparently having a hard time adjusting to the graveyard shift, the Bush punctuated every other question with a yawn so wide, it bordered on the obscene. Mother discreetly averted her eyes; I counted thirteen fillings.

We got Mrs. Turner admitted with Mother signing as her sister. The doctor on duty explained that Mrs. Turner had the flu and was suffering from dehydration.

"Don't worry," she reassured me, "your aunt will be up and at it and ready to boogie just as soon as we get some fluids into her."

They got an IV started and assigned Mrs. Turner a bed. When she got settled, we went in to say good-bye. Mother and I each carried a twin. Sir walked at my side, his sleep-heavy head resting on my hip, his feet moving on their own. I had to be careful turning corners; if we lost body contact, he'd walk straight into whatever was in his path.

"Sister Turner," Mother whispered, "we gon' leave now, honey."

Mrs. Turner opened her eyes wide. She seemed very alert. "Take care of the babies for me."

"Child, you know I will. You don't even have to ask. You just rest now, so you can get out of here as soon as possible."

"LaTreace get a hold of them, the county'll probably end up taking them."

"I know, I know," Mother reassured her. "We won't let that happen."

"Sir has the keys. He knows where everything is. There's another house key in the makeup compact in my purse. You better take it."

Mother opened Mrs. Turner's purse and removed the compact. The key was where she said it would be.

"Okay, honey, I got the key. You just rest now. I'll have them put your purse in the safe until you're ready to leave."

"No, give it to me. I'll keep it in bed with me here just in case I need it or something."

Mother pulled the covers back and stuffed the purse in close to her.

"Now, you get some rest, child."

Mrs. Turner smiled and closed her eyes.

It was five-thirty in the morning by the time we got back to Mother's and carried the sleeping twins into the house. Sir woke up and insisted on walking on his own. We placed the twins on Mother's vinyl-encased sofa, and they nestled together like yin and yang. Sir sat near them, glassy eyed, struggling to stay awake. I was beginning to feel like him. I was staying awake now through sheer force of will and nothing else.

Mother was in the back room sorting through boxes.

"I was collecting these things for the church, but I guess this is as good a cause as any," she said brightly, humming under her breath as she extracted a pair of pants here and a sweatshirt there.

Mother loves a crisis. She is at her best during disasters. The year floods nearly wiped out Strawberry Manor had been her brightest. She'd worked tirelessly collecting clothing, cooking meals, and finding shelter for those left homeless. She'd have rolled bandages had someone asked.

"This box of things here was donated by Mrs. Alston. I've never met her, but I know her by the stuff she gives. It's always so nice. It's almost like she went out and bought these things just so she could give them away. Take this shirt, for instance."

Mother held up a long-sleeved crew-neck shirt. I recognized it immediately. I'd know it anywhere. One hundred percent cotton, thirty-five dollars at the Gap. My son had a couple of them. I'd relented and bought them for him only after he had argued that they were a good buy because they appreciated with time. It was the cute, earnest way that he argued his harebrained case that actually persuaded me.

"Mrs. Alston, she's related to Bobby—Robert Alston who's running for mayor?"

"Uh-huh, she's his mother. She's also the lady Sister Turner worked for all those years, she and Doctor Alston. Those Alstons, they were some of the nicest people. Do you know they pay Mrs. Turner a pension and keep her health insurance up, too? How many domestics you know retired on a pension?"

"Not many."

"That's right."

Actually I don't know any domestics retired or otherwise except for Aunt Alice, but she didn't retire. She just worked until high blood pressure and diabetes got the best of her and her body simply wouldn't go the way it used to, and she quit. Everybody I know works for the county or the feds or the state, like I do. Mother did a little domestic work when she and Dad first married, but she didn't have the skills for it or the disposition. She retired after twenty-five years at Campbell's soup. Her long-term job there and Dad's job as a city garbageman had edged us into Sacramento's Black stable class if not middle class. Now Mother lives comfortably on her pension, a little bit of Social Security, and her widow's portion of Daddy's pension.

"Bobby went to Sac High," I said. "He and I graduated the same year."

"Did you know him?"

"Uh-huh, we had a few classes together from time to time. You know, he was kinda weird. His mother made him dress like Richie Rich or something. She was always coming to the school, bringing him his lunch, bringing his raincoat if the sky showed more than two clouds, arguing with teachers about his grades. You know that kind of stuff."

"Sounds like a pretty good mother to me."

"I don't know, there was always something kinda sad about Bobby. I suppose I'd have been sad, too, if I had to wear the mess she made him wear. It's funny, though, all that time I didn't know Mrs. Turner worked for her."

Mother was still working briskly. She didn't seem to be nearly as tired as I was. Since Daddy died two years ago, she's taken to staying up most of the night and sleeping well into the day. This was probably like high noon to her. She'd cared for Daddy at home for the last eight months before he died. Like a video run in reverse, he had forgotten how to feed himself, how to go to the bathroom, and even how to sit up on his own. Finally he was back at the beginning, lying curled in a fetal position in the rented hospital bed Mother had set up for him in the dining room.

Now Mother stays up nights and sleeps days, not because, as she claims, she got into the habit when she had to turn Daddy every four hours. That may be part of it, but the real reason, although she would never admit it, is because of fear. Quite simply the fear of being old and alone and the victimization that comes with it.

"How's Alston's campaign going? Is the Negro Women's Community Guild going to do anything?

The Negro Women's Community Guild was founded more than sixty years ago to provide suitable housing for respectable single Negro women. During that time, women of color coming to town to work or go to school couldn't find decent places to stay. Their only choices were to stay with relatives or, lacking such, to rent a room in one of the bawdy houses presenting themselves as hotels that ran along Front Street in what is now Sacramento's quaint and touristy Old Town. I believe the guild's first boardinghouse still stands somewhere on X Street. Mother lived in NWCG housing when she first came to Sacramento in the forties, and she has been a staunch supporter ever since. As times have changed, so has the guild, and it has branched off into other civic endeavors, oftentimes with Mother leading the charge.

"Oh, just fine. The NWCG has raised $500 so far. We've met with the campaign committee, and they're talking about opening a day-care center in Oak Park so welfare mothers who want to work will have someplace to leave their children. Of course, Mr. Alston can't do anything unless he's elected. I'm the chairwoman of the next fund-raiser."

"Great, what are you planning?"

"I don't know. But it's gotta to be better than Gartha Jackson's luau, or I'll have to listen to her mouth for the rest of the year."

We had sorted out a small mound of clothing from the various boxes. I looked at my watch. Either the hands were swimming about on its face, or my eyes were watering so badly I couldn't see. Either way, I couldn't tell the time.

"I think these should be enough clothes. Come on, let's get the children to bed before I fall down right here and you have to undress me and put me to bed, too. You know, I've still got to go home and get ready for work."

We went back to the living room. Sir had lost his battle with sleep and had keeled over next to the twins.

"Come on, Pookie, come on, baby. Time to go night-night," cooed Mother as she broke the vacuum seal the sleeping child's mouth had made on the vinyl and gently lifted her.

"Pookie?" I asked.

"Yes, and Nay-Nay."

"Why would anyone want to name such a pretty little girl Pookie? Life is hard enough already. What are their real names?"

"I think Nay-Nay's real name is Cenne. I don't know Pookie's."

We got the kids undressed and put them to bed. Even in his sleep, Sir resisted and fought, but we got him to bed, too. We put all three in Mother's double bed, and she bunked down in one of the twin beds in the room that used to belong to me and Carolyn. I had gotten my second wind by then and no longer felt as sleepy. I made myself a cup of coffee before heading home. Coffee cup in hand, I peeked out of Mother's living room window.

"You know, it looks like we left one of Mrs. Turner's back lights on."

"No, I'm sure I turned them all off," said Mother. "As expensive as electricity is, I certainly wouldn't leave her lights on. I hope no one's gotten in there. I better call her brother first thing in the morning and tell him his sister's in the hospital."

The sun peeked up over the horizon just enough to produce a promise of light. A few early birds twittered tentatively as I left. Mr. Aragon's semi was gone. The dogs were quiet, and my departure went unheralded. I felt good. I like my coffee strong, with lots of sugar. My first cup floods my system with caffeine and envelopes me with a sense of euphoria; also my fear quotient is much lower in daylight.

I took the freeway home, retracing my earlier route. The closer I got to home, the more my euphoria seemed to diminish. I'd left during the wee hours of the morning a good four hours ago. Although I'd left a note, there was no guarantee that Temp or the kids found it. What if Aisha had gotten sick during the night, or Shawn had a nightmare—the kind where you need your mother, only she will do—and I wasn't there? For that matter, what if Temp had awakened and stumbled up to bed and found it empty at three-thirty in the morning?

Temp and the kids are used to me taking off to Mother's or stopping by after work. But I'd never done anything like this before. I expected to be greeted on my return by some pretty anxious folk, and I wasn't looking forward to it.

Propelled by guilt and a certain degree of dread, I got off the freeway at Florin Road, an exit ahead of mine. I went through the drive-up window at Burger King and picked up a bag of those little breakfast sandwiches Temp and the kids are so crazy about. But by the time I got home around seven forty-five, they had already left for work and school. I ate a couple of the sandwiches halfheartedly and went upstairs to shower. Forty-five minutes later, impeccably attired in the best Liz Claiborne has to offer in size sixteen and accessorized to the bone, I left for work.

One of the good things about living in Sacramento is you can get to downtown, where I work, from just about anywhere in the city in about fifteen minutes. Unfortunately once you get there, if you survive near miss head-on crashes brought on by the wacky profusion of one-way streets, there's no place to park. On weekdays, I've solved the parking problem. I drive halfway to work and park in the lot reserved for state employees under Highway 80 on Sixth and W Streets. This takes me all of seven minutes. Then I take the shuttle bus—believe me, it's very aptly named—to within two blocks of the Resources Building and walk the rest of the way. The entire commute takes about twenty minutes.

If I took the express city bus from home to the stop directly in front of my building, I could cut my commute time in half. The bus has some advantages: you can read or even doze while you commute, and let's not forget the benefits to the environment. But despite the savings in time I might realize and the savings to the ozone layer and everything else, I prefer to drive. For one thing, the city bus people want to put you on a schedule—their schedule. I don't like the regimentation. I need the freedom to come and go as I please. You just never know when you have to leave unexpectedly; one of the kids may get sick or something. Then, too, I carry a briefcase and a tote bag for the things that wouldn't fit in the briefcase, and it's difficult lugging that stuff five blocks on foot from home to the nearest bus stop.

It was close to nine when I got to work. I'm the personnel officer for the Department of Environmental Equity, a small, relatively new state agency of about a thousand employees. The Department of Environmental Equity, or DEE, as it is known, was created by the governor, carved out of flanks of several larger agencies about four years ago. Although it has regulatory and research functions, DEE is primarily responsible for making sure that minority communities don't get more than their fair share of toxic disposal facilities, don't suffer more than their fair share of diseases related to industrial pollution, and that they do get their fair share of state and federal resources for prevention and mitigation. A rather daunting task.

Although it's nearly four years old, the department is still struggling to develop its own corporate culture. A lot of the scratching, clawing, and jockeying for position that takes place when people from several different organizations are thrown together and told to live as one big happy family is still going on. Also, when told that they were to lose positions and employees to DEE, some departments seized the opportunity to dump their less productive, more dysfunctional employees. So, DEE is somewhat of personnel gumbo. The highly sought after management and executive positions drew some of the state's best minds, creating a sort of brain drain for other departments. Some employees chose to come to DEE because of the challenge of setting up a new program, while others came in search of promotional opportunities. A few came as refugees from bad managers or progressive discipline policies gone awry. Others still, few in number but not in impact, the incompetent and the disgruntled, masters at "fomenting discord" came because no other department would have them. For them, DEE was the last stop before the unemployment lines or disability rolls.

It's my job as personnel officer to keep the department fully staffed so the various scientists and engineers can get their jobs done. I supervise a staff of fifteen, and I'm responsible for hiring and firing and everything in between.

I had just enough time to prepare myself for the Monday morning staff meeting at nine. These meetings are not happy affairs, so it is only right that they are held on Mondays. They start at nine, and I have never known one to go beyond nine-thirty regardless of what was on the agenda. It is the department's policy that all divisions hold regularly scheduled staff meetings. I think it has something to do with scientific management. So Division of Management Operations, which is where I work as personnel officer, holds these staff meetings where each manager halfheartedly reports the reputed highlights of the past week, notes any dubious accomplishments, glosses over any real problems, particularly those that could damage his promotability, and the meeting is adjourned. After that, a small core group repairs to the cafeteria, where the real reporting is done.

I glanced over the agenda that Miyako, my secretary, had put in a red folder and placed in the middle of my desk. The management information system project was on it again. DEE is involved in a massive automation project. When it is complete, each workspace, from the carpeted offices on executive row to the janitor's closet, will have its own computer terminal. The project was eighteen months behind schedule and a few million dollars over budget. This was the third time in a row that it had appeared as the kickoff item on the agenda. We were fast approaching the end of another fiscal year, and the funding would have to be rejustified. It looked like management was getting a tad bit nervous.

Brenda Delacore was also on the agenda, and this made me nervous. Brenda works for me as the manager of the classification and pay section. She is smart. I understand she has an IQ of 165. She's involved with the Black Repertory Theater group, the Historical Society, and a host of other community groups. But whatever smarts she has is all book leaning, as Mother would say. The child doesn't have an ounce of "mother wit." To make matters worse, she has a way of rubbing the average white male Homo sapien bureaucratus the wrong way.

I took two more gulps of coffee and left for the meeting. Brenda was striding down the hallway to the conference room when I caught up with her. Her short dreds seemed to bristle like tiny, articulated lightning rods, and I could smell a fight in the air. Another thing about Brenda—she loves a fight. The only problem is, I've never known her to win one. Maybe it's because she doesn't know how to pick them, or it could have something to do with her mother wit deficiency. I don't know. I have a hunch that she doesn't really fight to win; she just wants "them" to know that affirmative action or no affirmative action, she is here and she takes no mess. Sort of a way of marking her territory without raising her leg. Sometimes she makes me cringe. I'm from the "we shall overcome" generation, she's from the "get out of my face, mother" generation. I knew if there was a fight, she'd be right there in the middle of it.

"How's it going, Brenda?" I asked falling into step beside her and trying to match her long-legged stride.

"How's it going? How's it going? The stupid mothafuckas call me at three-thirty on Friday and tell me they want me to report on adverse actions on Monday and I spend all my fuckin' weekend getting ready and they call me five minutes before the meeting and say they may not have enough time to get to me. Fuck this shit. I don't need this."

"Okay, Brenda, chill out." I like to think of myself as Brenda's mentor, so I try to offer her sage advice whenever I can. Most of the time I'm reduced to saying something like, "Okay, Brenda, chill out." I don't know why I picked such an irascible pupil.

"Did you do a written report, Brenda, or did you just pull data together for your presentation?"

"Both. I have a presentation with overheads and shit and a written report."

"How long does the presentation take?"

"I don't know, about fifteen minutes."

"Why don't you hand the report out, do a three-minute summary, and tell them you will be available after the meeting to answer any questions?"

"Yeah, sure."

Brenda relishes a good fight, but she loses interest when things switch to a problem-solving mode.

Allen Warner, Management Operations Division Chief and my supervisor, was already in the conference room when we got there. He was seated at the head of the table and was deep in discussion with Tony Mateo, who is in charge of the Management Information Office. They looked up when we came in.

I greeted them, "Good morning, Allen, Tony. How were your weekends?"

"Much too short," replied Allen. Allen has a serene

air about him. A kind of karma that seems to put him at peace with himself and his surroundings. He is a vegan—a total vegetarian. He eats nothing that has a face, also no eggs, no butter, no milk, and no cheese. That may have something to do with his serenity. I've never seen it in any of the carnivores I know.

Tony just grunted. He doesn't interact very well with "humanware," but I've seen his eyes mist up as he rhapsodized eloquently about hardware and software and ethernets and token rings, whatever they are.

The other division managers were filtering in. Tyler Schultz from Labor Relations and Cheryl Tockenberry from Audits came in. Cheryl was resplendent in a lemon yellow outfit that looked somewhat like a nun's habit. She weighs close to 250 pounds but her quick, sharp movements give her the air of a predator. Her eyes darted around the room, as if she was memorizing our positions. Office folklore has it she can smell blood. She sniffed the air, mumbled a greeting, and settled in across the table close to Allen and as far away from me and Brenda as possible. This was not a good sign.

"Allen, I understand we may not be able to hear Brenda's full report this morning."

He nodded.

"Why don't we have her do a brief summary and make herself available for questions afterward?"

"Sure, that's fine. Let's get started now."

Tony was first on the agenda. He reported that the new management information system was proceeding right on target and should be installed in six months. We all knew the project was eighteen months behind schedule, but we all nodded and prepared to go on to the next agenda item—all, that is, except Brenda.

"Wait a minute. I don't want to cause a problem, but I believe I detect a slight contradiction here. Correct me if I'm wrong, but I think I remember reading a status report, oh, about six months ago, that indicated this project was a year behind schedule then."

Brenda was in rare form. She was using her ten-year-old white girl's voice. I could feel the tension ripple through the room. Tony snorted. I knew he wouldn't respond to Brenda's thinly veiled challenge or anybody else's. He never did. He had made his report, and he was finished. He responded to very little unless it was E-mail. Cheryl twisted her head to the side in a sharp, jerking motion so she could stare at Brenda from the corner of one eye. A faint smile played on Brenda's lips. Cheryl licked hers. Tyler began to fidget. Allen raised his hand in a Buddha-like gesture. The door opened abruptly, and Miyako stuck her head in.

"Excuse me. Theresa, you have an emergency phone call."

With a sigh of relief, I was out of there.

"Who is it, Miyako?"

"I don't know. She wouldn't give her name, but she insisted it was urgent, and I could hear sirens in the background."

I sprinted to my office, grabbed the phone, and punched the blinking light.

"Hello." I was panting from my short run.

"Yo, Theresa? This LaTreace. How you doing, girl?"

"LaTreace? LaTreace! What is it? Is something wrong."

"Say, listen, Theresa, I need some help real bad. It's Pookie. She got asthma, you know. And she had an attack this morning. And I need to get her medicine, but I can't 'cause I don' have no money. She takes this special kinda medicine, you know, it's kinda experimental and welfare won't pay for it. So can you let me have $79.62?"

"Seventy-nine dollars and sixty-two cents?"

"Yeah, that's how much it cost."

"It's experimental?"

"Yeah, it's experimental, but it works real good."

"LaTreace, tell me one thing."

"Huh?"

"Why'd you name the child Pookie?"

"Huh?"

"Why did you name the child Pookie?"

"Oh. Uh, I didn't name her Pookie, I just call her that. I was sorta sick when she was born and Mama named her."

"What did Sharon name her?"

"Uh, Andrea."

"Andrea, that's a beautiful name. Andrea. It fits her."

"Yeah, okay, uh-huh. Can you let me have the money?"

"Where's the medicine, LaTreace?"

"Huh?"

"What pharmacy?"

"Uh, Broadway Pharmacy. The one on the corner of Thirty-sixth and Broadway."

"I know where it is. I tell you what, I have to run by Mother's this evening anyway. I'll just stop by the pharmacy and pick the medicine up. I'm sure they'll take Visa."

There was silence on the other end of the line.

"LaTreace, I suppose you know your grandmother is in the hospital."

The phone slammed down in my ear.

Time passed, the rest of the day, in spurts and sputters. One minute I'd be riding high on caffeine, and the next minute my blood-sugar level would plummet so low, I could barely lift my mug to drink more coffee. I boycotted my slate of meetings and sent Brenda in my place, telling myself that tomorrow I'd patch up the broken relationships and soothe the hurt feelings she was sure to leave in her wake. Finally I knew it was time to go home when I wandered into the men's rest room by mistake and didn't even notice it until a fellow in wing tips settled into the stall next to mine.

I made it back to my office without bumping into the walls on the way, packed my bags, and headed out. I went to the reception area to tell Miyako I was leaving early. Miyako wears her hair in spikes and dresses all in black, but she has created her own oasis of grace, order, and elegance in the middle of drab surroundings. Mismatched partitions divide the rest of the office into eccentric little cubicles, furnished with gunmetal gray surplus furniture. Miyako's desk, however, is wood and old enough to be considered an antique. It's scarred and stained in places, but that only lends it an air of genteel elegance. Instead of the harvest gold partitions that lean haphazardly around other work areas, Miyako's area is defined by two screens with rice-paper panels.

"Miyako," I said, "at this time I feel compelled to quote that great philosopher, James Brown, when he said, "Sorry now I've gotta go. Money won't change it, I can't stay no mo'."" A little taste of the moon walk would have been appropriate here, but I could barely lift my feet, as it was.

Miyako shook her head and smiled.

"Brenda Delacore can act for me while I'm out," I said.

Miyako's smile vanished.

Chapter 4

The shuttle pulled up on its midday hourly run a couple of minutes after I got to the bus stop. I rode to the lot, picked up my car, and headed home. I avoided the freeway for fear of falling asleep while hurtling along at sixty miles an hour, taking Riverside Drive instead. I figured the constant stopping and going on the city streets would keep me alert, and even if I fell asleep, I'd probably stand a much better chance of survival doing thirty-five than I would doing sixty.

The Land Park area was lit up in a blaze of spring glory, but I hardly noticed. I was too busy biting the inside of my cheek, trying to use pain as a stimulus in order to stay awake. By the time I reached Shoreline Drive, I had turned the radio to a country-and-western station and turned the air-conditioning up as high as it would go in my battle to stave off sleep. After what seemed like hours, I came to Sandy River, hung a left, and quick right on Oyster Bay Way, and I was home.

I pulled into the driveway, nearly ramming the automatic garage door as it cranked up in slow motion. I went inside and went to bed, falling into a deep sleep almost immediately.

I probably would have slept well into the next day if it hadn't been for the sensation that I was being examined by a couple of pairs of coolly analytical eyes. Even in my semi-discombobulated state, I recognized the vibes before they even spoke.

"I say we wake her up. It's nearly ten o'clock, and she's been asleep since we got home. It's disgusting,"

spoke the one who has refined sentiments of disgust and
the taking of umbrage to an art form.

"No, let her sleep an' maybe when she wakes up she'll
be all rested an' she'll give us extra Nintendo time," said
the guileless one who mainlines Nintendo and other
technologies.

"You and your Nintendo. You're so disgusting.
There's more important things in life than some whack
game."

"Yeah? Like what, huh? Like some ole stupid Boyz
II Men concert, huh?"

"Sh, I know what. Let's set her clock to alarm in five
minutes. Then she'll have to wake up."

"Yeah."

I felt the air currents change as they grabbed for the
clock on my nightstand. I bolted upright, with both arms
extended straight out from my shoulders and my eyes
tightly closed, and they both screamed.

"Touch the clock and you die."

"Mo-ther," moaned Aisha with exasperation. Shawn
fell on the bed in a fit of giggles. Temp came in to see
what was going on. He was wearing an apron over biker
shorts and no shirt. Pink rubber gloves accented his
ensemble.

"I told you guys not to wake her up," he admonished
Aisha and Shawn.

"It's about time she woke up," said the unrepentant
Aisha. "Mother, I just want to know one thing. Why
can't I ever depend on you?"

"What is it now?" I asked warily.

"You were supposed to pick me up after practice, but
were you there? No-o-o. Everybody else just got into
their cars and drove away, but not me. I had to stand
there looking stupid for an hour."

Shawn pantomimed her speech behind her back. Temp
smacked him with a rubber glove.

Silently I debated lying back down and pulling the
covers over my head.

"I had to call Dad," she paused for dramatic effect.

"And he came looking like that."

Temp shrugged.

"I didn't have the apron on," he added as a point of clarification. I noticed he had on wing tips and black socks.

"Honey, I'm sorry," I said. "I got caught up in some things, and I forgot."

"That's just it. When it comes to me, you always forget," she wailed.

Shawn took a deep breath and recited in unison with her: "If I had my own car, you wouldn't have to worry about picking me up."

Aisha bestowed upon each of us in turn a look of profound disgust. Wheeling on her heels, she marched to the door, the short skirt of her cheerleader outfit marking time with each step. She walked the short distance down the hall to her room and very pointedly slammed the door.

Shawn was dancing on one foot and then the other. "Did you get it? Did you get it?" he asked.

"Did I get what, honey?"

"You know, the Game Wiz."

"The Game Wiz?"

"Yeah, the Game Wiz."

"I was supposed to get a Game Wiz?"

"You promised." Now it was his turn to wail.

"I'm sorry, honey. But I just don't remember."

"It was Tuesday. I asked you. 'Mom, will you get me a Game Wiz?' and you said, 'Yes.' "

"Was I doing something when you asked?"

"You were looking under the bed."

"Under the bed . . ."

"Yeah."

"Tuesday . . . looking under the bed." For the life of me, I couldn't remember what he was talking about, and then it dawned on me.

"Oh yes. I was late for work, and I was looking for one of my shoes. I'm sorry, honey, but I'm afraid our contract is invalid. You see, I was incompetent at the time I made that agreement."

"Does that mean I don't get it?"

"Let me think about it."

Shawn turned to Temp in appeal, but it was no use.

Shawn had come to me in the first place, in his quest for new and improved and decidedly more expensive technology, as an end run around his dad. Temp was showing no sympathy.

"It's time to finish up the dishes and go to bed, man," Temp said, handing him the rubber gloves.

"Aw, man," said Shawn. He leaned over, gave me a kiss, and left, dragging his feet, his head hanging almost to his chest.

Temp sat on the edge of the bed. He looked at me and sighed. I could almost hear the little wheels in his head cranking.

"What's going on, T?" he asked finally.

"I'm very tired. I hardly got any sleep last night."

I fought hard to stifle a yawn.

"Hey, don't play me. I asked you a simple question. What the hell is going on? I wake up this morning, and you're gone. I check the house. I check the kids' rooms. I check everywhere. You ain't here. I'm standing in the middle of the floor asking myself, 'What the hell's going on?' Then I see the note stuck on the TV. 'I've gone to Mother's'. What's that supposed to mean? I've gone to Mother's."

"Mother had an emergency . . ."

"Mother had an emergency," he said, mocking me. "Did she call the police? Did she call an ambulance? That's what you do in an emergency, T. Else she didn't have one. Every time I turn around, you over at your mother's house or you out running the street on something for her. I look up and you're gone.

"I'm telling you, T, this is no way to run a family. I'm trying to do my part and your part, too, and I'm getting just a little tired. You pay more attention to your mama that you do me."

"No I don't, honey," I protested.

"Yes you do," he said with more than a touch of Aisha's theatrics. "You know well enough that I'm trying to get the Trilux bid done. But I can't work for running behind you doing the things you supposed to do. When Aisha called me to pick her up at school, I was right in the middle of everything. I don't know how long it will take to get back on track."

He sighed again and sat glowering at me. I reached over and gently caressed his cheek. He slapped my hand away. I sighed and lay back down.

"What time did you leave this morning?" he asked.

"Around three-thirty."

"Three-thirty in the morning? Are you out of your mind? You realize how dangerous that is? You forget about your family when your mother calls. Do you lose your mind, too?"

I could see it was no use explaining about Mrs. Turner and the plants dying in her kitchen window, or about the locks on her cabinet doors and how wrong that was, or about Sir and the twins, so I didn't try. I turned over, pulled the covers over my head, and stayed that way until he left, slamming the door on his way out.

I got up early the next morning and fixed chorizo and egg burritos and fresh fruit with freshly ground coffee for Temp. I apologized to him and the children for my various failings over the past twenty-four hours. We were all overly courteous and somewhat distant with each other, but I knew that would soon pass. Speaking in well-modulated voices, we planned our various itineraries. Temp would be in the city of Folsom most of the day on one of his jobs, Aisha was going to the library after school with her study group but one of the other mothers would carpool the kids home, Shawn had soccer practice, and Temp, who was the team's assistant coach, would pick him up immediately after school and get him to the soccer field. That left me unencumbered after work. The unspoken understanding was I would come home and get dinner started so we could come together as a family at the end of the day as well.

I left for work with the unrealistic expectation that the rest of my day would go just as smoothly.

Miyako was waiting for me when I arrived.

"Theresa, Allen has called twice already this morning. You'd better call right away," she said by way of greeting.

"I will, just as soon as I get settled," I said, taking the messages from her hand.

"Also, a Ms. Penelope Troop is here to see you. She should be right back. She went to the ladies' room."

I went to my office, took my walking shoes off, replacing them with pumps, and settled in to contemplate what lay ahead for me. I had a pretty good idea why Allen was calling, damage control in the wake of hurricane Brenda. But Penelope? I hadn't seen her in years. She and I had attended Sac State together. We'd joined the same sorority, and somewhere along the line we'd gotten locked into a sort of low-key rivalry. Nothing really serious—she usually hit on the same guys who were trying to hit on me—that type of thing.

After graduation, Penny did a stint in Washington, D.C., and I went to work for the state. Penny came back to Sacramento about four or five years ago. The last I heard, she worked less than two blocks away at the capitol, where she was chief of staff for a senior member of the assembly. Our paths cross occasionally, but it had been a couple of years since I'd seen her. We ran in different circles. Penny tended to gravitate toward power and prestige, while I labored in the decidedly unprestigious mid-management trenches. I wondered what she could want with me now.

I examined my office. When the powers in executive moved the personnel office from sixteenth to the first floor so it could be "more accessible to rank and file employees," the room had been hastily constructed. It has a series of three windows across one wall, which almost make up for the fact that the walls do not go all the way up to the ceiling, stopping short about two feet from their destination, giving the room peculiar acoustic qualities. It's a kind of noise funnel. If you're not careful, everything you say is broadcast throughout the entire office.

Miyako discreetly tapped on the door and stuck her head in. "Ms. Troop is here. Shall I send her in?"

I nodded, thinking, "If you must."

The woman who entered was not the Penny I knew. For one thing, she looked too good. The Penny I knew had a jheri curl that was slowly evolving into something new and unheard of. Also, she was a woman of substance when it came to hips. The old Penny was bright, but she was just on the cusp when it came to the assimilation game. She always wore a confused look like she wasn't exactly sure what white folk expected of her, and she wasn't quite sure whether she was prepared to go on and give it up or just cuss them out instead.

I always liked the old Penny, in spite of her awkward ways. But that was the old Penny. The new Penny was svelte, weighing in at least forty pounds less than I remembered. The jheri curl had given way to a soft natural style conforming to the contours of her long, elegant head and accented with just a hint of gray. She wore an eggplant-colored suit with matching blouse, pumps, and handbag that was so fine, it nearly brought tears to my eyes.

"Girlfriend," she said, extending a well-tended hand.

"Penny, It's good to see you. And honey, you are looking good. Have a seat," I said pointing toward an orange vinyl side chair next to my desk. "What have you been up to?"

"Oh, nothing much, girl. Just a little of this and a little of that."

She said "dis" and "dat" just like the old Penny.

"Where are you now? You still over at the Capitol?"

"Un-huh. Senator Stinson chief of staff."

"You go girl. You survived the reductions, then."

"For the time being, yes."

She leaned over my desk and picked up the picture of Shawn and Aisha. Dust rose from it in a tiny mushroom cloud. She blew on the glass and brushed at it with her fingertips.

"These your kids, huh."

"Yes, those are my babies, Aisha and Shawn."

"How old are they?" she asked with a strange set to her mouth.

"Aisha just turned sixteen and Shawn is eleven."

"They look like nice kids. You don't have a picture of your husband. What's his name . . . ?"

"Temp."

"That's right, Templeton," she said.

"No, I don't have Temp's picture, he's too vain. No picture he's ever taken has been good enough, according to him. There's always something wrong with them."

"Girlfriend," Penny said ruefully, "you know, we just don't get together often enough. You got married, how long ago?" she queried.

"About seventeen years," I answered dutifully.

"Seventeen years ago," she mused almost to herself. "I was still in Washington then. You got married," she continued, "had children and they're just about grown."

"That's true," I said.

"You know, I met Templeton ..."

"Temp," I corrected.

"Huh?"

"Temp. Nobody calls him Templeton, we all call him Temp."

"Well, he introduced himself as Templeton. I met him at one of the Alston fund-raisers, the one at the Hyatt last Thursday night. Templeton Ford Galloway, that's how he introduced himself. I didn't even know he was married to you until someone told me," she giggled, looking uncomfortable.

I sat back in my chair and smiled. She may have upgraded her appearance, but she was the same old Penny.

"Penny, do you still have that vanity license plate that reads 'Do me,' " I asked.

"No," she said. "That was when I was young and foolish."

"Don't be no fool now," I said.

"No, I don't think I will," she said staring me in the eye. "I don't have much use for fools. You know what the old folks say, 'See a fool, bump his head.' "

I looked at my watch and stood up. "Girl, I got meetings stacked up. Why don't you give me your number and I'll give you a call?"

She reached into her purse and pulled out a gold card case.

"Here's my card," she said, handing one to me. "I'll be seeing you," she promised. "Kiss the babies for me. And ... take care of that man of yours."

She left, closing the door carefully behind her.

I pride myself on being a reasonable, rational woman. And, I love my husband and trust him, but I also knew Penny and what she was capable of. I had the phone up and was dialing Temp's cell phone number before she was completely out of the door.

Temp answered crisply.

"Honey," I said, "I'm sorry to bother you, but Penny Troop just left my office."

"T, I'm really busy."

"Penny tells me she met you."

"You know, you're getting more like your mother everyday."

"What's that supposed to mean?"

"It means I'm busy, T."

"This'll just take a minute."

"Okay, so now you're ready to talk, but last night you were too tired. Am I missing something here?"

"Temp, I just need to know what's going on, that's all."

"So do I, T, but right now I don't have time to deal with it."

He hung up. I sat at my desk staring at the door and the picture that hung next to it of a cow grazing on the grounds in front of the Capitol. A knot was tightening in my stomach. Miyako knocked on the door and stuck her head in. She looked at me quizzically.

"You all right?" she inquired.

"I'm okay," I answered. "What's up?"

"I've been holding your calls while you were in your meeting, and they're stacking up. Allen called again, so did Cheryl Tockenberry and an Anita from Accounting. Your mother also called three times."

"Mother called three times? Did she say what she wanted?"

"I couldn't quite make it out," replied Miyako delicately.

"Thanks," I said taking the messages. "I guess I'd better get to work."

Miyako turned to leave, "Are you sure you're okay?"

"Yes, I'm okay," I said offering her a weak, watery smile.

I shuffled through the messages trying to figure out what to do. Allen was my boss and returning his call took top priority. Also, I had a meeting in an hour with Cal Nguyn on a discipline problem he was having with one of his employees. I couldn't desert Cal now after he had done all the hard things that many supervisors shy away from, mainly supervise effectively. I needed to prepare for our meeting, review the employee's labor contract, take a look at his personnel file, things like that. Mother would just have to wait until I could get to her.

It was close to noon when I finally called Mother. She picked up the phone on the first ring.

"What took you so long?" she demanded right off. No hello, how are you doing, nothing. I just hate that.

"I called as soon as I could. This is the first chance I've had to even catch my breath."

"Well, never mind about all that. I need you to take some things to Sister Turner. She called this morning. She needs some things right away, but I can't take them because I have the children. So you have to do it."

"Look, Mother, I work for a living. I can't just take off anytime I want to go do errands for you and Mrs. Turner."

"Listen, miss, I know you work for a living. Your daddy and I worked long and hard just so you could get to where you are. So don't get so high and mighty, you forget where you come from and what other people did for you."

"Okay, okay," I moaned. I didn't have the stamina to listen to all twenty-two verses of Mother's version of that famous old classic, 'You Owe Me.' "What does she need?"

"Her Bible, some family papers, and some hair stuff."

"Mother, this hardly seems important enough for me to leave work. Couldn't I take it to her after work, on the way home or something?" I pleaded.

"No, I told her you'd bring it this morning, and it's already noon. The kids and I will go over and get it, and we'll have it ready when you get here," Mother said cheerfully and hung up the phone.

Mother's "little errands" have a way of expanding to consume all available time. A special meeting of the Deputy Directors' Personnel Advisory Board that I staff was scheduled for two-thirty. The allocation of the governor's most recent round of staffing cuts would be worked out at this meeting. I had to be there.

I dialed Allen again. His secretary put me through immediately.

"Allen," I said the minute he answered. "I'm afraid, I'll have to throw myself on the mercy of the court again. I really need to leave for a couple of hours, a family emergency. I'll be back in time for the advisory board meeting."

He sighed.

"Is it your mother?"

"Yes," I answered without elaborating. Most of my unscheduled absences have to do with Mother. At the end of the month when it's time to submit my attendance sheet, I tally up the absences and write "elder care" next to it. Mother would kill me if she knew that.

Allen had his first encounter with Mother about three years ago when she called for me and was told I was in a meeting. She demanded to be told who I was meeting with and was directed to his office. Unfortunately I had finished with Allen and had gone on to another meeting when Mother's call reached his office. Allen got off the phone forty-five minutes later after patiently taking down a list of sixteen items Mother wanted me to pick up at the store after work.

"Okay. I'll see you in a couple of hours. But, Theresa, have somebody act for you in your absence."

"Who would you like?" I asked.

"Anybody but Brenda Delacore," he answered.

I darted through the automatic doors just ahead of a woman in a wheelchair who flipped me the finger. My call to Allen had thrown my timing off, and I wasn't sure if I had missed the shuttle. If I had, I'd have to wait forty-five minutes for the next one. I decided to walk the eight blocks to the parking lot.

This could have been a pleasant walk if it hadn't been for the briefcase and tote bag I was lugging, the fact that I was wearing heels, and the Greek, an old man who has claimed the bench at the bus stop in front of the Social Services building at Seventh and P Streets as his parlor and political soapbox. The Greek spends the greater part of each day shouting at passersby in an unintelligible gibberish that sounds like Greek—hence his nickname. Today he was haranguing people in Swahili.

"Habari gani," he shouted at a man ahead of me who, with practiced skill, avoided looking in his direction.

"Habari gani."

The man didn't respond.

"Whole buncha' *gani,* motherfucka. *Izu Wazuri.*"

Still no response. The Greek picked a can from his pushcart, lowered his head, and studied it intently. Without looking, he lobbed the can at the man. His face still averted, the man did a little hop-skip step when the can hit him on the shoulder and quickened his pace, but he still refused to look at the Greek. The Greek threw another can and then another. In some parts of the city, aluminum cans are quasi-legal tender, the homeless's cowrie shells. The Greek was going to be sorry later on for squandering his riches. I knew better than to shop when I was hungry, and he had better learn to put his cans away when he was angry.

The Greek saw me.

"Izu Wazuri," he shouted.

"Use Afro Sheen," I responded.

His face softened, its contortions smoothing into a gap-toothed smile. He fell to his knees with his arms outstretched and professed his love for me.

I cut across the street and went into the Parks and Rec Building. The smokers standing outside were laughing. The Greek got up stiffly and ambled across the street after me, pushing his cart and loudly extolling my virtues. He came to the building and stopped at the double glass doors leading to the lobby.

"Come on back, my little why-toto wit' yo' fine self."

He closed his eyes, puckered his lips tightly, and fastened them to the glass door. His kiss was loud and heavy on sibilants. He swayed back and forth and rotated his rear provocatively. I left through the door on the other side of the lobby. The Greek was still engaged with his door and didn't see me go.

I fell into a syncopated rhythm, stepping to the swing of the tote bag I carried on one side and the slap of the briefcase against my leg on the other side. Soon I reached South Side Park, a pretty little patch of green in the middle of a sleepy residential area that has seen grander times. The Vietnamese, Hmongs, and other southeast Asians were out in large numbers fishing in the small man-made lake. I could see the parking lot from there, and I trotted to the end of the block, crossed W street, and made it to my car.

Mother's was about four or five miles away. It would only take me a few minutes to get there. That gave me just enough time to listen to Teddy Pendergast tell me how he was going to love me until the morning comes at least once before I got there. Teddy has a way of mellowing me out, and the one thing I was definitely in need of right now was a little mellowing. I slipped the cassette in, backed out of the parking space, and exited onto X Street.

On an impulse I decided to cruise by Emory Arceneux's house. I'd had a secret crush on Emory all during my high school years, and I used to get a rush every time I passed his house. Emory was a big, gentle giant of a fellow who turned down a starting position on the varsity football team his freshman year so he could work on the school's literary magazine. He wrote beautiful haiku back then. He's long since married and moved to Moreno Valley, where he drives a truck. Listening to Teddy Pendergast always made me think of Emory. I wondered if I'd feel anything of that old rush when I drove by.

To get to the Arceneuxs' house, I turned left on San Clemente Way instead of going down two more blocks to Mother's. The house was just as I remembered it, a pretty little pink cottage with white shutters and rose bushes lining the walkway.

Somewhere, a block or two over, I heard a car backfiring and someone screaming and more backfiring. Too repetitious, I thought, must be firecrackers.

A blast of rap music shattered the air, and before I knew what was happening, a car was bearing down on me on the wrong side of the street, guns extended from the windows. I threw my arms up in a futile attempt to shield myself. The car corrected itself, missing mine by inches and sped away. As the sound of rap faded, I thought I heard laughter.

I opened the door on the passenger side, crawled out, and vomited on Mrs. Arceneux's lawn. I got back into my car and turned the corner. This put me on Mother's street, one block away.

Now I heard screaming and dogs barking and one especially shrill voice crying, "Lord, have mercy," over and over. I began to pray. "Jesus ... Lord sweet Jesus ..."

There was smoke in the air. A crowd was forming in front of Mother's house, and I panicked. I stopped the car in the middle of the street, and got out and ran the rest of the way.

People were pointing at Mrs. Turner's house, not Mother's. I saw why. The windows had been blasted out and the door riddled with bullets. For about a sixteenth of a second, I was relieved that it was Mrs. Turner's house and not Mother's. Then it hit me, and before I knew it I found myself screaming, calling "Mother!" She was in there. Mother and the twins and Sir. I tore through the crowd and ran toward Mrs. Turner's yard. A man grabbed me.

"Hold her. Don't let her go in there," someone shouted.

"Poor child."

"Lord have mercy," the shrill voice cried.

Another pair of hands grabbed me. I tore away and dashed through the yard; losing my balance, I scrambled on my hands and knees before I righted myself and lunged toward the door.

The crowd fell silent. The two men who had tried to restrain me stopped a few feet away and watched me like spotters at a gymnastics match. I grabbed the doorknob and the door swung open. I stepped over splintered wood and broken glass and went in.

"Mother?" I called. Silence.

I checked the kitchen. The refrigerator and freezer were standing open. Dishes had crashed to the counters from open cabinet doors. Even the oven stood open. Every door in the house seemed to be open, including those to the cabinets on the service porch and the door leading to the backyard.

Slowly I retraced my steps to the front of the house. I was feeling a little more confident the house was empty, but I was still jumpy as I made my way to Mrs. Turner's room and the other end of the house. I passed the bathroom. The porcelain commode had been shattered by a bullet, and water was flooding the small room. The door to Mrs. Turner's room was closed. I tried the knob. It wouldn't turn. I shook the door, put my shoulder against it, and pushed. No use. It was locked. I thought back. Had Mother locked it when we left? I didn't think so. I know I hadn't. Why should we lock it as long as the doors to the outside were locked? Why was it locked now?

"Sister, you all right?"

It was one of the men who had tried to keep me from going into the house. He was standing at the end of the hallway looking nervous.

"I'm okay. I thought my mother and the kids were in here but they aren't, thank goodness. I just don't understand why this door is locked."

I could hear sirens in the distance.

The man said, "We'd better get out of here before the police come."

We went outside. Mrs. Turner's bedroom window was on the southern end of the house, facing the street. The window was completely shattered, and the curtains moved gently in the breeze.

"Give me a hand, will you?" I said to the man.

"Huh?"

"Give me a hand. I need you to lift me up so I can see in the window."

He looked up at the window, about five feet off the ground, and he looked at me.

I pried my shoes off.

"Come on," I pleaded. "Just a quick lift. I'm lighter than I look. Honest."

He sighed, bent over, and laced his fingers into a stirrup. I stepped into it and he hoisted me up.

A patch of sunlight cut through the darkened room and dust motes danced lazily in its beam. Dogs barked and somewhere, not too far away, I heard the insistent chirping of a cricket.

Mrs. Turner's bed had been torn apart, the mattresses cast to the floor and slit. Drawers hung from the dresser like protruding lips. The closet door stood open. Clothes and hangers were scattered on the floor. In some places, wallpaper hung from the wall in neat strips.

Mrs. Turner sat in an overstuffed chair. It had been shoved into a corner facing the window. She sat well back in the chair, her head leaning to one side as if she were tired, the other side of it was missing. I was screaming by the time I hit the ground.

Chapter 5

They tell me I was a mess, screaming and hollering and carrying on; it took Mother to calm me down. She ran out of the house, dragging half-dressed Andrea and Cenne with her. Mother had been washing their hair when the shooting started, and she'd grabbed them both and fallen to the floor. When the shooting stopped and her heart calmed down a bit, Mother climbed up from the floor, torn between getting the soap out of the girls' eyes and going to the window to investigate. She had just started to give them a quick rinse when she heard me screaming. When she reached me, sitting beneath Mrs. Turner's window, Andrea and Cenne still had suds in their hair.

A crowd grew. Children who should have been in school appeared on skateboards and bikes. Young girls pushing strollers gossiped among themselves. Several women Mother's age stood on the fringes and wept. Mother and the man got me and the twins into her house just as the police and emergency vehicles started to arrive.

"How did you know that was me?" I asked her later when we had both calmed down some.

"I just knew, that's all. Don't you think I'd know the sound of my own child anywhere?"

We sat quietly for a while. Mother put her head down and cried. I cried, too. The twins looked at us and sucked their thumbs. Outside, the mood of the crowd had grown festive. I could hear the incessant pounding of a boom box over the cackle of police radios. The police were barricading the area and trying to move back the curious. But the crowd was excited. It saw the bullet holes and havoc they wreaked; it smelled the pungent odor of cordite, and it wasn't moving, at least not very far, until it saw a body—it had better be a bloody one, too. The mothers of the neighborhood, the women Mother's age, the empty nesters and widows, the healers and soothers, returned to their houses and stood behind their barred windows and prayed.

Mrs. Turner's death had come so swiftly, so unexpectedly, and so brutally, I was having a hard time handling so many disparate emotions and incongruities. I turned to Mother for help.

"Something just isn't right. What was Mrs. Turner doing at home in the first place? I thought she was in the hospital. Isn't that right, Mother? When she called she was still in the hospital, and she wanted me to bring her Bible and some other stuff. Right?"

Mother dabbed her eyes. "She called from the hospital just after I got the kids fed."

"Are you certain she was calling from the hospital? I mean, could she have been already home or something?"

"No, she was calling from the hospital. Someone came in to take her breakfast tray while she was on the phone, and I could hear her telling Sister Turner she did a good job. Besides, why would she ask us to go to her house and find something and take it somewhere else, if she was already there in the first place?"

"Mother, this just doesn't make sense. What time did Mrs. Turner call?"

"Around nine-thirty."

"And you called me right after that. I got here around twelve-thirty and . . ." Mother was tearing up again. I went to her and put my arms around her.

"Sister Turner was such a good woman, such a kind, sweet, loving, Christian woman. She didn't deserve to die like that—just snatched away from here before her time."

Mother got up, went to the buffet, and picked up the family Bible she kept on top of it. It had been her mother's, who had passed it down to her, and before that it had belonged to her mother's mother, my great-grand-mother. Someday it would probably be mine. It was a humped-back volume, stuffed full of family papers, birth certificates, marriage licenses, old obituaries and, who knows, maybe even manumission papers. Mother sat down, opened the Bible to a passage, and read it silently. When she finished, she closed the book, clasped it to her chest, and sat with her eyes closed, rocking gently.

Tears welled up in my eyes again. Times like this always remind me of when Carolyn died. Carolyn had been three years my senior, but she was more than simply my big sister. She'd been a vital part of me, the right lobe to my left lobe sensibility. She was Carolyn the trail-blazer, the first one in our family to defiantly sport a natural, the first to go to college, and the first (and only one) to use the "f" word in earshot of Mother and live to tell about it.

Her death had come just as unexpectedly and as violently as Mrs. Turner's, but in a subtler, more insidious way. One moment, she was moving like a whirlwind, Miss pseudo-hippie, U. C. Berkeley coed; the next, she was home unexpectedly, announcing quite simply, "Mother, I'm so tired."

I believe, deep down inside, Mother saw Carolyn's death as a final act of defiance—the leukemia diagnosis, no matter how virulent the form, meant absolutely nothing to her. No child dies simply of being tired, at least not when a mother is praying as hard as Mother was, certainly not when a mother is making wildly aggressive statements of hope. But Carolyn did. She grew weaker and weaker until she was not strong enough to go on living, and she died.

And there I was, the hapless survivor, thrust into a stewardship I was hardly prepared for. In one fell swoop I became both the oldest child and middle child. I suffered the burden of a doubling in my filial responsibilities, yet I still felt compelled to continue to try harder. Jimmy opted out, joined the army, got stationed in Germany, and married a white girl. Now he only comes home for funerals. Most of Mother's other relatives are either down South or back East.

Carolyn's death and then Daddy's, and Jimmy's defection, created a huge vacuum in Mother's life that I felt compelled to fill. I ended up getting caught smack dab in the middle of the "sandwich generation," trying to juggle a career, raise a family, and be there for Mother, too.

Mother placed the Bible on the end table and stood up abruptly. "Theresa, we're going to find those little bastards who killed Sister Turner."

I was more shocked by her language than by her vigilantism. Mother simply doesn't go in for the hard-core cussing. Sure I've heard her say a "damn" now and then and a "hell" or two, but I'd never heard her call anyone a bastard before.

Her cursing disturbed me, but the direction things were heading scared me, and I remembered my New Year's resolution to stay out of Mother's messes. This time I was staying clear. She wouldn't get me caught up like she did last year when she nearly convinced me that poor old Mr. Samuels was really D. B. Cooper, and the hijack money was stashed in that old backpack Mr. Samuels wore everywhere he went. Or the time Mrs. Ortiz, three houses down, went to visit family in Mexico but Mother insisted that Mr. Ortiz, who was overly fond of the bottle, had killed her and plastered her body up in a wall. No, not this time. But I thought about Mrs. Turner sitting in that chair with part of her head missing, and I got angry. And I thought about that car bearing down on me on the wrong side of the street with rap music blaring and guns sticking out the windows, and I got angrier. Finally I thought about Sir and the twins, without a daddy and, for all intents and purposes, without a mother either, and the one person who loved them and cared for them brutally murdered. I got so angry, I was just about ready to sign up and join Mother's posse.

I looked around the room. I had never known Mother to discard anything. Everything she had ever owned was right here, in the living room, in the dining room, in the kitchen, in the bedrooms, in the bathroom, and on the service porch. It was piled on tables, stuffed under sofas, stacked on chairs. Maybe it had something to do with growing up during the Depression, I don't know. Over the years, intricate, indirect paths had been worn through to various locations in the house. The house had an air of controlled chaos that I found comforting right now.

Andrea and Cenne lay intertwined like two kittens, sleeping in a gentle swath of sunlight near the window. I surveyed the room again. Something was missing, but I didn't know what. Then it dawned on me—Sir.

"Mother, where's Sir?"

"Where is Sir? He was in the bedroom watching TV before . . ." her voice trailed off.

'Sir," I called as I hurdled over a laundry basket full of books and loose beads and headed for Mother's room. I checked the bathroom and the other bedroom as well as Mother's, but a part of me knew I wouldn't find him there.

I went back to the living room.

"He's not here."

"I thought he'd been sneaking out of the house. Just wait till I catch him. I'm going to tear his little behind up."

"Mother."

"What?"

"This is serious."

"Wait till I get my hands on that mannish little boy. I'll show you who's serious."

I was having difficulty breathing. I felt a tightness in my chest like when my hiatal hernia was acting up, only magnified a hundred times. I was struggling to speak above a whisper.

"Mother, listen to me carefully. I checked the house after the shooting. I was scared you and the kids got caught inside. But I'm not sure I checked really good. I'm not certain Sir wasn't in there."

I opened Mother's front door with some trepidation. I didn't know how I was going to finesse getting the information I needed about Sir without calling too much attention to myself. I had a feeling the police would not be thrilled to know I had gone through the house before they got there. One thing I knew, I had to steady my legs and get rid of the quirky things my voice was doing. They say police can smell fear. The problem is, they don't always identify it accurately—sometimes they confuse it with guilt.

New players had been added to the scene since I last peeked out of Mother's window. I saw Melinda Cropp with KCRA news and a couple of other people with video cameras. I also saw Malcolm Lyle from the *Bee*, his shaved head gleaming in the sun. Children cavorted on skateboards and did wheelies on dirt bikes. Some people in neighboring houses had moved patio furniture to the front yards and sat fanning themselves and watching.

I approached a police officer stationed in front of Mrs. Turner's house who was busy trying to shoo away a couple of kids who looked to be no more than five years old. I heard one call him a "cheese-faced mothafucka'."

"Excuse me, Officer . . ."

"Step back, lady," he barked. "Can't you people see this is a police barricade? Can't anyone around here read, for gosh sake? That says 'Police, Keep Out.' "

His ears were prominent and very red. His face was slick with sweat and exasperation.

"I came to get these boys," I said, and grabbed the two tykes by the wrists. They looked up at me as if to say, "I know you crazy."

I pulled them away from the barricade. They struggled against me, but I know a trick or two when it comes to restraint and control of sandbox ninjas—never grab them by the hand or by the clothing, for that matter, they just wiggle away. Grab them by the wrist, out of the reach of their little fingers, and clamp down. If they resist too much, tighten your grasp even more. They'll get the message.

"You guys oughta leave the police alone. Don't you see he has a gun? He could shoot you."

The one with the multiple lines carved in his hair sneered, "He ain't gon' shoot me. My daddy kick his ass."

"What's your name, little brother?" I asked still clutching them both tightly.

"My name Jamal," said the leader of the two.

If each Black boy named Jamal was given a number, this kid probably would have been number 900 million. It seems that somewhere along the line, probably in 1975, a secret message was sent out to Black mothers, "Name your child Jamal, and you shall be set free."

"My name Ndugu," said the other.

"I'm Theresa. Listen up, Jamal and Ndugu, I need your help. Did you see what happened?"

"Yeah," they both answered, nodding their heads vigorously.

"Well, what happened exactly?"

"They come and they shoot up the place. Bam, bam, bam, bam," said Jamal.

"Yeah, bam, bam, bam, bam," confirmed Ndugu.

"Did they come on the bus or in a car?" I queried.

They had to think about their answer. This was not a good sign.

"They shoot the place up in a car," answered Ndugu triumphantly.

I decided to take a different tack. "Do either of you know a brother name Sir?"

"Yeah, Sir live where they shoot up the house."

"Did you see Sir today?"

"Yeah."

"When?"

"We playing in the yard, and Sir come through his fence. And we say . . ."

"Wait a minute. What fence? Where do you live?"

"Over there." They both pointed at Mrs. Turner's house.

"You live in back of Mrs. Turner? Is that your house with the green roof?"

"No, not that one. That where Miz Fellow live," said Jamal. "She blind."

"Yeah, she can't see." added Ndugu. "She hit you wit' her stick if you mess wit' her."

"The other one next to it where we live," they pointed to the right.

"The one with the big tree?"

"Yeah. We have a swing an' a house in it an' everything."

"Okay. That's nice. Now tell me about when you saw Sir."

"We playing in the yard. Then the lady goes in Miz Fellow's yard and goes through the fence to Sir's yard. Then Sir comes out his yard and goes in Miz Fellow's yard. An' I say, uh-oh, somebody gon' git hit wit' that stick."

"What lady?" I asked.

"I dunno. She comes and she goes through the fence sometimes."

"What does she look like?"

"She real ugly."

"Yeah. She look like a witch."

"Okay," I said. I decided to throw in another trick question to test their reliability.

"Did you see Sir before the shooting or afterward?"

They gave a me look of incredulity tinged with pity. The kind of look the Greek often gets.

"Bee—fore," they dragged the word out for emphasis.

"Okay. Did you say anything to Sir when you saw him?"

"Yeah. We say, 'Hey, Sir.' An' he put his finger over his mouth an' he say, 'Be quiet.' An' we jump down from the tree, an' we meet him out front, an' we say, 'You gon get hit wit that stick,' an' we laughing. An' he say, 'That lady went in Grand's house.' An we say, 'Uh-huh.' An' we say, 'Did she see you?' and he say, 'Naw, I was hiding.' An' we say, 'You better go tell somebody,' and he say, 'It's okay, I hid everything.' "

"What did he hide?"

"Everything!"

"What did he do after that?"

"He went back to the other lady's house."

"What other lady?"

"You know."

"Oh, you mean my mother's house?"

"Yeah."

"Are you sure he went back? He's not there now."

"Yeah, we sure. We went with him 'cause he had to sneak back in, but he couldn't cause the door lock."

"We say, 'Oh, you gon' git a whupin' now.' He try act

all bad like he ain't scared. He say he got a black belt an ain't nobody gon mess wit' him.''

"I say you ain't got no black belt. I a yellow belt, stripe, and I know. An' I say if you so bad, do this. An' I do a twin crane extension and he can't do it, he don't even try. Just keep wiping his ole eyes like a baby.''

"He didn't go back in, then.''

"No, he say, 'I gon go find my mama.' ''

"An' we start laughing. We say yo mama have her high beams on. She be geeking and tweeking.''

"An' he start running. An' we run, too, but we laughing too hard, an' then we see T-bo an we ...''

"Wait a minute. Where did he go?''

"Where his mama is.''

"Okay, which way did he go?''

"He went up that way an' he cut through the churchyard, an' then we saw T-bo an' we went with him to the store.''

They pointed to toward Santa Ana Street. The nearest church, Mt. Pleasant Baptist, was two blocks over going toward Martin Luther King, Jr., Drive.

"An' did you see him anymore after that?''

"Naw. We went over to T-bo's house and played Nintendo, but his mama came home and she said T-bo supposed to be sick, and she take off work to see 'bout him and he up running the streets an' ...''

"Do you know where Sir's mother is?''

"No, but T-bo do. He say she be geeking and tweeking, and somebody gon' smoke her. They gon' blow her brains out.''

"Listen, this is important. If you see Sir or his mother, will you let me know? I'll give you five dollars each if you do.''

It dawned on me just then that I didn't have my purse. I'd left it in the car, and it wasn't exactly parked in a legal space. I craned my neck, straining to see if it was still where I'd abandoned it. It was, but a policeman was standing in front of it with his foot on the fender. It looked like he was in the process of writing a ticket.

"Wait here," I called over my shoulder to Jamal and Ndugu.

"Excuse me, Officer, I'll move it."

He waited a count of ten before he turned to look at me and another five before he spoke.

"This your car?"

"Yes."

"Let me see your ID, please."

"I'm sorry, but it's in the car. My purse is on the floor under the passenger seat."

"What's your name and address?"

"Theresa Nicole Galloway, 6562 Oyster Bay Drive."

He verified it against information he already had from running a check on the computer in his patrol car.

"All right, Mrs. Galloway, please remove your purse from the car and show me your ID."

I did. He verified my identity.

"We're running a check on every car parked on the street—standard procedure. Would you mind telling me why your car is parked in this manner?"

"I didn't actually park it. When I turned the corner and saw what had happened, I panicked. My mother was a friend of Mrs. Turner's, and I was worried that she might have been in the house or something."

"Were you in the vicinity when the shooting occurred?"

"No, I was a couple of blocks away, but I think I saw the car."

"Could you describe it?"

"It's kinda hard. I was on San Clemente Way when I heard what I thought were gunshots, and a car came hurtling around the corner from Santa Clara on two wheels, on the wrong side of the street. For the life of me I can't remember what the car looked like. I just saw guns . . ."

"What kind of guns?"

"I don't know. Terminator-type stuff."

"Were they handguns, automatic weapons, small, medium, or large?"

"Kinda large, probably automatic weapons. I don't know much about guns. All I know is I saw them, and I'll never forget that."

"Did you see the driver of the vehicle or the passengers?"

"Yes, but I didn't see them well enough to describe them. The only thing I remember is seeing a bandanna or two."

"What color?"

"Oh, a primary color. Either red or blue."

He looked up from his notepad. Without saying a word, he closed it, took out his ticket book, and wrote out a ticket. When he finished writing, he tore it out and thrust it at me.

"What's this?"

"Read it, lady. It's a ticket for abandoning your vehicle. You are also in violation of vehicle code 2440, and if it isn't taken care of pretty soon it's going to turn into a warrant. And next time don't play with me or any other officer of the law."

"But I wasn't playing, honest . . ."

"Just a minute."

He stepped away to talk to a man in a gray suit. They both turned to look at me. The man dug into his coat pocket and gave him a card. The officer came back to where I was standing and handed it to me.

"Please go by the police station tomorrow and make a statement. You should see Detective Rausher."

"Can I take my car now?"

"Be my guest."

"Officer, just one thing. During the excitement my nephew ran out of the house, and I don't seem to be able to find him. You don't think he could have run into Mrs. Turner's house, do you?"

He looked at me for a long time. I realized he was doing his version of Eastwood with the deliberate pauses.

"It's unlikely," he said, and walked away. He stopped and turned back to me. "Why did you say your mother *was* a friend of Mrs. Turner?"

"Well, I assumed that Mrs. Turner was . . . I saw the coroner's van and I just assumed . . ."

Satisfied, he said, "Well, just make sure you get that heap out of the way." He turned and walked away.

I got in the car. The keys were still in the ignition.

Miracles do indeed happen, I thought to myself. I backed up carefully and parked on the street. I got my purse and locked the door. I was mad. Not only had I gotten a ticket, but I had been insulted in the process. Calling my car a heap. Nobody with any sense would call a 325i a heap.

It looked like the coroner was getting ready to move Mrs. Turner's body, and a hush fell over the street. Fahsaad's Ice Cream and Frozen Delicacies lumbered into sight, followed by the tinny sound of canned calliope music. The handful of kids on the street shuddered with delight and scurried off en masse to the battered van. I followed, looking for Jamal and Ndugu. I found them and gave Jamal one of my cards. It said: Theresa N. Galloway, Chief Personnel Office, Department of Environmental Equity. It had my phone and fax number. I wrote mother's phone number on the back and told them to call me if they saw Sir or his mother. Ndugu stuck his lip out, and I gave him a card, too. I handed them two dollars to buy ice cream and headed back to Mother's.

From the information I'd been able to gather, I didn't think Sir had gotten caught in Mrs. Turner's house. But that didn't set my mind at ease any, because if Jamal and Ndugu were to be believed, he was somewhere far more dangerous.

Chapter 6

Mother was pacing the floor when I got back. I told her about my two informants, and she was skeptical, to say the least.

"Child, I send you out to see about the boy, and you come back telling me some trash those little Williams brats made up."

"Look, Mother, quite frankly, I think we should report Sir missing to the police. Maybe they can put out an all points bulletin or something. This is serious, and I don't think we should mess around with it. Now, as far as what Jamal and Ndugu told me, that's the best we have to go on. I know some of the stuff sounds pretty far-fetched, in fact, it bordered on fantasy, but I think I'm pretty good at picking out fact from fiction. What we need to do now is figure out where LaTreace is, where she crashes when she's not at Mrs. Turner's. But if we don't find him before dark, we'd better report him missing."

Mother shook her head.

"I just don't know. I don't want these children to end up torn apart and scattered in foster homes with strangers. We got to keep them together until we can get in contact with their people. We promised. Lord knows, I'm real worried about Sir, though. This city is no place for a little boy to be running around by himself. It's just too dangerous. And he's probably worse off if he's with that LaTreace, his so-called mother."

The phone rang and we both jumped. Mother had to find it before she could answer it. She traced the cord hand over hand to the hallway outside the bathroom, where she found it under a pile of towels. She must have a hundred-foot cord on that thing. I don't know why she doesn't just have an extension put in. Maybe it's the thrill of the hunt.

"Oh, Edna," said Mother, "you heard." Mother put her hand over the receiver and turned to me, "It's Edna. She heard about Sister Turner."

Edna is one of Mother's oldest friends. They both came to Sacramento from Shreveport, Louisiana, in the forties to work at McClellan Airbase during World War II. It surprised me that Edna had heard about Mrs. Turner so soon. But then again, it shouldn't have. Edna is one of those people who seem to have their fingers on so many pulses. She had a way of knowing things that was downright uncanny. They say Louisiana people can be funny that way.

Mother turned to me again, "Edna says, LaTreace has people over on Quintin Street, a cousin on her daddy's side. She says you should check over there and see if she's there or if she took Sir there."

"Okay, Quintin Street. What's the address?"

"She says it's the house near the corner, sits back some from the street, the people next door have a lot of old cars parked on the lawn. You can't miss it."

"Can't miss it. Mother, I hate to sound like the pizza deliveryman, but can't you give me a cross street or something?"

"Edna, what's the cross street? Uh-huh, you know how children are, they're so particular these days. Got to have everything laid out for them just so or they can't function. Uh-huh, oh yes, that's right."

Mother turned to me. "She says the cross street is Fourteenth Avenue. You'll recognize the house, it's the one used to belong to Mother Simms."

I knew of Mother Simms, although I wasn't one of her groupies like Mother and some of her friends who believe Mother Simms can stop headaches just by clasping your head between her hands. I know a lot of Mother Simms lore, I just didn't know where she used to live. Mother finished with Edna Thompson and hung up the phone.

I looked at my watch. It was a few minutes after two. I had to get back to work, and I was feeling uneasy about the escapade Mother and Edna had planned for me.

"I don't know, Mother. I still think we should inform the police that Sir is missing and let them apply some scientific search methods to find him. I think they stand a better chance of finding him than I do. Besides, I've got to get back to work."

"Child, all the police would do is what you're going to do except they wouldn't know to check with LaTreace's daddy's people because they wouldn't have sense enough to go talk to Edna and find out in the first place. Besides, if the police do find him, then what? The county gets him and probably the twins, too, and you know we can't let that happen. You have a jump on the police. You know LaTreace has other people here in town besides Sister Turner, and you know where they live. Now, all you have to do is go see if Sir is there. It won't take more than a couple of minutes."

"I can't go barging into somebody's house, demanding to see a child I have absolutely no legal rights to."

"Yes, you can, baby. Just show them one of those cards you always handing out and tell them you're from the county and you've come to get the boy."

"Mother, I work for the state not the county. I'm a personnel officer, for goodness sake, not a social worker or something. I can't do that."

"Yes, you can, honey. Nobody reads them ole cards anyway. Just do like I'm telling. It'll work."

"Suppose LaTreace is there. She knows who I am. She may be a junkie, but she's no fool."

"All the better if LaTreace is there. Just tell her you came to get Sir and to give her the money you owe her. You're right about one thing, the child is no fool. I guarantee you she will take the money and hand the boy over."

"That may work."

"Of course it will work. How much money do you have on you?"

I checked my purse. "Forty-two dollars, and some change."

"Here," Mother said reaching into her bosom and extracting a baby's sock, tied at the neck. Picking the knot open, she removed three twenties and a fifty dollar bill. "Take this, too."

"I think she'll settle for a lot less. Just give me the three twenties."

"This is not the time to haggle over the price of a child," Mother snapped, surprising me with her intensity. "Give her everything we have. We've got to make it easy for her."

I took the money from Mother, declining her offer of the safety sock. She reached under the cushion at the end of the sofa and pulled out a handgun.

"Here," she said, "take this with you."

"What's this?" I asked dumbly.

"It's for protection, just in case."

"Mother, where did you get that gun?"

"It was your daddy's, now it's mine," she said matter-of-factly as she slapped a clip of bullets into the handle and pulled the slide back, releasing it with a snap that made me jump. "Sig Hauer P230," she said, extending her arm and sighting the lamp in the corner of the room. "It's the kind the police use."

I stared at Mother mutely. I hate to admit it, but I think my mouth was hanging open. It's funny how you can live with a person for years and still not really know them. I never even knew Mother had a gun, much less knew how to use one. I really don't like these kinds of surprises.

"You don't think I'd sit up in this house by myself without some kinda protection, do you?"

"I can't take that. I don't know how to use it and, to be perfectly honest, Mother, I'm afraid of the thing."

"Aw, it's nothing to be scared of, just a little ole gun. There's a whole lot more things out there more scary than this. I don't think you'll need it, but I'll feel a lot better knowing you have it."

"I don't know how to ... operate it."

"Don't be a fool, child. You just take the thing, point it, and pull the trigger."

I was too tired to argue. Besides I worried about getting back to work in time for my two-thirty meeting, so I took the gun, stuffed it in my purse, and left to find the house where Mother Simms used to live.

The different sections of Oak Park are as varied as a patchwork quilt. Just about everybody on Mother's street owns the houses they live in, and it shows in the way lawns are cared for, the way houses are painted, and the way sidewalks are swept. Two blocks over in either direction is a different story. As older homeowners died or sold their houses and moved into rest homes, investors bought them or the children inherited them and rented them out. With the renters and absentee landlords came patchy lawns in baked-out front yards, discarded sofas in the gutters, abandoned cars, wild dogs, wild children, and loud music. That just about describes Quintin Street.

Zigging and zagging several times on its route from the freeway to Stockton Boulevard, Fourteenth Avenue changes names in a couple of places and identities in others. Quintin Street is a narrow, residential street, running not more than two blocks between Fourteenth Avenue and Truxton Way. I found it more by accident than by directions. Quinton Street was jumping with activity. Drivers paraded up and down the street, some stopping without regard to those behind them to talk to pedestrians or each other. I saw at least one other 325i on the street. Children rode skateboards and bikes with abandon. Several houses had cars parked on the lawn. The house I wanted was trimmed in blue, the walkway carefully edged in brick. It had a camellia bush in the front yard that was as tall as a small tree. Next door to it teenage boys sat on the rusted-out hulk of an old car drinking malt liquor from tall cans, laughing and pounding each other's fists.

Inside the house with blue trim, a child was screaming. It was a wild, hoarse sound, with a touch of vibrato and just enough screech to make my skin crawl. I wanted to run to the house with the blue trim and tear the door off its hinges and find the child and comfort it, but I couldn't because I was scared. I wanted to drive away as fast as I could, never looking back, and go all the way home and get both my children and put them in bed

with me. But I couldn't do that either. Sir might be in
the house with blue trim, and if not Sir, then surely somebody else's child. So I parked my car, got out, and
walked up the path edged in brick to the house.

The child began to scream, "Mama, Mama, Mama,"
almost like a chant. I heard the strong voice of a man
methodically talking himself through acts of mayhem.
"I'm—gon'—fuck—you—up—bitch," each word accented with the sharp sound of flesh being struck and
the ripe thud of something heavy striking the wall.

I got to the door, stopped, and looked over at the boys
on the car. They watched me intently. "Call the police,"
I said to them. They looked at each other and burst out
laughing. One threw his heels up in the air and rolled
down the hood of the car, he was laughing so hard.

I turned back to the house. The front door stood open.
It was a standard hollow-core entry door, painted blue
to match the trim on the house. A screen door with
ornate scrolls blocked my entrance. It was held shut by
a thin hook latch. I grabbed the screen door and shook
it hard. "Open up," I barked with as much authority as
I could muster.

The boys on the car started to laugh again, and I
whirled around to face them. I shouldn't have ever
turned away from that door, I know that now, but that's
hindsight and you know what they say about hindsight.
Before I could vent my anger and fear on the boys, their
laughter was silenced by a flash of light so brilliant it
seemed to freeze the comical expressions on their faces.
It was followed by a noise so thunderous, I cast a furtive
glance to the sky, fearing for a second we were being
bombed from above like in Iraq.

That's about as far as my intellect will take me. I remember the events and can recount them for anybody
who asks, but it's more like retelling a story that somebody else told me, that I've heard enough times to tell
convincingly. There are parts that I can't explain. No
matter how hard I try, I can't articulate the funky odor
of fear, the base taste of my own blood in my mouth,
and the knowledge, the brain-numbing knowledge that I
almost killed a man. I came so close to shooting another

human being, right in front of his little girl and his wife with three ribs kicked in and some boys on an old rusted-out hunk of a car who were cheering.

The woman came through the screen door without unlatching it, nearly taking it off the hinges and pinning me between it and the outside wall. She stumbled and went down on her hands and knees, still clutching a gun, her head lowered as if in prayer.

"Run, Mama," urged the child from the doorway.

The woman looked up groggily, but before she could react, the man came out after her. His shirtsleeve was torn, and there was blood on his arm. He reached her in three strides. Stopping just short of where she crouched, he took a hop step on one foot and kicked her solidly in the stomach with the other. His kick lifted her off the ground, and he shook her off his foot and stood hunched over, panting. She doubled up retching. Her dress came up—she had a pin in the waistband of her panties. There was dirt in her hair. The child screamed and ran at him, her arms extended in weird angles, her fingers bent into claws. But I beat her to him.

I went for him without thinking, without even considering that I was overweight and overage and unused to unnecessary physical exertion, particularly street brawling. I forgot all about the Anne Klein I was wearing, the fiberglass nails, and the $90 I'd given Thomas at the Hair Doctor to make me look like Naomi Campbell.

I grabbed his head with both hands and yanked downward, twisting it at the same time and smashing it into my knee as he went down. He fell forward, a witless look of astonishment on his face, mine registering something similar. But it was not going to be that easy. As he went down, he grabbed me by the legs, just below the knees, and by the time I hit the ground he was climbing my chest, choking me with both hands and banging my head against the concrete walk. He was killing me. I was dying but I wasn't scared and I wasn't sad, I was angry. I was angry for being there in the first place, angry for rushing him when I had a gun in my purse, and angry enough to kill him if I ever got loose.

He continued to bang my head and choke me. Suddenly he stopped and turned his head slightly to the side as if someone almost beyond his range of hearing was calling him. Then he clasped his head with both hands and fell over, making a shrill keening noise. When he fell, I saw the child standing there holding a brick like the ones that edged the walkway. The woman was back up on her hands and knees, patting the ground around her. One of her eyes was swollen shut. Bloody spit bubbled from the corner of her mouth each time she exhaled.

"Help Mama find the gun, baby. Find the gun," she called to the child.

The man stirred. I looked around for the gun, too, scrambling about on my hands and knees. The boys on the car shouted, "You gettin' hot. Naw, naw, now you gettin' cold." I ignored them. The man was up on his knees now, and I was desperate to find the gun first and crazy with fear about what would happen if I didn't. The child stood frozen, unable to do any more than she had already. I saw a blue-green glint of light near the camellia bush and lunged for it, the man lunging for me. But I was quicker that he was, and I grabbed the gun, rolled over to my side and raised myself to a crouch, pointing it at his chest. It was heavy, so I held it with both hands. He froze, staring at the barrel.

"Shoot the mothafucka'," said the woman with unnatural calm. "Kill his ass."

I wanted to. I knew how. Mother said, just point it and pull the trigger. It seemed so easy, a fitting act of closure for this contest. The boys began to chant, "Smoke the mothafucka'."

"Shoot him," the woman said again through clenched teeth.

A crowd had gathered. The man stood up straight and so did I, the gun still leveled at his chest. His eyes darted from me to the woman and back again. He parted his lips and smiled. It was a slow, shag-nasty smile, full of evil. It made me want to spit, but it produced a peculiar surge of energy in the woman, who turned one way and then the other, searching for something. The child stood frozen between the man and the woman. He took a step toward me, and I tightened my grip on the gun. Adrenaline pumped through me like some wild sex hormone.

"I will shoot," I said to him.

He smiled again and took a step backward.

The woman ran to the side of the house just as the man grabbed the child, a split second before I decided to shoot him. I relaxed my finger on the trigger. The gun was greasy with sweat. I didn't know what to do, and I was scared now.

"That's whack, man. Put the kid down, mothafucka'," shouted one of the boys.

But before he had a chance, the woman came back. She was holding a shovel in both hands high over her head, and she brought it down with all her strength on the back of his. He relaxed his grip, and the child slid to the ground. Dazed, he turned to the woman, and she smashed him in the face twice before he finally crumpled. A "ooh" went up from the crowd, the boys started to cheer, "Hey, ho, hey, ho . . ."

She wanted to continue to beat him with the shovel, even after it was obvious he wasn't going to get back up, but I stopped her.

"Have you seen LaTreace? She inside?" She wasn't tracking. I grabbed her by the shoulders and spoke into her face. "LaTreace, Sir, do you know where they are?" She nodded. "They inside?" I repeated. She shook her head no. The child was sitting where she had been dropped, breathing so rapidly she appeared to be hyperventilating.

"Come on," I said to the woman. "I'd better get you to the hospital." I retrieved my purse by the front door, where I'd dropped it, and searched futilely for my other shoe. They're Jourdans and I really wanted to find it, but I gave up after a while. The crowd had thinned, and the boys had wandered off and were talking to two girls with babies in strollers. The man lay where he had fallen. The woman picked up the gun from where I had dropped it and went into the house. A moment later she came out carrying her purse. I didn't see the gun.

"Come on," I said as I limped to the car in one shoe. The woman and the girl followed meekly. I stuck my hand into my purse to fish out my keys, and a jalapeño pain shot through my thumb. I jerked my hand out and examined it. The fiberglass nail had almost been torn off. Had it been the old-fashioned, low-tech kind, the tip would have simply broken off unnoticed. But these were ultrachic, lightweight, guaranteed to last a lifetime, fiberglass. Chemically bonded to the nail surface, a thin layer at a time, until a very good facsimile of a long, elegant, perfectly shaped nail is created; fiberglass nails are just about indestructible. The only problem is they don't breathe and they don't give. I was frugging with pain.

I managed to get the door open and us loaded in the car. The woman sat in the front, the child refused to get in the back and sat huddled in her lap. They ignored my announcement that seat belts were required. We pulled off from the house with hardly a notice from the street circus. I barely made it to the end of the block before I was overcome with chills. Then a wave of nausea washed over me, and I got hot and I had chills again all in a matter of seconds. I turned on Fourteenth Avenue, but I couldn't go any farther, so I pulled over in front of a house with a "FOR RENT" sign in the window. I put my head down on the steering wheel. Reality fought its way through the receding adrenaline, and I began to shake uncontrollably. What had I done? Had I really been rolling around on the ground in the dirt like some common streetwalker? Had I really come this close to killing a man? Was I losing my mind? My head was pounding. I opened the door, spit out blood, and began to retch. Now, I thought to myself, I'm puking on the side of the road like a drunk.

I straightened up, closed the door, and pulled away from the curb. Turning to the woman, I said, "I'm taking you to the University Medical Center. That okay?" She nodded.

"What was that all about? Why'd he jump on you?"

"I called his mother a ho'."

"You called his mother a ho'?" I said with disbelief.

"I got tired of him messing wit' me," she said stubbornly.

"You called his mother a ho'," I repeated dumbly.

I looked down. My suit was streaked with dirt, a button was missing from the jacket, and one of the pockets hung from a single thread. I had on one shoe. My head hurt so bad I was seeing double. All because I had risked my life for a fool, and I still didn't know where Sir was.

"Can I turn the radio on?" the woman asked.

"No!" I screamed, startling her, the child, and myself. We drove in silence for a couple of blocks. The only sounds were a hissing noise the woman made as she breathed, punctuated by the child's muffled sobs.

I was still grappling with what I'd done just a short while ago. Had I reverted, like a bad press and curl, to a me I didn't even know? I've been accused of thinking I was "better than people" usually by those same social analysts who accuse me of "sounding white." I have long since come to grips with those criticisms. I don't necessarily think I am better than anybody, but I am better behaved than many. There are just some things I wouldn't dream of doing. I can't see myself hurting a child, for any reason. I know some people believe the best way to teach is with pain. A friend of mine, not a very close one, more like an acquaintance, taught her three-year-old to recite the alphabet by drilling him over and over, stinging his bare legs with a switch each time he made a mistake. I've seen people beat children for bad report cards, wet beds, rolled eyes, minor misbehavior, something as vague as a bad attitude, whatever. I guess we beat our children because our parents beat us and we came out all right, and their parents beat them and you go so far you find yourself right back in slavery with somebody standing over you holding a whip.

Also, I can't see myself being disrespectful to an old person. I don't know, it just doesn't seem right. I can't even prep my mouth to say anything discourteous to anybody twenty years older than me. As for infidelity, it's out of the question. I don't believe in it and even if I did, I don't have the energy for it. I'm loyal, trustworthy, and friendly. If I were a dog, I'd be Lassie, never a bitch. So, how do I account for today? How do I separate myself from them—those other folk out there who aren't as good as I? I'd calmly held a gun in my hand, extended from my body, supported with both hands, and I had contemplated—no, planned, prepared, was ready—to shoot a man. I was twisting and turning in my guilt and shame, and I just couldn't get comfortable. I turned to the woman.

"You were trying to kill him, weren't you?"

"No."

"Yes, you were. You had the gun and you tried to shoot him, then you tried to get me to shoot him." I almost pointed my finger at her and screamed, "It's your fault! I'm going to tell!"

"He the one. He tried to shoot me."

"You had the gun," I corrected.

"I had Baby . . ."

"Baby?"

"The Browning."

"Huh?"

"The piece, the ghat, the gun, shit. I had the gun, but I was just trying to keep him off me, that's all. I wasn't going to shoot him."

"No, you didn't need to, not with me there eager to come to your rescue, eager to do your bidding."

The woman closed her eyes and rested her forehead on the top of the child's head.

"You shot at him," I said. "You shot at him while you were inside the house. He was probably acting in self-defense or something. Just trying to protect himself from you." I almost said "the likes of you," but I didn't think that would go over too good, so I didn't.

The woman raised her head and sighed.

"He shot at me with that piece'a gun he made, supposed to shoot potatoes and shit. It blew up in his hands, stuff burnt me all in my face. Must'a burnt him, too, but he don't feel nothing anyway—nothing but his buzz."

This woman must really think I'm a fool. Potato gun. Nobody in their right mind would believe such nonsense, "such out-and-out folderol," to quote Mother. Pretty soon she'd be trying to bump my head. In spite of my doubts about her truthfulness, I studied her more closely. Her face was a landscape of tiny blisters.

"I couldn't see nothing," she continued. "The next thing I know, I was outside on the ground."

"But you left your baby," I said, referring to the child.

"No, honey, I had Baby right there in my hand."

"You left the child," I repeated, my voice rising.

"I wasn't thinking about no kid."

"No, I don't suppose you were."

"What the fuck that's supposed to mean?"

I was silent.

"Look, I don't need this shit. You ain't my mothafuckin' mother. Stop this mothafucka, I'll get out and walk."

I shook my head. She'd used "mothafucka" two times in as many sentences, once as an adjective and another time as a noun.

"I said, stop this mothafucka so I can get out."

I still didn't know where LaTreace and Sir were. I couldn't let her go until I at least found out what she knew about them.

"Look, you don't have to walk. I said I'd take you and I will."

"I don't take shit off nobody," she responded.

I nodded and a sharp pain shot through my head.

We drove the rest of the way to the medical center in silence. I pulled into emergency-room parking and turned to the woman.

"Look, I really need to know where LaTreace and her little boy are."

"Why you looking for her?"

"Her grandmother died today, and I don't think she knows. She left something for LaTreace, and I want to get it to her."

"What happened? Was she sick or something?

"No, she was shot to death."

"Somebody broke in her house and shot her?"

"Somebody drove by her house and shot it up and killed her."

"A drive-by?"

"Yes."

"Was she 'in the life'?"

"No, I don't think so. She was retired and trying to help raise LaTreace's children."

"Shit, Trey Dog. Somebody better tell LaTreace quick."

"Trey Dog?"

"I told LaTreace not to fuck with him. She messing 'round, come up short on her account. She better give the nigger his money or get outta Dodge quick. It's probably too late now, anyway. She just better go somewhere quick before they be looking for a box to put her in, too."

"Who is Trey Dog? She owes him something?"

"Yeah, she owe him something, all right. She owe the mothafucka' some money; now she probably owe him her life 'cause I know she don't have no money. She always talking large, 'um gone do this, 'um gone do that. Don't do shit. Smoke the mothafuckin' profits up, that's what she do." She began to cry. Tears struggled out of her swollen eyes and ran a broken path down her dirt-streaked face. They were muddy by the time they reached her chin.

I waited quietly, trying to absorb this new information. Mother was right, Mrs. Turner's death was part of La-Treace's mess, after all. But it looked like it wasn't over yet. LaTreace still owed Trey Dog money, and he was inflicting pain on anybody close to her until he either caught up with her or got his money.

"She come by with the boy, but Trey Dog looking for her, so I say she better stay somewhere else. 'Sides, Calvin acting a fool and I didn't want no mess."

"Where did she go?"

"Rose Garden Motel."

"Where's that?"

"Stockton, between Forty-eighth and Fiftieth."

"You sure that's where she went?"

"That's where she said. I give her my last twenty. She say she have plenty of money soon."

"You think she's there now?"

"Yeah, she there, 'less she out trying to make tomorrow's rent."

I dug my walking shoes out of my tote bag and went

in with them. The woman wrapped her left arm around
her chest and took small, careful steps. Her breathing
sounded like a bellows with a hole in it. The child cast
an anxious glance at her every couple of steps.

The Med Center's waiting room looked more like a
fast-food establishment than a hospital. Four admission
windows each with a line served its customers. Bright
lights glared down on brightly colored molded plastic
chairs bolted to the floor. It differed from a burger joint
in its prominent security. I saw two armed guards patrol-
ling the area as video surveillance cameras winked down
from the ceiling.

"Will you call my job and tell them I won't be in
tonight?" asked the woman.

She made the request like I was a friend she'd known
for years, not for less than an hour. Like I was the kind
of friend you shared insignificant intimacies with and did
favors for, favors that might involve a slight shading of
the truth.

"Tell them I had ... a ... accident. But I'll be in
tomorrow."

She wrote a phone number on a corner of the admit-
tance form and handed it to me. "Ask for Carla," she
said.

I looked at the paper. She'd written all in caps using
the neat, legible, style drafting people use. I realized I
didn't know her name. I simply thought of her as "La-
Treace's cousin on her daddy's side." That wouldn't do
if I were calling her job.

"What's your name?" I asked.

"Dorothy, Dorothy Barns."

"This looks like a state number. Where do you work?"

"DMV."

A bank of public phones were on the far wall. I turned
toward them.

"By the way," said Dorothy, "thank you for helping
me, us." I nodded. I wanted to scream obscenities at her,
but I just nodded.

I called Dorothy's job and did more of her dirty work.
At least this time she wasn't asking me to kill anybody.

When I finished, I ducked into the women's rest room to assess the damage.

My hair was standing up on my head like some wild fright wig. Some grass clippings were in it and a piece of string. I picked the larger pieces out and used my comb to get the rest.

I took off my suit jacket and used it to brush my shirt off as best I could. Then I took one of the rough, buff-colored paper towels and some liquid hand soap and washed the dirt and grime and Mary Kay off my face, and rinsed twice to get rid of the soapy residue.

My lower lip was split and swollen, giving me a lop-sided pout. Bags were forming under my eyes, and claw marks were visible on my neck where the man's nails had dug in while he choked me. Both earrings were missing. It's a good thing I'm dark, or I would have been a multicolored sight to behold. Fortunately my coloration hides a lot of excesses and abuses. My adrenaline had settled, my muscles cooled, and I was sore all over.

I wondered what had happened to the man. Was he still lying there in the yard, or had he dragged himself up wondering about his sudden and severe headache and gone inside to get a beer and fall asleep in front of the set? If someone had finally called the police or an ambulance, he would most likely be brought to the Med Center for treatment, and I did not want to be here when he arrived. It's a good thing they have security guards, armed ones at that.

I pulled myself together the best I could, but I didn't think it would matter a whole lot where I was going. I was still probably overdressed for the Rose Garden Motel. In fact, the last time I saw LaTreace, she'd been wearing a housedress with a jogging suit jacket over it.

My toiletries finished, I left the rest room and talked a triage nurse into giving me a bandage for my thumb. Then I left to find LaTreace and Sir before Trey Dog did.

Chapter 7

Stockton Boulevard goes from staunch to raunch and back again in a matter of a few miles. Anchored on the northern end by the U. C. Med Center, and the southern end by a thriving medical complex that includes Kaiser and Methodist Hospitals and a host of smaller medical institutions, the area between Broadway and Florin is the purest form of a honky-tonk strip Sacramento has to offer with the possible exception of Marysville Boulevard. They say you can get anything you want on Stockton Boulevard, and I believe them. If what you want can be found in a Black club, a soul food café, or a fast-food joint, you'll find it there. Also, if you're looking for a kosher burrito or Thai food, a generous sprinkling of storefront churches, male or female companions for rent by the hour, small strip malls anchored by K mart or the 99 Cents Store, motorcycle gang clubhouse, and a cemetery, all within walking distance of each other, best head to Stockton.

Until now I had been unaware of Stockton's series of residency motels dotting both sides of the street. A few were freshly scrubbed, recently painted, homey kind of places; the majority were down on their luck, don't give a damn 'bout no paint, weekly rent due in advance kind of places. Regardless of their condition, enchanting names abounded. There was the Rose Garden, Cedarwood Manor, Greenbrier Inn, and my favorite, By-d-by Motel.

It was close to five o'clock, and traffic was heavy. My headache had graduated to a full-fledged migraine, and

I could only see out of my left eye. The right one, caught in a pulsating vise of pain, was just about useless except for a steady stream of tears that trickled down my cheek. I was squinting like Popeye. The odor of rancid grease spewing from the soul food joints, the exhaust fumes, and the stop-and-go traffic had my stomach churning like an old wringer washer Mother had when I was a little girl. I was rapidly becoming more dysfunctional with each surge of pain. I knew the signs. I needed two Butalbital tablets and about eight hours curled up in a quiet, dark room. No visitors, no phone calls, complete sensory deprivation, if you please.

But being a middle child, I struggled on. I'd already blown the afternoon including missing an important meeting at work. There was nothing left but to go home and go to bed. As soon as I find the Rose Garden and talk to LaTreace, I'll go home and get in bed, I told myself. "Home, bed," I repeated like a mantra.

As I progressed through the Thirties, I started to watch the streets more carefully. Since I didn't know what side of the street it was on, I had to pivot my head from one side to the other in order to see both sides with my left eye. I could feel the pain mass shifting with each pivot. The Rose Garden Motel reared up suddenly between Thirty-eighth and Thirty-ninth Streets on the left side. If I had relied on Dorothy's directions and hadn't started looking for it early, I would have missed it. I pulled over into the turn lane and waited through sixty-seven surges of pain for an opening in traffic so I could make a turn. A Regional Transit driver, noticing my dilemma, stopped and waved me through. I squinted at him and waved. He thought I was winking and winked back.

The Rose Garden Motel was built in a U shape with a pool in its crook. The registration office sat between the two arms of the U like a tollbooth. Cars went in one side, around the pool, and out the other side. A cyclone fence encircled the pool, which, devoid of water, had become a receptacle for the detritus of broken families. Old tires, mattresses, broken furniture, and a bicycle frame filled the pool to the brim. Someone had painted crooked parking slots with white bathroom gloss in front of the units. Women lounged in some of the doorways awkwardly trying to strike poses from movies of the forties. One woman, obviously into collectibles, wore hot pants and platform shoes. A small group of men and a lone woman played a noisy game of cards on a rickety card table outside a unit near the office.

From what I could see, the Rose Garden had no garden and no roses. Nothing seemed to grow there at all except for junk and a gaggle of raggedy little children who wandered about, poking in trash like a desolate flock of urban fowl.

I drove in the right side, made my tour around the pool looking for LaTreace or Sir. Finding neither, I stopped near the card players and got out. Maybe they could tell me about the comings and goings of this place. One of them might know LaTreace. As I started toward the cardplayers, a Vietnamese woman bolted from the office and ran toward me, gesturing wildly.

"Oh, no, you no come back. You go away. You no come back. I call police. You no come back."

"I beg your pardon." That's all I could think to say. "I beg your pardon."

At the sound of my voice, she paused and contemplated me more closely, knitting her brows and pursing her lips. She teetered for a moment in uncertainty, but she shook her head and shoulders like a boxer shaking off a blow and grabbed a broom and started to shoo me like a chicken.

"You no come back."

The woman got up from the card table and ambled over to us. She was big. Not fat, just big. Her pants were so tight, I could see all of her stuff, her lips, everything. Her hair was combed over one eye and curled under at chin length. The other side was cut short, fading just above the ear. She examined me closely. Turning to the woman with the broom, she said, "She ain't Oretha, Vu. Put the broom down."

"Oh, no, she no come back," repeated the woman with the broom.

"Oretha dead, Vu. Put the damn broom down."

Vu took a step back, then another. She backed to the

office. Reaching behind herself, she opened the door and backed in. "You no come back," she yelled a final time and jerked the door closed.

"Goddamn, you sho' look like Oretha," said the woman examining me closely.

"Oretha?" I asked.

"Yeah, she was a good friend of mine. Used to give Vu and them hell. Skipped out without paying her last week's rent. Went and got herself killed. Vu hasn't forgiven her."

"I can tell."

"Hey, my name is Sweet Pea. You can call me Sweet, everybody does." She extended her hand and I met hers with mine, careful to keep my thumb out of her grasp.

"Theresa."

"Nice to meet you, T."

"No," I corrected, "Theresa. Nobody calls me T but my husband."

She cradled my hand in both of hers. Hers were pudgy with dimples. They were soft and warm. Her blunt cut nails were painted a pink like the inside of a cheek.

She reached up toward my cheek, stopping just short of touching me. "What happened to you, baby?" She asked with a silky gentleness that made me want to lay my head on her full, bread basket of a bosom, and cry and tell her everything.

Instead I answered, "I got in a fight."

"I hope you put whoever the mothafucka was in the hospital," she said with a crooked smile. Her hand dropped to my shoulder. I turned just enough to force her to move it, but not enough to appear rude or, worse yet, jumpy. Especially since I was very jumpy. I don't like people touching me and taking liberties when they don't even know me. Even though I'm pretty assertive in other ways, I didn't want to tell her out and out to get her hands off me. I was also getting tired of so many "motherfuckers." I'd heard that word more today than I had in my entire life. Motherfucker this, motherfucker that, I was sick of it.

"Come on. Let me put something on that," she said, speaking so softly I had to strain to hear her. "I got something that'll soothe you, something that'll move you, something that'll make you feel all right." Her voice had taken on a singsong quality.

I knew it was time to go. I wanted to get out of there before I hurt somebody or they hurt me.

"I'm looking for somebody," I said.

"So am I, T."

"I don't think you understand . . ."

"Baby, I understand just fine."

She reached up to touch my face, and I brushed her hand away, but she grabbed my wrist. The muscles in her arm tensed. They were as clearly defined as her labia in her tight pants.

I looked around to see if there was anyone who would help me. The people at the card table elaborately pretended not to notice us. One of the men snickered. The children had found a three-legged dog and were chasing it around the pool. The woman with the broom was gone. I hoped she had called the police like she threatened.

"Let go of me," I said through clenched teeth.

She looked at me and smiled. "What you say, baby?"

"Get your filthy hands off me."

"Oh, I'm filthy now, huh, baby? Do you think I would be so filthy if I drove a ride like yours? Maybe I need to wear as much Red as you do and smell right sweet. You think that's it, huh, baby?"

I planted my feet and forced my arm up to shoulder height, trying to break her grip. She tightened her grip and forced it back down.

"Oo, girl, what happened to your thumb?"

She started to touch it, and I jerked my hand out of her grip with strength I didn't even know I had, but lost my footing in the process, stumbling backward. Sweet stepped to the side and caught me around the waist as I was going down. It was the kind of move a matador might make. She broke my fall, leaned over me, and pressed her lips against mine. I caught my breath, pressed my lips tightly together, and swung my head left to right trying to avoid her.

She let go of me abruptly, as if an alarm had sounded and my time was up. I staggered backward, nearly falling,

trying to regain my footing. She turned from me and
swaggered back to the card table, where the players were
not pretending to ignore us anymore.

She slapped five with one of the men and said,
"Gimme my money, nigger."

"Yeah, but did you stick it all the way in?" he asked.

"To her tonsils, mothafucka. I could have fucked the
'ho if I wanted to."

I got out of there. I just left. I didn't try to talk to Vu
or anybody else or ask about LaTreace and Sir. I was
out of my element. Way out. The streets were just too
mean for me.

Chapter 8

During one of their rare periods of rapport, Aisha and Shawn made a sign for me that reads, "Danger! Keep Out. Migraine In Progress." I found that sign when I got home, hung it on my bedroom door, and climbed into bed in my bra and panties. I felt gritty. I needed a bath badly. But everything else was secondary to appeasing the throbbing pain over my right eye. Curling into a tight ball, I waited for the two Butalbitals I'd taken to kick in. The phone started to ring. I got up slowly, felt my way to it, and snatched the cord out of the wall by its plastic root. I could still hear the muffled treble of the downstairs extension, and I briefly weighed the prospect of launching a search-and-destroy mission for it, too, but it stopped ringing abruptly. I crawled back into bed, fell asleep, and didn't wake again until nine o'clock the next morning.

I awoke fighting the dual demons of a Butalbital hangover and a guilty conscience, and it was hard to tell which was worse. All the things I hadn't done the day before paraded before me like the credits at the end of a particularly ignoble film. Not only had I missed an important meeting at work, I hadn't even gone back after lunch. AWOL. People have been fired for that, and I'd signed the papers, too. I dreaded facing Allen, and I could only hope my staff hadn't degenerated into an orgy of backbiting as they are prone to. Facing Allen would be a piece of cake, though, compared to Temp and Aisha. Shawn forgives everything, but Temp and Aisha hoard hurt. They're like tobacco chewers, picking off odd pieces

of old hurts to savor in the corners of their mouths. I
crawled out of bed, called Allen, told him of yesterday's
events and my involvement in them, and asked to take
the day off to recuperate. Allen is compassionate and
understanding. He really tries to be there for me as a
supervisor, but even he has his limits. He was silent for
a long time after I asked for the time off. Finally he said,
"Okay, but you and I need to talk when you get back."
We discussed who should act for me while I was out. I
reminded him that Brenda Delacore was the only choice,
since she was the highest-ranking employee in the
branch, after me, at least until Phil Wyckoft's promotion
went through. He reluctantly agreed. I got the time off.
I should have felt relief, but I didn't. I felt like a rubber
band of uncertain quality that was being stretched in too
many different directions.

I hung up the phone and called Brenda. After ringing
three times, the call rolled over to her section clerk who
told me Brenda could be reached at my desk. I hung up
and dialed my number. Brenda answered on the first
ring.

"Brenda Delacore, personnel office."

"What are you doing at my desk?"

"Theresa. Hey, what's up?"

"I said, what are you doing at my desk?"

"I'm acting for you."

"Brenda, acting for me doesn't mean you assume my
identity. You do not sit at my desk, nor do you drink
from my coffee cup. If Temp forgets I'm off and calls,
you do not talk to him about how good last night was.
Got that Brenda?"

"What's your problem, sister-girl? I'm just trying to
watch your back while you're out. You got some real
problems. Don't nobody do no work around here, and I
caught Dieter—that Aryan nation motherfucker—doing
up his flyers on the copy machine. But don't you worry,
I handled it."

"Brenda, I just want you to go to my meetings for me.
Okay? Miyako will give you all the necessary background
material. Just go to my meetings, sign the administrative

stuff that comes in, that's all. Don't try to handle any disciplinary problems. Okay, Brenda?"

"Yeah, sure. Wait until you see how I've rearranged your furniture."

I hung up and retreated to the bathroom.

The master bath is the one place in the whole house that I call my own. The kids each have their own rooms, Temp has the guest bedroom that he's converted to an office, and I have the master bath. I all but bled dry the allocation for the rest of the house when it was being built, so I could afford Italian marble and whitewashed oak in "my room." Decorated in grays and peach with a profusion of green plants, it is my temple. It is where I come when I need to meditate or when I'm tired, or depressed, or when I just want to relax and mellow out. I do a lot of my reading and some of my best thinking in the sunken, jetted tub that seats two.

I opened the skylight, leaned over the counter toward the mirror, and began my inspection. My eyes were puffy and so was my lower lip, but not nearly as much as I had expected. It was nothing that a little Mary Kay, skillfully applied, couldn't handle. I had slept, most of the night, on my left side, and a cross-hatching of welt-like sleep marks were embossed on my cheek and forehead. A good soak in the tub should take care of those. Next, I carefully examined my teeth and gums. Ever since my dentist told me I had early-stage periodontal disease, I've been preoccupied with them. Sometimes I even have nightmares, dreaming that my teeth are breaking off at the gum line like the teeth of a comb. My gums looked all right. They didn't appear to have receded much since the last time I checked yesterday morning, but my teeth looked mossy, and my mouth tasted like somebody had been striking matches in it all night.

I started a bath, and as it ran, I brushed my teeth and pasted a mask on my face. Searching the cabinets, I found a new Band-Aid for my thumb. It was flesh-colored, undoubtedly intended for raw flesh, since its shade of "peeled pink" certainly didn't match the mahogany tones of my skin.

Stepping into the tub, I submerged myself up to my

neck. I lay my head back on the vinyl, inflatable pillow Aisha and Shawn gave me for my birthday, and I worshiped like that for a good forty-five minutes, replenishing the hot water when the bath started to cool.

When I couldn't justify staying in any longer, I opened the drain and watched the water swirl away. Staying in until the very last moment, I abandoned the tub, only when there was less than an inch of water remaining. Hoisting myself out, I grabbed a towel and crossed the floor to the shower. The shower is another of my indulgences. A freestanding structure fashioned of glass brick that forms three curved walls with an opening between each one, it is a work of art. It has something to do with angles, but even though it is an open structure, the water is contained completely within its confines and doesn't splash out. I like to watch Temp shower early in the morning, just when the sun is rising and natural light is funny. Then the glass columns look like crystal. They become a crystal crucible forging me a man who emerges shiny and wet and new.

I turned both the upper and lower level shower jets on and reveled in the gentle message of the pulsating currents. When my hair was suitably wet, I poured on a generous amount of shampoo and scrubbed vigorously, careful to keep my thumb out of the way. I rinsed and lathered and scrubbed repeatedly until the bottle was empty and I finally felt clean. I finished with a cold rinse that set my skin to tingling. Temp was there when I stepped out of the shower, holding the towel just beyond my reach, waiting for me. I stepped into his arms. He closed them around me and buried his head in my wet hair.

"Smell so good," he said in a voice a couple of octaves lower than usual. I was wet and getting him wet, too, but he didn't seem to mind. He nuzzled my ear, and the tingles started up again. He kissed me at the base of my throat and leaned back a little as if to admire his handiwork. He lips were slightly parted, and I could see the tip of his tongue in the corner of his mouth. It's always been like that; that look, the lips and tongue excite me almost beyond endurance. They are my undoing. Temp allowed me to undress him. I worked slowly and methodically, first the buttons on his shirt, then the belt, and finally the placard on his pants. We were silent, but the sound of our breathing filled the room. I lifted his shirt off one shoulder, and he turned slightly freeing the other. Then I loosened his pants and pulled them down, and he stepped out of them. There was nothing between us now but a few cubic centimeters of air, and then that was gone.

I meant to ask Temp about Penny Troop, but somehow I got distracted. After lovemaking, I like to doze, off and on, and speak in lazy, hushed tones, thick with contentment. Temp, on the other hand, is into snacks, so for him après sex is synonymous with appetizer. Gently disentangling our limbs and blowing me a kiss on his way out, Temp trotted down to the kitchen in the buff. He returned carrying my purse that I had dropped on the kitchen counter last night in one hand and a tray laden with whatever he could rummage up in the other. In this case, it was sliced kiwi fruit and bananas, smoked oysters, water crackers, a handful of walnuts in the shells, and a jar of lemonade. After carefully placing the purse on the dresser, he turned to me and offered to share his snack. I took one look and begged off.

As I lay there listening to him grind and crush and slurp and suck, I congratulated myself on refusing to allow a TV in the bedroom. Temp likes a little TV with his meals and a lot of TV with his snacks. This way I don't have to contend with flashing lights and car chase sounds well into the wee hours of the night. Crumbs in the bed used to drive me mad, now they are a thing of the past.

Temp was poking at the kiwi with his fork. He stacked a kiwi slice on a banana slice and followed it with another slice of banana. Alternating kiwi with banana, he stacked the fruit in a wobbly tower until the whole thing toppled over. His face was tight with concentration as he started again, this time stacking banana on kiwi. I watched with morbid fascination.

"By the way, where the hell were you last night, T?"

he asked with studied casualness as he deliberately stacked fruit slices.

"Well, honey, it's a long story . . ." I began hesitantly, as I wanted to keep Mother, LaTreace and Sir, Dorothy, the man and all the rest, out of it.

"Damn sure is a long story. You left here yesterday morning, and I don't see you again until this morning. I come in last night, and you had that funky little sign on the door."

"Temp, Mrs. Turner, Mother's friend from across the street, was killed yesterday, shot in a drive-by."

"Aw, baby, I'm sorry," he said with genuine compassion. "Your mother all right?"

I nodded.

"I know she's taking it hard."

"She is, very hard."

"You know, I heard something about a shooting on the news, but I didn't pay much attention. It was in Oak Park, too, come to think of it. What happened? It had to be some kind of mistake, or was it a stray bullet or something?"

"I don't know exactly. They shot up her house and some cars on her side of the street. It was a miracle no kids were out playing or anything. As far as I know, no one else was hurt. I didn't get a good look at the car, so I can't . . ." I didn't say, "uh-oh," but the look on my face said it for me. I could tell Temp was mad 'cause his ears and nose turned red. That's one of the problems with being light-skinned, it's harder to hide your emotions.

He said, "Let me make sure I got this right. You were at your mother's house yesterday . . . What time was it? When did all this happen?"

"Around noon."

"Around noon," he continued. "T, I thought you were somewhere safe, like at work dealing with the humbug, shuffling papers and shit. I just don't even know you anymore. You're not where you supposed to be, doing what you supposed to be doing. 'I didn't get a good look at the car,' " he mimicked me. "For all I know you could've shot Mrs. Turner. No, I think robbing 7-Eleven's more your style."

"Aw, come on, Temp," I said, desperately trying to ride this one out.

He got up, stalked over to the dresser and grabbed my purse.

"What is this?" he demanded, his voice rising. "Huh? What is this?"

Temp is somewhat of a neat freak, but this was going a bit overboard, even for him. Besides, he put the purse there himself. Without waiting for an answer, he turned the bag upside down over the bed and let the contents tumble out.

"Say, if you're talking about that condom, I can explain," I said with mock alarm.

"Don't play with me, T."

"Just trying to lighten things up a bit. If you'll pardon my saying so, I think you're overreacting."

Temp scattered the contents of my purse with the palm of his hand, picked through it, and withdrew Mother's gun.

"What is this?" he demanded again, holding the gun in the palm of his hand.

"Oh, that. That's Mother's."

"What is it doing in your purse? What are you doing with it?" he asked patiently.

"Mother gave it to me for protection. By the way, how did you find it in the first place? What were you doing in my purse?"

"You have a habit of just dropping your things anywhere. It was on the floor, behind the door in the laundry room. Everything fell out when I picked it up. But the point is, I thought you were afraid of guns. At least that's what you told me. Isn't that right? You can't stand to be around guns. They scare you to death."

We were at a critical juncture in this discussion. The signs were unmistakable: he was starting to quote me. Temp only quotes me when he has spotted an inconsistency in reasoning and he smells blood. He was circling for the kill. I don't like guns. That's true. And I am afraid of them, particularly when they're in somebody else's hand and pointed at me. But the real issue here was not whether or not I was afraid of guns. The real issue was my refusal to allow Temp to bring a gun into the house. This is a long-standing sore point with him. But I had been adamant about it. I had become even more adamant after Shawn was born and his kamikaze character began to reveal itself. I tried to explain.

"I didn't want the thing, but Mother insisted. Said it was Daddy's. I only took it so I could get out of there. Otherwise she would have kept me there all day."

Temp was barely listening. He stood, turning the gun over in his hands, examining it. He's into gadgets, any kind of gadgets, and he had that gleam in his eye, that tampering look.

"You know, T," he said absently, "this is not a bad piece, not a bad piece at all. Yes, sir, a Sig Hauer P230. Where's the clip?"

"Huh?"

"The clip, the thing the bullets come in. It does have a clip, doesn't it? Or did your mother advise you to throw the thing and run?"

"Oh, that. It's in there somewhere."

"Baby, first of all, you're a little too casual about things. If you're going to carry a gun, you got to know what you doing. You got to know how to use it and how to take care of it."

"I know how to use it. You just point it and pull the trigger."

Temp threw his head back and laughed. "That sounds like something your mother would say."

I rolled my eyes at him. He grabbed my hand and tugged me upright.

"Come on," he said.

"Come on, where?"

"Downstairs. I'm going to show you how to take it apart and clean it."

"But, honey, I don't want to know how to clean it. I don't even want it. I'm giving it back to Mother."

He was all but bubbling over with the prospect of instructing me in the fine art of dismantling and cleaning small arms. His true calling is really teaching. He loves it and is good at it. I've seen him with the children patiently explaining the function of a carburetor or discoursing on the works of Henry Tanner Turner or Zora Neal Hurston. He suffered through law school, the bar, and years working in the Legislative Counsel's Office only to come to the belated realization that he hated law and he hated politics and he most undoubtedly hated what he was doing. He chucked the whole thing three years ago. Quit his job, exchanged his suit and tie for a pair of sweatpants and a T-shirt, and sat at his computer for three weeks devising plans for a new life. At the end of the three weeks he gathered Aisha, Shawn, and me around the dining room table and pitched "Second Generation" to us. Second Generation's a cleaning business specializing in the commercial markets. Mother Alma, Temp's mother, had worked as a domestic until his oldest brother, Lonnie, completed his internship and got his practice started. Then he and Temp bought her a small home and "sat her down." In a way, Temp was paying homage to his mother by naming his business Second Generation, but she hated it. She liked being able to brag that she had a son who was a doctor, another who was a lawyer, and a daughter who was a professor of religion. She was fond of saying, to the consternation of the other women in her seniors group, that she had a child to take care of any eventuality. If the doctor couldn't handle it then the lawyer most assuredly could, but if neither of them could, then it was time to call on the good offices of the professor. When Temp quit his job and abdicated his exalted social standing, he had, in her eyes, diminished her social standing as well by at least one third. For weeks she could not bear to show her face at Sweet Valley Baptist Church. Now she had a doctor, a domestic (as she called it), and a professor, and somehow it was my fault. The first time Temp told her about Second Generation, she sat frozen for a good three minutes. I was beginning to think she'd had a stroke until she turned to me and asked accusingly, "How could you let him do this?"

I'm waiting for Temp to find his true calling and go into teaching. I prod him every once in awhile, but I know too much prodding can backfire, so I'm patient. Now he was dragging me to the door, eager to teach me something I did not want to know. I dug my heels in.

"Wait a minute, honey. At least put some pants on. Let me throw something on and do something with this hair, and I'll be down."

When I got downstairs, Temp had spread a tea towel on the table and arrayed his makeshift cleaning tools around it. There was a box of toothpicks, a can of sewing machine oil, a small round brush with a handle, and one of the old cloth diapers I use for dusting. I don't know where he found those things. I haven't sewed for years. I didn't know we still had sewing machine oil in the house. The gun was lying in the middle of the towel, and Temp stood by beaming. I took a seat across from him, and he sat down and got started.

"The Sig is one of the finest semiautomatics around. It is both a simple instrument and an exceedingly complex one. Fortunately, they are so well constructed as to require very little maintenance. This one seems to have been well cared for, but all guns, as with any other fine instrument, must be cleaned every once in a while. Now, T, I want you to pay attention. I going to show you how to dismantle it. First, remove the clip and take the round out ..."

My eyes started to glaze over. I stifled a yawn.

"Next, you press the breakdown lever to remove the slide. Are you listening, T?"

I nodded yes, too paralyzed with boredom to speak.

"Okay. Remove the spring and there you have it. It's as simple as that."

I nodded and lifted my eyebrows to indicate awe.

"Now we will concentrate on a few basic areas. You want to clean the barrel to remove any power residue, etc. Ordinarily you would use a gun cleaning solvent such as Gunslick, but for the purpose of this demonstration, we use just a tiny bit of this."

He took the diaper, tore off a small strip, and wrapped it around the brush. He put a few drops of oil on it and inserted it in the barrel and swabbed it out.

"You must be careful to remove all excess oil. Now the toothpick." He picked it up and held it out in front of himself. "What do you think we're going to do with the toothpick?"

I offered up an elaborate shrug. Not a disdainful, disinterested shrug, but an "I'm stumped. Please tell me the answer" kind. He was only too willing.

"The toothpick is used to clean crevices." He cleaned every crevice he could find. Then he held the gun up, minus the slide, the spring, and the clip, peered through the barrel, and admired his work.

"Now, T, watch carefully as I reassemble it. First, replace the spring. Got that?"

I nodded, pursing my lips, trying to yawn discreetly.

"Okay. Now, you replace the slide and lock the breakdown lever. Following me so far?"

"Yes."

"That's good. We're just repeating the steps we took to dismantle, only in reverse order. Now, you push the de-cocker down. It puts the hammer in the safety position. Insert the clip and, to put a round into the chamber, simply pull the slide back and release it. Now remember, as long as the de-cocker is depressed, the hammer is in the safety position and it is impossible to fire without actually pulling the trigger. It can't accidentally fire. Got that?"

I nodded, raised my eyebrows, and bit my lower lip pensively. I was hoping he didn't ask me anything else 'cause I was running out of gestures. Pretty soon I would have to nod head, raise eyebrows, bite lip, and wiggle ears.

"Good. Now I want you to take it apart and put it back together." He clapped his hands together and stood there beaming down at me.

"That's all right, honey, I can practice some other time."

"No, T, I want to see you do it now. Just follow the steps I showed you."

I picked it up. It felt heavier than I remembered. I turned it over in my hands.

"How do I get the bullet out?"

"You weren't listening, were you?"

"Of course I was listening, honey. Just show me how to get the bullet out."

"I tell you what, T. Why don't I just take it apart for you again?"

In a few swift movements, he had it completely broken down.

"Now, you put it back together. If you're going to use it, you're going to have to reassemble it."

He got up from the table and went to his office. I sat there looking at the parts of Mother's gun, the spring, the slide, the clip, and the other part, whatever it's called. I got up, went to the kitchen, and got a large Ziploc plastic bag. Returning to the dining room, I picked up the pieces of Mothers' gun, put them in the bag, took them upstairs, and deposited them in my purse. I'd put it together some other time, or wait until Temp was in a better mood and get him to do it. Mother might even know how to reassemble it. Anyway, learning to dismantle and clean a gun was right up there on my list of priorities with learning to lube my car and skin a 'possum.

LaTreace, Sir, and dead people were the last things on my mind. In fact, I'd pushed them so far to the back of my mind, it took me a couple of moments to figure out what Mother was talking about when she called, ignoring all rules of telephone etiquette, as usual, and launched right into her harangue.

"What are you doing there?" she demanded, the indignation fairly crackling in her voice.

"I live here, Mother. This is my home. The other people who live here, too, tell me they are my family. I recently learned that I am contractually obligated to spend a certain percentage of my time here, with these people who claim me."

"Well, Miss Lady, while you sitting up there at home, lollygagging, LaTreace is dragging that poor child every which way through the streets."

"Dragging who?"

"Have you lost your mind or something? Sir. You

know, the one you went looking for last night. And why didn't you at least call me to let me know what happened?"

"Mother, believe me, you don't want to know."

"I take it, you didn't find them. Oh, well, when you coming over?"

"This weekend."

"This weekend? And what am I supposed to do in the meantime, with people coming paying their respects and all? I need some help here with these girls. Mother Iola watched them this morning while Edna, Kaylene, Ella, and I went over and cleaned up Sister Turner's place and packed up her stuff. Lord, they just about drove that poor woman crazy. Wait just a minute."

I heard the receiver on the other end drop. Then there was a swell of rustling noises. Mother returned abruptly.

"Okay. Now, say hello, girls," she cooed.

"Heh-wo. Heh-wo, Teesa."

"Mother, don't tell me that's the twins."

"Uh-huh, that's them, all right, Andrea and Cenne— my girls."

The last time I saw "her girls," they'd worn filth-starched rags and communicated with sad little whimpers. Their chirpy little hellos were a big improvement.

"How'd you get them to talk?"

"I laid down the law, that's all. I told them if they wanted something, they had to speak up and ask for it."

"And it worked?" I asked with disbelief.

"Of course it worked. They walking, too."

"No, they aren't!"

"Yes, they are. I sat them down and talked to them. I said, 'Look at you. You half grown and round here crawling on your hands and knees like babies.' I said, 'Won't be none of that in my house, no sir. From now on, you want to go somewhere, you get up off your little bottoms and walk like regular folk.'"

"And they got up and walked?"

"No, they sat there and looked at me like I was a fool, but I didn't waver. Then they looked at each other. I saw I'd gotten my point across, so I moved everything back out of the way so they could have room. And I reached my hands out to them, and they looked at each other again, and then they took my hands and we practiced for a good while last night and this morning, too. We walked back and forth, back and forth. Didn't we, girls? They still a little wobbly, but they can walk a few steps now without holding on."

"I don't believe it."

"They just needed somebody to take a little time with them."

Mother inserted a canny pause.

"By the way, how you and Shrimp getting along?"

"First of all, it's Temp, Mother. Temp. You know his name perfectly well by now. Secondly, we're getting along just fine, thank you."

"Just wondered."

Another pause.

"I met a fine young man here the other day. Just as polite as he could be."

"Mother, I am not looking for a man, fine or otherwise, impolite or not. I am married and happily so."

"He has a good job."

"Temp has a job."

"But this one has a good job. Detective, Sacramento police. Can't do much better than that. Good steady work."

"Mother, I thought you liked Temp."

"Oh, I do, baby. Temp's a nice boy. I was just checking. Anyway, he wants to talk to you."

"Who?"

"Pay attention, baby. The detective, that's who. Wants to ask you some questions about Sister Turner. They interviewing everybody on the street. He came by yesterday just after you left.

"Mother, why didn't you just say so."

"I did. By the way, LaTreace called."

"She did? When?"

"Not long ago, just before I called you."

"What did she say? She got Sir?"

"I'll tell when you get here."

The disconnect buzzed in my ear like a swarm of flies.

Chapter 9

Any reasonable person would simply have hung up the phone and gone about her business. A reasonable person, that is, not a fool. I was getting sucked in again, plain and simple. Sucked into another of Mother's messes. As if Dorothy and her man and the potato gun weren't enough. As if Sweet and her stuff weren't enough. I could feel the apron strings tightening around my neck. Struggling would only make it worse, hasten my demise, so to speak. I sighed and got dressed.

Temp had left while I was on the phone. I would have hell to pay later on, but I left a sticky note in the middle of the TV screen, grabbed my purse, and left.

Cars lined both sides of Mother's street. I hadn't seen so many vintage automobiles since I toured the Towe Ford Museum last year with Shawn's Jack and Jill group. I had a hard time finding a parking space. Everybody else seemed to have avoided the space directly in front of Mrs. Turner's house and I did, too, for a while. Finally, in desperation, I backed into it and parked. I stared at the house. Someone had nailed a couple of planks across the door, and they stood out like keloids. The house looked so abused. Mouth nailed shut, eyes put out, shattered. Soul dead. A thick, ungiving despair rolled over me. Poor Mrs. Turnip. Grabbing my purse, I checked to make sure the doors were locked and headed across the street to Mother's.

A leathery old man in a plaid leisure suit pulled the door open just as I raised my hand to the knob.

"Praise the Lord, you come right on in, child," he

exclaimed. "I'm Brother Cummings. You must be Sister Barkley's girl."

I admitted as much, shook his hand, and inquired about his health. He assured me all was well, except for a little irregularity now and then, nothing he was inclined to complain about as long as the good Lord made prunes.

I hardly recognized Mother's house. Most of the boxes were gone. The few that remained had been placed in strategic locations near chairs or at the window, covered with lace doilies and magically transformed into occasional tables. The floor had been vacuumed, and all that remained of the recent jumble were dark spots on the carpet where boxes had sat. Plastic flowers, recently dusted, bloomed everywhere. A Mahalia Jackson tape played softly in the background.

Kaylene Simmons, as elegant as ever, sat in the armchair across from the sofa, and Ella Agnew, who taught school up until a year ago, sat near the window. Bea Greer was there, too, and so was Mother Iola, who, in her mid-nineties, was partially blind and close to being deaf. I didn't see Mother or the twins.

"Will you look at what the wind just blew in?" declared Edna Thompson.

"Come here, baby, and give me some sugar."

Edna was partially hidden behind the door, and I didn't see her at first, but I'd seen a brand-new Lincoln Town car parked out front, and I knew it could only belong to her. I went to her and extended my hand in greeting. Ignoring it, she enfolded me in a hug. She was wearing Giorgio. Holding me at arm's length, she exclaimed, "Let me look at you. Look at her," she said to the others, "didn't she grow into a fine woman?"

"Put on a little weight, too," added Sister Ella. "Who would have thought that skinny little girl would ever have any kinda' hips?"

"Put on her woman's weight," added Mother Iola admiringly.

"Come on over here and give me some sugar, too, child," admonished Kaylene. "Don't act like you don't know me."

I made my rounds, and each of the women put down

her teacup and held my hands or kissed me and asked
about my family. Each, to a person, exclaimed in astonishment when I told her Aisha was sixteen and Shawn
was eleven.

"Lord, where does the time go? asked each in one
variation or another. "It seems like just a little while ago
you were only eleven yourself." And I could tell, by the
way their eyes would mist up, that they were thinking of
Carolyn, then I would gently move on to another.

By the time I finished my hellos, my eyes were misting
up, too. I was glad when Mother flounced in carrying a
tray of cookies with Andrea and Cenne, resplendent in
dotted swiss and patent leather, toddling along on either
side of her.

"Mother, they really can walk."

"Of course they can," she said, handing the tray to
Brother Cummings. Bending down, she cajoled, "My
girls can walk, can't they?" The twins giggled. "And they
can talk, too, can't they?" More giggling. "Say hello to
Theresa," suggested Mother. They buried their heads in
the folds of her skirt, giggling. "Come on now, say hello,"
she coaxed.

"Heh ... wo!" shouted Andrea, "Teesa," chirped
Cenne, collapsing in a fit of giggles. Mother picked her
up and handed her to Ella. Edna got Andrea. Kaylene
gave Mother the armchair and joined Bea and Edna on
the sofa.

"So these the babies," said Ella. "They sure some
pretty little things."

"Yes, and just as sweet as they can be," answered
Mother.

"To think, LaTreace tried to get rid of them. But,
Sister Turner stopped her. Good thing, too."

"I don't know where people get off talking about freedom of choice and all this mess. Just killing babies, that's
all," snorted Mother.

"Women need to be able to control their own bodies,"
I interjected foolishly. Not that the belief itself is foolish,
but tactically speaking, it just wasn't the right place or
time. This was their party, not mine. And here I was,
trying to interject reason and logic. Silly me.

Mother glared at me.

"And how many babies have you gotten rid of?"

"Why . . . none," I answered.

"And how many do you plan to get rid of in the future?"

"I hardly see how that's important . . ."

"Answer me."

"None."

"Okay, then."

She turned back to the women and Brother Cummings with a flourish. She didn't slap five, but she didn't have, too. She'd "put me in my place" quite nicely, and the others looked at her with approval. I tried not to sulk.

"This one here's the spitting image of Sister Turner," announced Ella. "See here, look at the way she does her mouth."

"Uh-huh, she's got Sister Turner written all over her," agreed Edna.

The music stopped, and a pall of silence fell over the room as each person, in her own way, savored a special memory of Sister Turner.

"Where'd they send the body?" asked Kaylene.

"They haven't released it yet. They have to do the autopsy and stuff. They'll send her to Gaston-Monroe when they finish," replied Mother.

"How long will all this take? When will she be ready for viewing?"

"I don't know. There's still a lot of decisions to be made, decisions her people should be making. I just don't know what to do."

"Sure is a shame," said Bea, barely above a whisper. "Lord, Lord, Lord."

Brother Cummings, in a seat by the door, rocked gently, tapping his foot and humming to himself. Every once in a while he would mouth some of the words. I caught a few snatches of "Precious Lord," and I had to steel myself to keep from crying.

"The Lord is a good God, he is a merciful God. He will not give you more than you can bear," declared Mother Iola, her head resting on the back of the sofa. Her eyes closed in prayer.

"Yes, yes," whispered Bea.

Sister Kaylene stared into the distance, clenching and unclenching her hand around a delicately embroidered handkerchief. Ella held Cenne close to her, gently patting her back. They all showed the strain of grief, Brother Cummings and the women. All but Mother and Edna. Mother sat dry-eyed and resolute while Edna paced the floor with nervous energy, the sleeping Andrea fixed to her shoulder like a corsage.

Brother Cummings got up and went to the door. A minute passed and nothing happened. No one rang or knocked, and I was beginning to wonder if he wasn't a little dotty when, with a flourish, he pulled the door open and ushered in Robert Alston, his mother, and Penny Troop.

"Praise the Lord, come on in," intoned Brother Cummings.

Mother advanced to the door to welcome the new arrivals.

Robert greeted her with a hug, mouthing condolences. His duty done, he turned to the women with him.

"I'd like you to meet my mother, Margaret Alston, and this is Penny Troop, my campaign manager."

Mrs. Alston wore a Chanel suit, a pillbox hat, and white gloves. Actually she wore only one glove. She clutched the other in her gloved hand. Hers were strong, capable hands deliberately denatured with white gloves. On first glance she appeared to be a diminutive woman, with champagne blond hair, watery brown eyes, and a certain air of hesitancy and uncertainty that usually comes from living in the shadow of a powerful man. But she wasn't small, she only thought of herself as such. She looked to me like a big woman who had lived a lifetime squeezed into a small woman's space.

Mrs. Alston took Mother's hand with both of hers. "I want you to know how deeply saddened we are by Louise's death, she said. "She was very dear to Bobby and me."

"Thank you," said Mother. "I really appreciate that. We loved her, too. Please, come in and have some refreshments. You, too, Miss Troop."

They moved deeper into the room. Mother made the introductions, and everyone except Mother Iola greeted the new arrivals. She, under the license of old age, refused to interrupt her prayer. Brother Cummings gave his seat to Mrs. Alston and went to the back of the house to get more chairs.

I stood where I was, put my hand on my hip, bowed back one leg, and gave Penny a long, hard look. She was up to old tricks. Stalking. Not me so much as Temp. But first she had to put me on notice. She'd invaded my office, and now my mother's home. My bed was next. Only this time she wasn't jacking around a young, naive college freshman. She was dealing with a grown woman who knew a trick or two herself. I decided not to confront her now. It was too early. She'd simply change her tactics. But Temp—I had to get him in check right away.

Penny moved over to the piano, pulled out the bench, carefully brushed it off, and sat down. Robert, his tie loosened and his hair artfully mussed, was shaking hands with everyone old enough to vote and kissing those too young to protest. He worked the room like a third-rate lounge performer while his mother sat smiling primly in her Chanel suit, pillbox hat, and single glove.

I ducked into the kitchen under the pretense of getting more refreshments, but actually to get a better fix on the changing dynamics of the room.

"You can run, but you can't hide."

I turned to find Robert Alston leaning in the doorway, one hand resting on the jamb a little above his head, the other stuck casually in his pants pocket, his feet turned out to a ballet dancer's second position.

"I didn't get a chance to bid you good tidings," he said, a roguish grin of practiced charm spreading across his face. His eyes were intensely blue, much bluer that I remembered. A sort of "baby doll vinyl" blue.

"Bobby Alston," I said. "Fancy meeting you here, in Mother's kitchen, of all places."

He crossed the floor to where I stood.

"How've you been, Terrie?

His calling me "Terrie" jolted me. I haven't been called that for a good twenty years. Which is just fine with me. It's been that long since I came to the realization that I absolutely, unequivocally, hated the name Terrie. I don't know, there's just something about that name. It has a certain element of frivolity, it's a bit too giddy for my liking. I just don't like it. Besides, my mother named me Theresa, not Terrie.

"Oh, not bad," I answered. "And you? How's the market for mayor these days?"

"Oh, not bad," he said, mocking me. "But, we'll know for sure in November."

"Don't the polls have you out ahead of the pack?"

"The polls. The oh-so-fickle polls. I was doing all right—good name recognition, positive image, a little bit of charisma. But this abortion thing . . ."

"What's abortion got to do with a nonpartisan mayoral race?"

"Nothing. And everything."

"Hey, wait a minute, did you become a Republican or something when I wasn't looking?"

He chuckled and shook his head.

"I do have to be mindful of my constituents . . ."

"Just tell me, Bobby—are you fo' it or agin' it?"

"It's not that easy, Terrie. I only wish it were. I'm for freedom of choice, but I also believe very strongly in the sanctity of human life."

"Yes, but are you fo' it or agin' it?"

"I think my stance on this issue if perfectly clear . . ."

"Come off it, Bobby. By the way, I go by Theresa now," I said. "I almost didn't know who you were talking about when you called me Terrie.

"That's funny, I've always thought of you as Terrie. You just seem like one to me."

"I'm surprised you even remember me," I said. "We weren't exactly in the same group."

"You're being kind. I wasn't exactly in any group, but you were. And I remember you. You were sassy and smart, and very, very pretty . . ."

"Wait a minute, I think you got mixed up with some other colored girl."

"No, I remember you, girl. Remember how you and Doritha and Barbara used to call each other girl, all the time? 'Gir-r-r-l, guess what ...' I used to love to hear that."

"You did? I'm beginning to think you deserve more credit for being weird than I've been giving you."

"No, come on. Do you remember the dances we used to have and all the Black kids wanted soul music and the steering committee played a record by the Beach Boys and someone unplugged the sound system and all the heads kept right on dancing?"

"No."

"Come on."

"I don't remember that, honest."

"Okay, do you remember ... a vest you had? It was something like suede, and it had long fringe all the way around it. You used to wear a miniskirt with it and platform shoes, but from the back it looked like you only had on the vest 'cause the skirt was so short?"

"You are weird."

"Well, what do you remember?"

"I remember being out of step and always worrying about being too something—too short, too tall, too fat, too thin, too dark, too smart."

"And me. You remember me."

"Yes, Bobby, along with the other too's I remember you."

"Why didn't you ever go out with me, Terrie?"

"Cause you were a white boy and a wimp ... and ... you never asked me due, undoubtedly, to the first two conditions."

He threw his head back and laughed.

"What if I asked you now?"

"Bobby, Mother is voting for you and I probably will, too. So, chill a little bit, will you, honey? You're working way too hard."

"No, come on, I like a challenge ..."

Penny had entered the room at some point during our bantering. She stood just inside the door with her arms folded across her chest.

"Bobby, I think your mother is getting tired," she said dryly.

"Oh, yes, thanks," he said over his shoulder.

She did not move.

He turned around and said very pointedly, "I'll be right out."

She held his gaze for a moment in some sort of duel, but he didn't back down, and she turned abruptly and left the room.

He turned to me, back in character.

Well, Terrie ... Theresa, I've got to go, but I'll be calling you to arrange that date."

"Can I bring my husband and kids?"

"Sure, Penny'll put them to work stuffing envelopes and walking precincts."

We laughed and hugged, holding each other for maybe a second longer than was necessary, but he was weird Bobby and I'm big on charitable work. I patted his back the same way Ella had patted Cenne, and I looked up, over his shoulder, and came face-to-face with Mother, the Goddess of Anger.

She shot me one of those "just wait till I get you alone" looks, and it was all I could do to keep from looking guilty. I quickly suppressed the impulse to jump back from Bobby, smooth my skirt down, and pat my hair to make sure it was in place. I'm grown. I don't have to go through those kind of changes anymore.

I patted Bobby's back one final time, and Mother spoke.

"Mr. Alston, I believe your mother needs you," she said with a tight smile.

He thanked her with a smile—his calculated to dazzle. Turning back to me, he said, "Remember, I'll be calling you," and left.

"I thought I raised you better than that," snapped Mother the minute Bobby's shadow had squeezed through the doorway after him.

"What?"

"Don't play the fool with me. You know what I'm talking about."

"Oh, Mother ..."

"Don't 'oh, Mother' me either," she snarled. "And don't disrespect me. I will not have that in my house.

You know what I'm talking about. Him all over you, and you just a skinnin' and a grinnin'."

"Mother, it was just a friendly hug . . ."

"I don't care what you call it, you hear me. I will not have that kinda mess in my house. You respect me or at least respect my house."

She was getting wound up, and I knew from experience that there was nothing I could do. I would just have to ride it out. I sighed and shifted my weight to the other foot, trying to find a comfortable position.

"You can sigh all you want to and you can dance around and roll your eyes if you want to. But I'll tell you one thing, if you play with a puppy—it'll lick your face. Mark my words. You've got to carry yourself in such a way that people, particularly white boys, won't take liberties with you."

I knew better than to respond. I should have just kept quiet until she ran out of steam, or got tangled in a tangent, but she was getting under my skin and I foolishly allowed myself to be baited.

"Give me a break, will you? This is 1993 not '43."

"Oh, you think so, do you?"

"Yes, I do. Besides, I'm getting sick and tired of your double standards. Look at Jimmy, he didn't stop at just hugging one, he married one, and I don't hear you saying anything about that."

"But Jimmy didn't do it in my sight, and he didn't do it in my house. He went halfway 'round the world to do something like that, and I appreciate that . . ."

She teared up at the mention of Jimmy and his German wife, and I felt guilty. I hate to see Mother cry. I can withstand almost any torture, other than watching her cry. I tried to hug her, but she brushed me away.

"Oh, you can talk so high and mighty," she sniffed. "Well, let me remind you, Miss Lady, you have a husband, too. While you 'round here grinning in some man's face, you better check out what your own man is doing."

"Mother, you can just leave Temp out of this."

"Oh, no, you so grown, you think you can say anything you want to me without regards to my feelings, then you just listen to what I have to say, too. Where were you last night when women were crawling all over 'your man'?"

"What do you mean?"

"I ask you again 'Where were you?' Wherever you were, you weren't where you should'a been, that's for sure. I know that as a fact. I never would have let your father go to something like that without me. I'd have been right there, yes, ma'am, to protect my interest. Girls today don't know nothing about how to keep a man."

Now it was my turn to get mad. She knew good and well where I had been last night—out on a harebrained mission she and Edna cooked up. This is it, I swore to myself. This is it. No more of Mother's messes. "Find LaTreace, find Sir." They can find themselves for all I care. I'm running hither and yon, getting choked, getting beat, being assaulted and sexually harassed, neglecting my family, neglecting my job, and for what? For someone who doesn't appreciate it and who doesn't respect me. I don't care if she is my mother, this is it.

"Mother, what are you talking about?"

"Don't ask me," she responded coyly. "Ask your husband."

Chapter 10

"There's a boy at the door. Says he wants Theresa," announced Brother Cummings.

Mother and I dashed through the house for the front door, both thinking the same thing—Sir. But the boy holding the puppy in his arms was too big to be Sir.

"You Theresa?" he said directing his question with dangerous boldness to Mother.

"It's Mrs. Barkley to you," she snapped. "And don't you dare try to bring that mutt in my house."

"She said she wanted it," responded the boy. He was a chubby kid with sleep still in the corner of his eyes.

"Who said she wanted what?" I asked.

"This here Theresa, she said she wanted a dog, and she would pay five dollars for one."

"I'm Theresa, and I did not ask for a dog."

But I knew before I even spoke that this was the work of my two informants, Jamal and Ndugu.

"I'm looking for a little boy named Sir," I explained. "You know him?"

He nodded.

"Have you seen him?"

He shook his head.

I sighed.

"I don't get the money?" he asked.

"I'm sorry."

"But they said you wanted a dog . . ." he whined.

"Here, son, have some cookies," said Brother Cummings, extending the tray to him.

The boy cradled the puppy to his chest with one arm

and grabbed as many cookies as he could with the other hand.

"And here's a dollar for you," continued Brother Cummings.

The boy's hands were full of puppy and cookies. He weighed putting one or the other down but, glancing over at Mother, changed his mind. Brother Cummings, seeing his dilemma, stuck the bill halfway down the neck of his T-shirt, folding the other half down like an ascot. He took the boy by both shoulders and turned him around to face the street.

"God bless you, son," said Brother Cummings as he closed the door on the boy's retreating form.

"Brother Cummings," I said, "you certainly have a way with children."

"Indeed, I do," he answered, beaming.

Andrea and Cenne had fallen asleep and had been put to bed by a committee of three. Mother was chatting with Bobby and his mother. Penny ambled over to where I was standing.

"Who was that?" she asked.

"Just some neighborhood kid trying to sell a puppy."

"I heard you ask about Sir. There's something I need to talk to you about," she said, casting a quick glance over her shoulder at Mrs. Alston. "LaTreace has been calling Mrs. Alston, upsetting her, asking for money."

"When?"

"Off and on over the last two or three days. She knows her grandmother used to work for the Alstons and how good they were to her, and I guess she figured she could touch them up for a few dollars."

"Did she say anything about her little boy, Sir?"

"I'm not sure. I believe she told Mrs. Alston she had sick children, and she needed money to buy medicine. As you might imagine, this is very upsetting to her. Of course, she wants to help in any way she can, but it's still very upsetting. You know, I really don't think her health is very good. She tries to hide it from Robert, she doesn't want him to worry. But she's really not very strong. I've advised her against getting personally involved. From what I understand, this LaTreace is on

drugs, and she could be dangerous under the right circumstances. You know people like that will hurt their
own mothers to get at some crack. Anyway, Mrs. Alston
insists on trying to help her, and she's asked me to line
up some services for her. You know, emergency food,
clothing, lodging ..."

"Police protection," I said under my breath.

"What?"

"Nothing," I lied.

"Well, anyway, if I could get in touch with her ..."

"We don't know where she is. Mother wants to keep
Sir until she gets this straightened out, and I've tried to
find her but I haven't had any luck."

"Where does she live?"

"She's at some residency motel on Stockton."

"Which one?"

I didn't want to remember. I'd just about washed that
bad memory out of my head.

"I believe it's called the Rose Garden," I said.

"The Rose Garden," she repeated.

"It's not what you think," I told her. "It's worse."

"How do you know what I think?" she quizzed with
a smile.

"Trust me, it's worse than anything you could
imagine."

"By the way, I didn't get a chance to tell you how
sorry I am about your ..."

"Aunt," I lied.

"Yes, your aunt. When Robert asked me to accom-
pany him to the home of one of Mrs. Turner's relatives,
I had no idea we were coming to your house."

"This is my mother's home," I corrected.

"Oh, excuse me," she laughed, casting her eyes about
as if she were taking mental measurements. "I thought it
was a little small for you and Templeton—Temp, Aisha,
Shawn, and your mother. By the way, your children are
dolls, absolute dolls. Why didn't you tell me Shawn was
fluent in French? And that Aisha, she's quite a beauty,
and a cheerleader, too."

"What are you talking about?"

"Oh, didn't Temp tell you, the naughty boy. He's volunteered to work on Robert's campaign. I'm after him to head up one of my committees."

"I bet you are. When did all this happen?"

"Last night at the Black Chamber fund-raiser. And where were you girlfriend? I expected to see you there, too. Honey, if I had a man as fine as yours, ain't no way I'd let him out of my sight. You know, some of these political groupies out there can be absolute piranhas."

She all but nudged me in the ribs with her elbow. The smirk was there, all she needed was a short, stubby, cigar. I was fighting off the urge to slap that silly smirk off her face when Mother called me over to where she was with Mrs. Alston. Penny removed a day planner from her briefcase and went over to where Bobby was talking to Brother Cummings.

"Theresa, LaTreace called Mrs. Alston."

"Yes, dear," said Mrs. Alston in a wee, little voice. "She called, out of the blue, asking for assistance. I'm sure you can imagine how distressing this was to me, coming on the heels of the dreadful news about poor Louise. She was rather excited, and I tried ever so hard to get her to slow down so I could tell her where she could go to get help. I wanted her to know that I would have Miss Troop personally see to it that she got everything she needed. But she just wouldn't listen. All she wanted was money. You know, I kind of got the feeling she thought I owed it to her. Money, you know."

"Mrs. Alston, did she say where she was, where she was calling from?" I asked.

"No, and that's the strange part. She kept asking for money—well, demanding it, actually. But she wouldn't tell me where she was or where she was calling from. I don't want to appear rude, and you'll forgive if I say so, but I'm afraid the young lady is somewhat unbalanced," she said delicately.

Penny abandoned Bobby and joined us.

"Who's unbalanced?" she asked.

"This dear lady's ... what did you say your relationship to Louise was, dear?"

"We're, uh, distant cousins ... by marriage," answered Mother.

"Yes, I do notice some family resemblance," said Mrs. Alston.

Penny was smirking again. But I refused to give her the satisfaction of letting her know I noticed.

"This dear lady's young cousin," continued Mrs. Alston. "You know, I never knew Louise had so many relatives, at least, not here in Sacramento. There's her brother and his children in Forest Hill, but they weren't very close. There's her daughter, the poor child, her granddaughter, and probably a slew of great-grandchildren. I don't think she was ever married, at least I don't remember a husband."

Mother bristled.

Mrs. Alston continued blithely, "And she never mentioned you, dear. To think, you lived right across the street from her all these years. Oh yes, there was something else I wanted to ask you, and my mentioning living across the street reminded me. My goodness, my memory is getting so bad, I'm beginning to think I must have a touch of Alzheimer's."

She tittered girlishly, covering her mouth with her gloved hand.

Mother was just about in need of restraints.

Mrs. Alston suddenly gasped.

"Oh, my goodness, what about Tonton?" she wailed. "Who's caring for Tonton?"

"Who?" asked Mother.

"Tonton," she replied. "The German shepherd. Who's caring for him now that Louise is ... is ... dead?"

"Oh, you mean the dog," said Mother, deliberately giving the word dog two syllables. "He's all right. Long's he's got plenty to eat, a little bit of water, and a place to mess, he's all right."

"But leaving him over there like that borders on abuse ..."

"I agree," said Mother. "And I tell you what, you take Crouton, whatever his name is, and that'll solve your problem and mine."

"Are you sure?" queried Mrs. Alston. "He is a magnificent animal. I wouldn't want to offend anyone. What about the rest of the family?"

"I think I can speak for them on this. Take him."

"Well, thank you. I'm delighted. But are you sure?"

"I'm sure," purred Mother. "He also has about fifty pounds of food in the shed. You can take that, too."

Mrs. Alston turned to Penny. "Mrs. Barkley has graciously consented to our taking Tonton. Please be sure to take him when we leave." Penny glared at her, and she returned the glare with a smile so sweet, it rivaled Mother Iola's.

"Have you been able to locate Louise's personal papers?" asked Mr. Alston as she fiddled with her glove in her lap.

"What do you mean?" said Mother.

"Oh, you know," she said without looking up, "old letters, birth certificates, deeds, things like that."

"No," responded Mother cautiously. "I believe her brother would want to do that."

"Well, I only ask, because I believe Louise had a will, in fact, I'm almost certain she did. And I'm not so certain she'd want that brother of hers handling anything for her after that dreadful business with his—"

"Mrs. Alston," interrupted Mother. "I don't think we need to go into all of that."

Mrs. Alston looked up from the wadded glove she was so carefully kneading, and for a second I saw something in her I hadn't seen earlier. It was like when an old person burst out laughing, tossing her head back, and for a second you realize how fine she must have been in her youth and you're dazzled by the ghost of that youthful beauty. I caught something like that in Mrs. Alston's glance, only the flip side. I saw a flash of fire, an unleashed look of such scathing intensity that a for moment I was frightened. I believe Mother saw something, too, but whatever she saw made her angry. Mrs. Alston prattled on like a woman who strolls about in a public place unaware she is dragging six feet of toilet tissue behind her.

"But, of course, you probably already know that, don't you, dear?" she continued. "I also believe she owned another house somewhere here in the city."

"No, I didn't know that," answered Mother stiffly.

"Oh yes, I don't know where, exactly. You might want to check with the county recorder or county assessor's office. They have records, you know."

Out of the corner of my eye, I saw Brother Cummings heading for the front door. He was halfway there when the bell rang.

"My goodness," he muttered to himself, "I nearly missed that one."

He pulled open the door to reveal yet another boy. This one was wearing high-top athletic shoes that were so massive, they dwarfed everything about him including his rather large, oddly shaped head.

"This the house . . . ?"

"Son, say 'hello' first," admonished Brother Cummings.

"Hello," said the boy.

"Hello," answered Brother Cummings. "Now, ask how I'm doing?"

"How you doing? This the . . . ?"

Brother Cummings held up a finger, silencing the boy.

"I'm fine," said Brother Cummings. "How are you?"

"Um fine, Um fine," said the boy. "Can I have my five dollars now?"

"Why, of course, young man," said Brother Cummings as he pulled out an ancient wallet, laboriously removed the three rubber bands holding it together and extracted a five dollar bill, seemingly as ancient as the wallet.

"There you go."

The boy handed him a bottle and turned to leave.

"You forgot to say thank you," Brother Cummings reminded him.

The boy sighed, said, "Thank you," and darted out of the yard.

"You're very welcome," said Brother Cummings, standing on his toes and craning his neck to catch sight of the boy as he ran a broken path down the street. Brother Cummings closed the door and turned back to the room with a satisfied smile.

"Nice young man. Just needs to learn a few more manners. See how well he took to just the little bit I taught him?"

"Yes sir, Brother Cummings," I said. "You undoubtedly have a way with kids. What's in the bottle?"

He looked at the bottle absently.

"This? Oh yes, it's, uh, syrup."

"Syrup? Why on earth did he bring you a bottle of syrup?" I asked.

"I'm going out back and get me a peach tree switch, and I'm gonna light up the next one comes to that door," announced Mother.

"Go right ahead," I said, "if you're that keen on doing some time for child abuse."

Brother Cummings raised his hand to interrupt.

"Mr. Alston," he said, "I believe that's for you."

We looked around trying to figure out what he was talking about.

"What?" snapped Mother. Mrs. Alston had chipped away at her good humor, and her patience was waning fast.

"That," said Brother Cummings standing erect with pride, pointing toward the door.

We were wondering what "that" was when a car horn started to honk short, staccato blasts.

"My car phone," shouted Bobby as he ran to the door. "Mother, I think we'd better get ready to leave."

Penny put the day planner back in her case and snapped it shut. She went to help Mrs. Alston from her chair, but she waved her away.

"Mrs. Barkley, I have something I want to give you," she said, opening her purse and removing her checkbook. "You may use this as you please. I'm sure there are expenses, what with the little ones and all."

Slowly and laboriously she wrote out a check with the ungloved hand and handed to Mother.

"Thank you, but you really don't have to," said Mother, taking the check. She glanced down at it and raised her eyebrows.

"Are you sure you want to give this much?"

"Absolutely," responded Mrs. Alston firmly.

"Well, thank you."

"Now, dear, there is something I would like you to do for me. Louise had some family papers that belong to me. I would very much appreciate if it I could get them back."

"What are they?" asked Mother.

"Oh, there's no need to go into all of that now. You'll know them when you see them. Good night, dear," she said to Mother, patting her on the hand. "I think you and I understand each other." Turning to the others in the room and waving like she was in an open car cavalcade, she sang out, "Good night, everyone. I had a lovely time. Remember, vote for Bobby."

Chapter 11

"Some funky shit's going down somewhere," announced Bea, in her quirky basso profundo voice. A small woman, a little under five feet, with freckles and inch-long nails who'd somehow managed through hook or crook or Clairol conspiracy to hold on to the sandy blond hair of her youth, Bea stood in the doorway like the Colossus with her hands on her hips and her eyes squeezed into slits.

Mother shook her head in disbelief.

"How much is that check for, again?" asked Edna.

"One thousand dollars," said Mother, "that's a good piece of change."

"One thousand dollars to show her sympathy? Uh-uh, naw," said Bea. "Something else's going on. That bitch ..."

Mother shot her a look.

"Okay, okay, that heifer thinks she's talking to a bunch of fools. 'She has some papers that belong to me' bullshit. She trying to get her hands on Sister Turner's house."

Mother is used to latching onto an idea like a pit bull, the more outrageously harebrained the better, and not letting go of it until she's shaken it to death. But she was clearly having a hard time getting a grip on Mrs. Alston.

"I certainly didn't appreciate some of the things she said, but then again, I don't think the poor woman's wrapped too tight," said Mother. "You sure that Penny child's not her attendant?" she asked hopefully.

I shrugged.

"And all this talk about family papers. I knew Sister

Turner, and let me tell you, she wouldn't take anything that didn't belong to her, and that's the truth. I wouldn't be surprised if Miz Alston's not looking for a bunch of old receipt cards or something. It probably dawned on her that she can't find the recipe for her favorite cottage cheese and ketchup casserole, and now she thinks Sister Turner lifted it some twenty years ago."

Edna, Kaylene and Bea chuckled. But something was bothering me.

"Mother, did Mrs. Turner really have a will?"

"I don't know, baby. That's not the kinda thing you go around talking about, especially when you have a junkie living right there in your house."

"It's just that she seemed so worried about her Bible and some kind of papers. Isn't that what you told me? Weren't those the things I was supposed to take to her at the hospital?"

"I can understand why she wanted her Bible. I wouldn't want to be in the hospital without the comfort of mine. And that's probably where she kept her important papers. What's still bothering me, though, is how she ended up at home when she was supposed to be in the hospital," said Mother.

"You know how Sister Turner was. Maybe she just upped and walked out," suggested Kaylene.

"No," said Mother, "she was too weak. She couldn't hardly stand up when we got to her. They carried her out on a stretcher."

"She was at Mercy?" asked Bea.

Mother nodded.

"Maybe somebody should check with Ester Chatway's girl, Peaches. I believe she works at Mercy."

"Peaches ... Cynthia works in accounting," I reminded them. "I don't see how she would know anything about all of this."

"You never can tell," said Bea, "I'd check with her anyway."

"That's right," said Edna, "it sure can't hurt."

"There's just too much that doesn't add up," said Mother. "Ain't nothing ever got the best of me the way this has. But, Lord, I'm forgetting my manners. Is anybody hungry? Can I get you all anything?"

We were all full with the events of the last two days, and no one wanted to eat.

"Okay," said Mother, "let's sit down and sort this mess out. I'm beginning to feel about as batty as 'Po' Miz Alston."

"Honey, don't let her fool you," said Kaylene. "Mark my words, the woman's putting on an act. All that 'poor little ole helpless me, my mind's failing, I can hardly write my own name' mess. Did you see the shoulders on that broad? She's a tough ole hammer, and I'd trust her just about as far as I could throw her."

"And who's this Penny child, come flouncing 'round here like she owned the place?" asked Mother. "You sure she's not Miz Alston's attendant?"

"Penny Troop's the Alston-for-Mayor campaign manager," I answered.

"Penny Troop? What kinda name is that? Who's her people?" asked Mother.

"I don't know. I met her at Sac State years ago. I think she's from Weed or somewhere like that."

"Weed?" said Ella. "I have people up there. What did you say her name is?"

"Troop, Penny Troop. She did an internship at the capitol right after graduation and went on from there to Washington. I heard, at one time, she worked for Clarence Thomas, and he complained about harassment."

"Aw, girl, quit," laughed Edna. "So you and this Penny good friends, huh?"

"About as good as they come. Right now we're considering a little husband-swapping arrangement. Only Miss Penny ain't got no husband, if you know what I mean."

"I believe I do. In fact, I worked out a similar little arrangement with a certain Miss Arlene Butter Beans Stoddards and my second husband, Mr. Charles."

"Second husband?" I said with astonishment. "I thought Mr. Steve was your second husband."

Edna winked. "Honey, there's a lot you don't know about me. I could teach you a thing or two. 'Follow me, and I will make you fishers of men'—but you've got to promise to throw the small ones back."

"You all better stop that blasphemy," cautioned Mother.

But Edna was just now hitting her stride. "And while we're on the subject of husbands and ex-husbands, where were you last night, baby?"

"Oh no. Not you, too," I cried in mock distress that was close to being real.

"I saw Temp and the kids, but no Theresa. I looked high and low, but couldn't find a trace of you."

"Edna, I think if you and Mother put your heads together and thought real hard, you could come up with a reason why I wasn't there."

"All I know is, ya' snooze, ya' lose, honey. Take it from someone who knows. Don't let no one or nothing come between you and your man."

I closed my eyes and swallowed. That's a sort of symbolic gesture I picked up from high school biology. Frogs can't swallow with their eyes open; they have to close them, and that action helps push the food down their throats. I close my eyes and swallow like a frog when I'm having a hard time dealing with situations where reason or even logic would put me at a disadvantage.

Edna called to Mother, "Lorraine, she's doing it again."

"Ladies," interrupted Brother Cummings, "I believe I will take Aunt Iola on home now. She is feeling a mite poorly."

"Thank you so much for coming to sit with me, Mother Iola," said Mother. "You, too, Brother Cummings. Now, Mother Iola, you know you're welcome in my home anytime. You just get this nephew of yours to bring you on over, or you pick up that phone and call me and I'll come get you. You hear?"

Mother Iola smiled, and she and Mother hugged.

"Here," said Mother handing her a foil-covered dish. "Here's a little something for your dinner. No need to go home and try to cook when we have plenty here."

"Lord bless you, child," said Mother Iola. "You find that baby, now. Hear?"

"We will. We got a pretty good idea where LaTreace took him. We just gotta catch up with her, that's all."

"Remember, it's just as easy to swallow a wet rag as a dry one," said Mother Iola nodding sagely.

Mother furrowed her brows reflectively, then her face brightened, and she smiled.

"That is true, so very true," she said.

Brother Cummings led Mother Iola to the door. Stopping just short of it, he turned to Mother.

"I think we'd better wait until those bad boys leave."

"What boys?" demanded Mother.

"The ones in the car. Been driving up and down the street like they looking for trouble. They out there now."

Mother, Edna, Bea and I crowded to the window and pulled the curtains back. Brother Cummings stood behind us, peering over our shoulders. We saw nothing unusual, just a sleepy little street with too many cars parked on it and a couple of little kids on bikes.

Mother sucked her teeth in frustration and whirled around to confront Brother Cummings.

"Cleotis, I'm getting sick and tired ..."

I nudged her in the ribs.

"Mother, look."

She turned back to the window just as a silver 4X4 cruised into sight, slowing down to a crawl as it neared Mrs. Turner's house. Rap music with the bass pumped up to a bone-jolting boom rattled Mother's windows. We strained to see who was in the car, but the tinted windows blocked our view.

The two kids on bikes had circled the block and came back now, pedaling furiously, their heads down and their ears back like puppies. It dawned on each of us at the same time—they did not see the silver car, almost at a standstill, in front of Mrs. Turner's house. A burst of psychic energy jolted us, but it was a split second before anyone moved. Then Mother, Kaylene, and Edna, turned as one and charged the door.

"Wait," cried Brother Cummings, and they came back to the window panting as if they had run a mile. Just then the boy in front lifted his head and saw the car. He stood up on the brakes, locking the wheels, trying hard to stop. The bike skidded forward, its speed barely checked, tires squealing. At the last moment, just before impact, the boy jerked the handlebars sharply to the left, turning the bike in a half circle and leaning into the turn. He skidded to a stop, landing in a heap on the ground with his head just underneath the car's back fender.

The door opened on the passenger side, and a boy got out. It was one of the boys from outside Dorothy's house the night before. He held a tall can of malt liquor in his hand, a cigarette dangled from his lips. The crotch of his baggy pants sagged past his knees. He walked with an exaggerated swagger to the rear of the car and checked the fender for damage. Apparently seeing none, he reached down, grabbed the little boy by his shirt, and dragged him to his feet. The little boy stood looking up at him bright-eyed with fear and perhaps even admiration. He shook his left hand, loosely from the wrist, as if it had been burned.

The boy from the car said something to someone inside, and they burst out laughing. Reaching down, he grabbed the little boy's hand and poured some of the liquor over it. The boy jerked his hand back and shook it furiously, dancing in place. The other boy laughed again, slapped the can of liquor into the little boy's hand, got back in the car, and it drove away.

The little boy looked at his friend and then at the can of liquor. He cast his eyes about to see if anyone else was looking, and then he put the can to his lips and threw his head back.

I had made it to the door by then.

"Ndugu!" I shouted. "Put that can down this moment!"

I'd flung the door open, darted out to the street, and stood looming over him with both hands on my hips before he had a chance to swallow.

"Boy, don't you ever let me catch you trying to drink alcohol, you hear me. I'll tell your mother."

"Un-uh, you don't even know who my mama is."

"I'll make it my business to find out."

"You don't know her name."

"Yes, I do. It's Mrs. Ndugu."

"No, it ain't," wailed Ndugu. He and Jamal fell in a heap, giggling uproariously.

"Theresa, come on in the house and leave those mannish little boys alone," demanded Mother from her porch.

"Come on," I said to them, motioning toward the house.

"You want us to get in the mean lady's house?"

"Yes, I want you to go in the mean lady's house."

"Un-uh."

"Come on. She won't hurt you, I won't let her."

Mother stood on her porch with her arms folded across her chest.

"So, you gonna bring Mr. Man and his little henchman into my house," she said, surveying Jamal and Ndugu as if they were day-old chitterlings someone forgot to refrigerate.

"Yes, ma'am," I said.

Bending over from the waist so she could get right up into their faces, she said, "I don't appreciate you throwing those tomatoes up on my roof."

They nodded timidly.

"And," continued Mother, "the next time you want some peaches, you come and ask me. I don't want you up in my tree breaking limbs off. You hear me?"

They nodded again.

Mother straightened up, still holding a bead on the boys.

"Now, what do you think you should say?"

"We sorry," said Jamal.

"Ma'am," added Ndugu for good measure.

"I accept your apologies. And you don't have to keep calling me ma'am either. My name is Mrs. Barkley."

The boys introduced themselves. Mother graciously ushered them into the house and offered them refreshments. Mother Iola and Brother Cummings left, and Bea, who was the newlywed of the group, having married Mr. Clarence only six weeks after retiring, was packing up and preparing to leave, too.

"Her man called and asked for her home," said Edna with a knowing smile.

After settling Ndugu and Jamal in the kitchen, Mother returned to the dining room table to finish the sorting out process. Ella took a leather-bound notebook from her purse and flipped through the pages until she found a clean one. At the top of it she wrote "things to do" with a slender gold pen.

"Okay, ladies," she said, "let's get busy."

Under things to do she listed, "Find Sir" and under that, as a sort of subtopic, she put "Find LaTreace."

Mother brought us up-to-date on LaTreace's call. LaTreace said Sir was with her and they both were okay, but she refused to tell Mother where she was staying. She had, however, asked Mother to get her AFDC check when it was delivered and hold it for her. Mother attempted to bait her in by telling her she was holding some money for her, but LaTreace wouldn't bite. She said she would be by in the next couple of days to pick it up.

I gave them a sanitized recounting of my search for LaTreace, and Ella wrote another subtopic, "Check with Dorothy again." I also told them about Trey Dog, the money LaTreace supposedly owed him, and his threats.

"It looks like Trey Dog shot up Mrs. Turner's house gunning for LaTreace," I said.

"Like I said before, this was all LaTreace's mess. If it wasn't for her, Sister Turner would be alive today," said Mother.

"We still have a problem," said Kaylene. "As long as LaTreace owes this triple-dog person money, she's still in danger, and that means the baby's in danger."

"We gotta come up with something," said Edna.

"We pay him off," said Mother. "That's the only way," she said in response to our raised eyebrows. "We take Miz Alston's check here and cash it and use the money to pay off Mr. Dog. That way we keep LaTreace alive until we can find her and get Sir."

Kaylene was struggling with the idea.

"Somehow, it just doesn't seem right to deal with a person like this down on his own level. I'm afraid we may be biting off more than we can chew."

"What choice do we have?" said Edna. "We gotta try

something." Turning to me, she asked, "How much does she owe him?"

"I got the feeling it was a couple of hundred dollars, four or five at the most."

"Well, a thousand should more than cover it. I'll get this check cashed first thing tomorrow and take the money to Dog Man," said Mother. "Write that down, Ella."

"Excuse me, but who's going to take the money to Trey Dog?" I asked.

"Why, I will, of course, baby," said Mother. "Who else."

"I got a better idea," I said. "Hire a process server."

"Quit your teasing, Theresa."

"I am not teasing."

"Quit your joking, then."

"I am not joking, and you're not going. Look, don't you see this could be dangerous? In all likelihood, Trey Dog killed Mrs. Turner. I don't want you to be next."

Ella patted my hand.

"The child's right, Sister Barkley."

"Oh, she's just making a mountain out of a molehill," said Mother. It's a simple little thing to take the money to the boy and leave, that's all."

"You don't even know where he lives."

"That Dorothy probably knows."

"No, she doesn't," I said adamantly.

We heard a shuffling noise and looked up to find Jamal standing in the doorway to the kitchen with his hand raised high over his head like he was in school.

"What is it, honey?" asked Mother.

"I know where Trey Dog live."

"No, he doesn't," I said.

"Uh-huh, T-bo told me. Him and Fat Daddy Mack ..."

"Wait a minute," I said. "Before you listen to this ... this ... kid, remember he's the one who sent the boy with the puppy here and the other one with the syrup, and they both got paid for nothing. This kid has an overly active imagination and a strong mercenary sense. I should know, I'm the one who discovered him."

Mother cut me off. "Where does he live, honey?"

"Him and Fat Daddy Mack live over by Manny's."

"And where is that?"

"It's way over past Tosh's and you go by the freeway and there's a big tree."

I looked at Mother and her cohorts. Incredulously they were nodding their heads as if what Jamal was saying made sense. Then again, he was talking their language. That's the way they give directions, too. They're perfectly comfortable telling you to go 'a few houses down from where Sister So-and-So used to live.' Conventional things like addresses and street names mean very little to them and neither, apparently, did Mother's safety.

I'm an easygoing, good-natured type of person, slow to come to a boil, but I was getting angry. Here I was, sitting in a room with four women, each one old enough to be my mother and each taking on that role from time to time, and not one child from their collective brooding in sight. Just me. Where were all the rest? And who elected me proxy for my mother's friends' absentee progeny? I know I sure didn't volunteer.

I could get up and walk. I could just say 'later for this' and go home to my kids and my man they're so keen on me keeping. And I could close my eyes and cover my ears and hope that everything came out all right, hope that I didn't see their faces on the six o'clock news, and hope that I could still sleep at night.

But, as they say about parenting parents, "It's a dirty job, but someone's gotta do it." The streets are just too mean to turn your own mother loose on them, and I'm the only one here. So I guess it's my job.

"Mother, why don't I deliver the money?"

"No, baby, I don't want you messed up in this end of it. You just find the child."

"Mother, you don't seem to understand, you could be walking into something. This is dangerous."

"That's all right, baby. You just let me worry about it. I didn't get this old being a fool."

I definitely didn't want to go wandering around the city looking for the kid who might have killed Mrs. Turner. But I couldn't let Mother do it either. I couldn't live with myself if something happened to her.

I stood up, planted both hands firmly on the table, and leaned toward Mother.

"Listen to me, I will not let you do this. Do you hear?"

The women looked at me and then each other, and smiled as if to say "isn't she cute." Mother patted my hand.

"I'll tell you what, Theresa. You can take me to the bank tomorrow—I'll need some help with the girls. Then we'll decide how to get the money to the dog boy."

I agreed. I hadn't gotten her to back down, but at least I still had some time to reason with her.

"Once you start something like this, it's going to be hard to get out of it," cautioned Ella. "What's to stop every little snotty-nose gang banger from knocking on your door, demanding you pay off some real or fabricated debt of LaTreace's? What's to stop you from ending up like Sister Turner once you become associated with LaTreace? I don't know, ladies. I'm not sure we're thinking this thing through."

"My sentiments, exactly," I affirmed.

Ella's voice of reason was like a dash of cold water in the women's faces. It was the last thing they wanted to deal with right then. They sat silently, their enthusiasm for the scheme of the moment wilting by the second.

"I'll go an' show her where Trey Dog live," volunteered Jamal, desperate to regain the warm glow that came with being the center of attention.

"Now, you hear that, Theresa?" said Mother. "Everything's okay, the baby will show me the way."

Edna and Kaylene chuckled. Jamal didn't like being called a baby, but being the authority on anything seemed to agree with him, and he was all too willing to show Mother where Fat Daddy Mack and Trey Dog lived.

"Ladies, if you insist on going through with this, I want it known that I did my best to dissuade you," said Ella. She wrote on her list, "Deliver money to Dog."

"Jamal'll have to get his mother's permission first," I said. "Anyway, why aren't you guys in school?" I asked him and Ndugu, who had joined him.

"We in home school."

"Who's teaching you, then?

"Wanda."

"And who's Wanda?"

"She our grandmother."

"Why're you in home-schooling?"

"Our daddy says kids in regular school too bad. He say, he gon' put us in Elite Day School when they get vouchers."

"Is that so? Then, why is it I see you guys outside riding bikes and messing around every time I come over here during school hours?"

They looked at each other.

"Oh, that must be nap time."

"If it's nap time, how come you're outside?"

"No-o-o, Wanda's nap time. We come outside when it's Wanda's nap time, and we go back in when she wakes up."

"I give up. Don't tell me anymore," I said.

"What else is on the list, Ella?" asked Mother.

"Well, we still need to find out how Sister Turner got home when she was supposed to be in the hospital. Someone has to check with Peaches on that."

Mother nodded.

"I guess we should also check on whether she had other property."

"Hey, wait a minute," I said. "What about Mrs. Turner's papers? Did you find anything when you did the cleaning?"

"Just some bills and stuff. Edna has what was there."

I turned to Edna. "What did you find?"

"Just some bills and stuff."

"The key to everything may be somewhere in those papers."

"I am well aware of that," she snapped.

I looked at her, wondering why she was getting so testy. She returned my gaze. I shrugged and continued.

"Maybe we should just go through it right now. We might find something that'll help us put this whole thing in some kind of perspective."

"I took it home," said Edna. There was an edge of challenge to her voice.

"But that doesn't make any sense."

Edna leaned back in her chair and looked around the table. "Somebody better tell this child to read First Timothy, chapter five, verse one—'Rebuke not thy elders.' "

A couple of the women chuckled. Mother didn't. "Leave her alone, Edna," she said.

Edna shrugged. "Anyway," she said, "the first thing we oughta do before we go messing around in Sister Turner's business is notify her people."

"I tried calling her brother but he's unlisted, all I have is his address," said Mother. "I even called Western Union and sent a telegram by phone, asking him to call me, but so far nothing. I know he got it. I just don't understand why he hasn't called or anything."

"You know, they say there was some bad blood between them."

"I don't care how bad the blood, she was his sister. That ought to count for something."

"What happened between them?" I asked.

Mother sighed.

"It just doesn't seem right to stir up old mess, especially when the person is dead and can't defend herself. I'll tell you like I told old lady Alston, 'Let sleeping dogs lie.' Oh, I heard the rumors and I heard the lies. I probably was closer to Sister Turner than anybody else in this room, but not once did I ever insult her by bringing any of that mess up. 'Let sleeping dogs lie.' That's what I say."

"But it might have something to do with all this," I insisted.

"It has nothing to do with anything. The child died, isn't that enough?"

"What child?" I asked, perplexed by the seemingly non sequitur.

I saw the warning signs, but I don't think anyone else did. I saw Mother's eyes scrunch down so tight, the little laugh lines at their corners looked like they'd been cut in with a knife. I saw the muscles in her neck cord up and her ears turn red. So when she brought the palm of her hand down on the table with such force, it jarred the knickknacks on the buffet. I didn't jump like everyone else. My eyes didn't bug out like Jamal's either. I was relatively calm, considering the circumstances.

"Girl, what's the matter with you?" sniffed Edna. Have you lost your mind?"

"I will not have you destroy Sister Turner's good name. When a child dies, people start looking around for somebody to blame. And who is the first person they point their fingers at? The mother. If the child gets run over by a car, the mother should have watched him better, a child had rheumatic fever and his heart plays out, the mother should have taken him to the doctor more often, a child died of TB, the mother should have kept a cleaner house, should have given him cod-liver oil. Sister Turner was a mother to that child. It was not her fault, and I will not have you destroy her good name, not here in my house."

"Well," sighed Ella, "what's done is done. Let's go on to other things."

"We need to make sure her brother knows. Somebody needs to go up there and let him know. Where does he live?"

"Forest Hill," said Mother. "His name is Walter Gillian. I have his address here, but I kinda feel I should be the one to go talk to him."

"Well, we'll just put down 'Notify relatives,'" said Ella. "And we can work that out later. Are there any more relatives?"

"She has some people in Oklahoma, and there's the child at the Women's Correctional Facility in Stockton."

"She should be notified, too," said Edna.

Ella tore out the "things to do" list and handed it to Mother, who handed it to me.

"I'm going to be leaving now," said Ella. "But you let me know what I can do to help."

Kaylene also packed up and left. Edna got ready to leave and pulled me aside. Without preamble she asked: "What did you take out of Louise's house?"

"What?" I asked, my astonishment robbing me of all rhetorical grace.

"When you searched it. Don't tell me you didn't

search it," she said in response to my look of dismay. "You were in there too long. I know you searched it."

I looked at Edna carefully. She was Mother's closest friend, and I'd grown up with her. But she'd always had a certain edge to her. She seemed to push the envelope just a little farther than the rest of Mother's friends. As a kid, I wouldn't have been surprised to learn that she had secret tattoos in private places. But I wasn't a kid anymore.

"I didn't take anything," I protested, my voice rising a little more that I would have liked. "How do you know how long I was in there anyway?"

"That's all right how I know. You just be sure you didn't take anything?"

"Wait one minute. Time-out. With all due respect— First Timothy and all that stuff—who the hell do you think you're talking to?"

Edna smiled. There was a slight shifting in her demeanor, an almost imperceptible altering. If I hadn't known her so well, I wouldn't have seen it. She hugged me.

"I'm sorry, baby. But you don't know what you might be getting messed up with, that's all. I don't want you to end up getting hurt. Lorraine's heart's in the right place, but all she sees is the good in people. Somebody killed Louise, and we think we know who it was, but we don't really. It could have been anybody for any number of reasons. If you have something of hers, you could be walking around with a time bomb on your hands and not even know it. You just have to be careful that's all."

Edna hugged me again and left. I watched her go, shaking my head—crazy old woman. I sent Jamal and Ndugu home to Wanda. That left me and Mother alone. We sat facing each other across the dining room table, drinking coffee in an easy, companionable silence. Mother got up, went to the kitchen, and returned with two generous servings of pound cake.

"You must have been reading my mind," I said. "Speaking of such, what's with Brother Cummings? He supposed to be psychic or something."

Mother laughed.

"Supposed to be's a tall order for Brother Cummings."

"What do you mean?"

"He was blessed with a gift—that kinda thing seems to run in Mother Iola's side of the family—but he didn't do anything to develop it and the Lord didn't bless him any further."

"What runs in Mother Iola's family?"

"Seeing."

"Is that kinda like Mother Simms?"

"Mother Simms' a worker."

"What's the difference?"

"Mother Iola can tell you things."

"Kind of like a fortune-teller?"

"No, baby, there's not very much fortune in it. That's Brother Cummings's problem, he got sidetracked looking for fortune. Mother Iola can look beyond the surface. It's kinda like she sees the inner working of things from a spiritual perspective. Now, Brother Cummings, on the other hand, played with his gift and ran around chasing women, drinking, and gambling."

"That old man?"

"He wasn't old all his life, honey. He made a mockery of his gift, trying to pick horses that would win, mess like that. They tell me, he even worked in a carnival at one time. Called himself Swami something or the other. But God don't like ugly. The Lord fooled him, turned his gift on and off, on and off, like a lightbulb. He didn't know when he was true and when he wasn't, but he kept on trying to act like he could see. Pretty soon people come looking for him, wanting their money back. And they wasn't asking nice like, some of them wanted to let their guns and knives do the talking, if you know what I mean."

I didn't quite know what she meant, but I was following along the best I could. Mother had finished her cake and was playing with the crumbs left on the plate as she spoke in a low, mellow, relaxed tone.

"He finally came to his senses a few years ago and came back home to help his aunt."

"That's all there is to it?"

"That's all there is to it."

"What about all that business with the door and the phone?"

"Parlor games. Just like the carnival, he loves to entertain. It doesn't mean anything, though, not like Mother Iola."

"How come I can't understand what she's talking about?"

"You got to listen real hard. You got to study up on what she says. You got to think on it, and sleep on it, and pray on it before it means anything. Sometimes, unless you put it in the right context, it doesn't mean anything at all."

"Is that what Mother Simms does?"

"Mother Simms has gifts, too. She helps you work things out, helps you fight back. Things are revealed to her when she prays."

"Maybe we'd better talk Mother Simms into helping us find Sir."

"You can laugh if you want to, but I've already talked to Mother Simms about this mess, and she's told me some things."

"What kind of things?"

"That's all right, it'll all come to pass."

"And Edna. What was with her today. She seemed awfully testy, didn't she?"

"You mean about Sister Turner's papers?"

I nodded.

"You know Edna," she said with lightness that seemed almost forced. "Edna is a scrapper. She's gotta feel she's in control of something. She's gotten worse since Mr. Steve died and left her high and dry. She gets a little hotheaded sometimes—that geeche blood in her."

"I never got the full story on what happened with her and Mr. Steve. I thought he was rich?"

"He was well-off. Edna thought she'd finally found her gravy boat, latching onto an old man like that."

"How old was he?"

"He was pretty old. Must have been close to ninety. One foot in the grave and another on a banana peel a slippin' and a slidin'—that's what Edna use to say. She thought all she had to do, to use her words, was rub his head a time or two, make sure he had plenty of Attends, and sit back and wait to collect his insurance."

"What happened?"

"He had the last laugh. His kids got everything."

"Everything? All the property, the business? Everything?"

"He had everything wrapped up in a trust so tight all she got was that little house she lives in."

"What about Mrs. Turner? You know, the child she lost. What happened?"

Mother carefully balanced her fork on the edge of the plate before looking up. "Nothing. Her niece was staying with her. She came down sick and died."

"That's it?"

"That's it."

"Then why did you make such a big deal of it and everything?"

"Because it ain't nobody's business."

"What did Mother Iola mean when she said 'It's just as easy to swallow a wet rag as a dry one'?"

"Damned if I know."

Chapter 12

I was ready for Temp when I got home. We were going to deal with the Penny Troop issue before things got out of hand. I hadn't worked as hard as I had to build a life with this man just to have some woman walk in and destroy it all with her cheap innuendos and petty manipulations. I was ready—but Temp had left by the time I got there.

I retreated to the bathroom and did the soak and shower routine again as I planned my opening salvo in the Penny War. I was blow-drying my hair when Aisha bounded in and tickled me in the ribs. I turned and kissed her on her forehead. She has a prominent forehead like Temp's, and she's usually a little self-conscious about it and wears bangs. But today she had her hair pulled back in a single French braid that ran down the back of her head. She looked very sophisticated for a sixteen-year-old.

"Hi, baby. How's school?"

"All right. What're you doing here?"

"I took the day off—mental health."

"You still coming to the game?"

"Of course."

"Mom, you said that the last time."

"I wrote it down on the wrong day the last time. This time I got it straight, Friday, this week, three-thirty p.m."

"Right."

"Besides, I'm bringing Mother. She wants to see your new cheers, and she won't let me forget."

"I see you had another migraine last night."

"Uh-huh."

"Well, you missed a real good one last night, Mom. The social event of the year, according to Dad."

"What was that?"

"Some ole whack political thing Dad made us go to. Bunch of tired old people standing around drinking wine, acting phony. Everybody treating you like a baby."

I believe it is unethical to pump a child for information about her parents. Ordinarily, under different circumstances, I would never stoop so low. But I needed to know how deep Penny had been able to burrow into my life. So I broke one of my cardinal rules and sought information from my child about her dad.

"Did you happen to meet a woman named Penny Troop last night?"

"Penny? Oh yeah, the one in the tight dress. She's nice."

Her answer was disquieting. "What do you mean?"

"Well, she wasn't like the rest. She talked to me like I was a person instead of a kid. Although she did seem to hang on to Daddy a lot." Aisha paused thoughtfully. "Mom, you know, I kinda think a lot of the women there thought Dad was cute or something." She shuddered. "But Penny was nice. Even when Dad tried to clown me about the wine, she was nice."

"She's not nice," I wanted to tell Aisha. "Stay away from her." But Penny was my problem, not hers. I struggled to pick up the strands of our conversation.

"You still trying to convince your dad to let you have wine?

She nodded.

"I take it you tried again last night."

"I only wanted a little, but Dad started running 'round snatching glasses and stuff. The French and Italians do it all the time, you know, let kids have wine. You guys makes such a big deal out of everything."

I was trying to stay on track with Aisha's conversation, but Penny was weighing heavily on my mind.

Aisha continued, "I didn't want to go in the first place. I had tons of homework, but Dad didn't care. All he could say was 'Get off the phone ... Get dressed ...

Where's your mom?.' Shawn went along, just like a puppy, wagging his tail and everything, letting old ladies pinch his cheeks and kiss him and stuff. You should have seen him, Mom. He had on that too little suit from last Easter, looking like the geek of the week. And he spoke French all night. French! *Wee, wee, monsieur. Wee, wee, madame.* Everybody thought it was so-o-o cute. Mom, it was embarrassing. I've never been so embarrassed in my entire life."

Embarrassing? I was struggling to keep from laughing out loud. Aisha caught me.

"Mom, if you want me to, I can go out. I know how bad gastric upsets can be."

I burst out laughing. "Honey, don't leave. It's just that, it's so funny the way you described it. I can just see Shawn."

"Mom, it's not funny. He's already a nerd and now he's becoming a . . .a . . . a geek. If I were you, I'd take him out of Lawrence Academy before it's too late and put him back in public school."

"Honey, there are worse things in life than being a nerd."

"And a geek?"

"And a geek."

"You say that now, but wait until he has to be around Black people and he doesn't know how to act. You don't know how hard that's going to be on him. Brothers and sisters will dog him, Mom. You just don't know."

"Was it hard for you, honey?"

"Kinda. But I didn't stay at Lawrence as long as he has, and I'm not like him. I know how to listen and check things out. I know how to get along. I don't go around getting in people's faces, annoying them like Shawn does."

"You really believe it's going to be that hard for him?"

"Mom, face reality. The boy is hurt, and it's only going to be worse when he leaves Lawrence and has to deal with real people, Black people.

"But there's a whole church full of Black folk at Mount Calvary, and you guys have Jack and Jill. That's why I joined, pay the dues, go to the meetings, so you guys could have some sort of positive interaction with other Black kids."

"That's not the real world, Mom; church on Sundays and Jack and Jill on the second Saturday. The real world is everyday, all the stuff in between Sundays and second Saturdays. I'm telling you, Mom. Just wait until he starts bringing home white girls."

Ka-pow! She hit me where it hurts, and she knew it. How had this become "trash Shawn day"? Something heavy was weighing on her mind, and it wasn't Shawn's social skills.

I abandoned my hair and went into the bedroom. Aisha followed and plopped down in the middle of my unmade bed. I sat down next to her.

"Mom, there's something else we need to talk about."

Aisha was fingering the satin binding on my blanket, something she used to do when she was little. She'd started off a blankie kid, but by the time she was three, she had refined the habit until a strip of satin binding was all she needed. Right up until she kicked the habit a few years ago, she always went to blankie when she was stressed.

"And I don't want you to get all bossy, or sarcastic, or flippant, or try to make fun of me. Okay?"

It's funny how people see you, especially your own family, your own children. I am rather passionate about certain things I believe in, but bossy? I see myself as having a healthy sense of humor. Maybe I am a bit over enamored with irony, but I'm never flippant, hardly sarcastic. With Temp maybe, but with my children, the little darlings, the lights of my life, never.

"Honey, you can always talk to me about anything. You know that. I'll give you my complete, undivided attention, and I promise not to be sarcastic."

"I think it's time you and I talked about birth control," Aisha said with solemn dignity.

"For me or you?"

"Mom!"

"Okay, okay. Are you, uh, planning on becoming sexually active?"

"Mom, you don't have to make it sound so clinical."

"All right, what's a better way of saying it? What would you say?"

"Well, I don't think I'd ask. I'd just assume if a person wanted to talk about birth control, the person either was or was seriously considering to."

"To what?"

"Mom!"

"Well, what do people say nowadays when they decide to? What is the current terminology?"

"Oh, Mom."

"No, come on, tell me."

"What do you and Dad call it, huh? Answer that."

"Okay. You watch Nickelodeon, right? You've seen that little old man on *Laugh-In*, goes up to the old lady? Well, Dad says the same thing the little old man says."

"He doesn't."

"Wanna see my walnetto? Honest, that's what he says in the same kind of gravelly voice. 'Wanna see my walnetto?' "

We laughed and Aisha lay back staring at the ceiling. I lay staring at her. She is a beautiful child and most of the time she is the sweetest, most caring person I know. I've been madly in love with this child from the first time I caught a glimpse of her image on the sonogram in the doctor's office.

"Who is the boy, anyway?" I asked. "Don't tell it's that ole chuckleheaded Mark, Mark Wesley Talbot."

"Mom, I love him."

"In that case I take back the 'chucklehead' part."

"It's just that I'm not sure I'm really ready . . ."

These were my sentiments, exactly. I was literally biting the inside of my lip trying to "actively listen."

"It's really no big deal. Everybody's doing it."

Active listening lost out. "Everybody who, honey?" I gently queried.

"Oh, you know, everybody."

"DeShanna and Laura?" I prodded.

"No, not my friends, but everybody else. Melba Benjamin."

"Mark's old girlfriend?"

"Uh-huh."

"Honey, this shouldn't be a competitive thing."

"Mom, you promised not to get bossy."

"So, I had my fingers crossed. Honestly, sweetheart, this is a decision only you can make. I know that, and I trust your judgment."

She smiled weakly.

"You know how Dad and I feel about young people and irresponsible sex. And you've listened to us and Pastor Miller often enough to know our feelings on morals."

She nodded.

"Good. Now, it seems to me, what you got to work out is how you feel. Not how I feel, or how Dad feels, or how Mr. Mark Wesley Talbot feels. If you were to ask me, I'd say wait. No, not for the reason you think. I'd say wait until you find someone who is at least your equal. Someone who balances you out. Someone who is as smart as you are, someone who is as kind as you are. Someone who is about something."

Aisha closed her eyes.

"I'm getting too preachy, aren't I?"

"No, that's all right, Mom. I know you can't help it."

We sat silently. Aisha scooted up to the head of the bed and leaned back against the headboard, crossing her legs at the ankles and drawing them up close to her. Her fingers worked the binding like a rosary.

Warnings flashed through my mind like images in a light show. There are diseases, I wanted to warn her. Really horrible things like genital herpes, syphilis, gonorrhea, crabs, chlamydia, not to mention AIDS. And don't forget to factor in good old-fashioned unwanted pregnancy. Then there's logistics. They've closed all the drive-ins down, besides chucklehead doesn't have a car. And you can't just go check into a motel. Parks are unsafe; Lover's Lane is more like Mugger's Lane now. And if that boy so much as goes a foot beyond the living room the next time he is here, I will find Mother's gun, reassemble it myself, and shoot him in his little butt. So, my dear, I thought to myself, I guess you'll just have to call the whole thing off.

I was getting carried away and so, for that matter, was

Aisha. This boy, with his weak little pressures, wasn't the only boy in the world.

"What happened to Kalid?" I asked. "I thought you kinda liked him."

"Oh, Mom, Kalid is into white girls."

"He is? Kalid? Does his mother know? Well, what about Jason, Jason DuBois?"

"Asian girls. Little petite, shy ones, not the ones who run track or are on the debate team."

"Well, I always liked Darryl, despite what Temp and Shawn said. What about Darryl?"

"Hispanic girls and salsa music."

"What? I can't believe this. Do boys really specialize these days? You know, when I was young . . ."

"Yes, Mom, I know. When you were young, girls didn't 'court' until they were eighteen and then only with written approval from both parents and the maternal grandmother."

That's another thing I like about this child, her biting wit.

"What I was going to say, when I was so rudely interrupted, is in my day, boys specialized in girls who 'did' and girls who 'didn't.' I don't remember all this stuff about race and music. Which ones go for the regular, down to earth, R and B, hip-hop-type sisters?"

"Aaron Mosberg . . . and he's taken."

"It's pretty bad, huh?"

She shrugged.

"What are you going to do?"

"I don't know. I haven't decided yet."

"Well, that's a good sign. *You* haven't decided. Just as long as you are making the decision and you don't do anything just because you're scared or pressured or you want to keep up with the Melba Benjamins of the world. Understand?"

She nodded.

There should have been a swell of syrupy violin music right about now, and the image of the wise and understanding mother offering guidance to the young girl hanging on to her every word would fade into a commercial for Massengill Medicated Douche. But this was real life, so instead of a Massengill moment I got Mother. I was just about choking on the "active listening, nurturing, supportive mother, you make your own decisions" stuff anyway when the "Mother tapes" started playing in the back of my mind.

"You tell that girl to keep her dress down and her legs closed, and maybe she'll get somewhere in life. She's too young to court, anyhow. I told you that. But do you listen to me? You don't need no little boys sniffing 'round your house. You tell that child, the easiest thing in the world is to get a boy to lay down with you, and the hardest thing in the world is to get a man to stand beside you. You tell her that, you hear?"

Mother always was bossy.

Aisha and I were sitting in contemplative silence when the door flew open and Shawn burst into the room like some machine from hell.

"Mom-m-m," wailed Aisha. "He always spoils everything."

"Mom, Mom, Mom," hiccuped Shawn. "I got it. I got it. The letter . . . they wrote me back. I got a letter from Sega." He had on clothes I didn't recognize.

"That's good, honey. Where'd you get those clothes?"

"Oh, I had a little accident. Somebody caused the aquarium to spill all over me. These are spares from school."

"Mom-m-m," complained Aisha.

"Shawn, Aisha and I were having a little talk . . ."

"A little talk, thanks a lot, Mom. I'll just leave now and let you and the dunce raptor here have a little talk."

Shawn looked at her and shrugged as she ran from the room. He barely winced when her door slammed. I sighed and turned to him.

"Now, what's this about Sega, honey?"

"They answered my letter, Mom." He fluttered a piece of paper in my face. "And they said I couldn't get a job testing their games yet 'cause I'm not old enough, but I can when I'm 'round sixteen or seventeen. And they said I have to study math and science and computers, and I have to learn these computer languages."

Shawn is my expressive child. He dances and pantomimes his way through most discussions. He danced through this one, not hip-hop stuff, but expressive in the mode of Katherine Dunham.

"That's wonderful, Shawn." I hugged him, and he beamed up at me.

"Shawn, honey, I need to ask you something."

"Be my guest," he said in the cartoon courtly manner of his.

"Honey, what kind of man will you be when you grow up?"

"Well, I'm gonna be kinda like Dad."

"Kinda like Dad?" I queried.

"Yeah, Dad is way cool. He can drive with one hand, one finger even. And once he had this gigantic burp that lasted for three whole minutes."

"That's impressive."

"I'm gonna kinda be like Chung Li, too. She can turn upside down and do this whirly-bird kick, and Ryu, he throws fireballs, and Vega, he moves hecka fast."

"Wait a minute, are these real people?"

"They're Street Fighter II."

"Oh," I said, not quite sure whether I was relieved or not. "What type woman do you think you will marry?"

Shawn looked around cautiously. "Promise not to laugh and not to tell anyone?"

I promised.

"Well," he said, "I have decided to marry DeShanna."

"You have good taste, boy. She's smart, beautiful, and from what I know of her, she is of sterling character."

Shawn allowed himself to breathe. "That's exactly what I think," he said with relief.

"How long have you felt this way about her?"

"Oh, a long time, since I was ten, at least. You won't tell her will you?"

I promised not to tell, and he went to his room to play. I went to Aisha's room to play some "Mother tapes" to her.

I knew Temp was home when I started hearing doors slam downstairs—first the door leading from the garage to the laundry room, next the bathroom door, and then it seemed like every cabinet door in the kitchen.

It was time for me and him to talk Penny. I should have dealt with the issue this morning, but Temp had distracted me with his lovemaking, and he'd been distracted, in turn, by Mother's gun.

I went downstairs. Temp stood in front of the open refrigerator staring. He made no effort to take anything out.

"Honey, we need to talk."

He turned and stared at me and then walked over to the dining area and sat down. I closed the refrigerator and followed him.

"Honey, I know things have been difficult lately. I've dropped a few balls. The thing with Mother. Everything. But I love you."

I reached over and took his hand. He let me.

"I'm going to sort out everything so I can concentrate on what's important to me—you and the kids. I guess sometimes I forget that. Thanks for reminding me this morning." I squeezed his hand and smiled. He didn't respond. I continued.

"That's why we really need to talk about Penny Troop."

He withdrew his hand, put his elbows on the table, and buried his face in his palms.

"I was one minute and sixteen seconds late," he said, "and they closed the door in my face."

"What?"

"The Trilux bid—I didn't make it. They wouldn't accept it. I was late."

He got up, kicked the chair out of his way, and stood with his back to me staring out of the window.

"I needed that contract. I really needed that contract."

"Honey, I'm so sorry."

He swung around to me.

"You're sorry? What have you done to keep from having to be sorry? Have you done anything to help? Have you picked up the kids when you were supposed to? Have you even been here when you were supposed to?

Do you live here or at your mama's? You're sorry. You know, T, you're not half as sorry as I am."

Temp grabbed his car keys from the counter and headed for the door.

"I'm getting out of here," he said. "I need to think."

Chapter 13

Temp got home around one in the morning muttering to himself and smelling of smoke. He crawled into bed, turned his back to me, and promptly went to sleep, snoring softly. It wasn't as easy for me. I'd been worried, more than I like to admit, when he stormed out. Now that he was home I was relieved, but still worried. He needed me, but because he didn't trust me to be there for him, he was turning away from me. I saw it all clearly now in the early hours of the morning. I only hoped it wasn't too late for me to make a change. I had one more obligation to keep tomorrow, deliver the money. After that I was removing myself from the whole thing. I would notify the police and let them handle finding Sir. From now on, I would concentrate on the most important people in my life: Temp and the kids. I tossed and turned a couple more hours before falling into a shallow, fitful sleep.

I got up early the next morning, just like it was a workday, and dressed for the business transaction with Trey Dog. I am not very much of a pants person, but I thought I might have to make a few fast getaways, and pants are the most functional getaway clothes I know. I dug out a sand-colored pair from my Willi Wear days and put them together with a chocolate blouse and a persimmon, sand-washed, silk flight jacket. Aisha lent me her Doc Martens to complete the look.

I was almost ready for business, but first I had to call Allen and ask for one more day off. Allen had given me an inch, and now I was asking for a mile. He expected me to be at work today, and I knew I needed to be there, especially with Brenda acting. But I had this final obligation to fulfill. I had to pay off Trey Dog, redeem LaTreace's life, and then things would go back to normal.

I dialed Allen's number and was informed by his secretary, Lillian, that he was in a meeting. I took the easy way out, and asked her to inform him that I was taking another day off due to family matters. I only hoped I wasn't eroding an already seriously damaged relationship. Allen was a friend and a mentor. I could afford to lose neither.

I called Brenda next.

"I shut down that gambling ring," she announced. "And I put the Tupperware and Avon peddlers on notice, too."

"Gambling ring? What gambling ring?"

"Greta's over in payroll transactions."

"It was a baby pool. They were guessing when LaDonna's baby would be born."

"It's still gambling. I shut it down."

"Brenda, I've been gone one day. One day. I asked you to go to my meetings and take care of the paper flow. That's all."

"You can't ignore something like that."

"Brenda, no more changes. Okay? Just go to my meetings. Okay? Now, is there anything out of yesterday's meetings I should be aware of?"

"I didn't make them."

"What do you mean you didn't make them? That's all I asked you to do."

"I didn't have time. I was trying to deal with this gambling thing."

It was no use trying to reason with Brenda. The only thing I could do was get back to work as soon as possible and try to salvage my career. I should have known better than to give her that kind of power. The last time I'd taken vacation and left her in charge, I'd returned to find the Latino Employee group pitted against the Disabled Advisory Committee, the Black Employee Support Group wearing red, black, and green and chanting in the corridor outside the director's office, and Brenda smiling like the cat who swallowed the canary. When I went back to work this time, there'd probably be more than a few fence-mending meetings to attend, hurt feelings to sooth, egos to massage, and probably a couple of letters to the governor's office to answer. But, I couldn't worry about that now. I forced it to the back of my mind so I could concentrate on the task at hand.

I kissed the kids good-bye—Temp sullenly turned away from me—and told them I was going out in the field at work. It was easier that way. The day was going to be trying enough, and I didn't need the added stress of arguing with Temp or having him and the kids worry about me. Besides, I'm grown.

Mother was ready when I got there, her eyes burning brightly behind her glasses.

"Okay, then. Let's go."

Mother took her glasses off and wiped the lenses on the hem of her skirt and put them back on. Then she stared at the alarm, in what seemed like a contest of wills, for nearly a minute before she began slowly punching in the numbers. She finished entering her code and waited. Beads of sweat rimmed her hairline. After ten seconds there was no ear-piercing blast of sound, just the reassuring beeping noise the alarm made as it armed itself. Mother let her breath out.

"There," she said triumphantly.

"You have any problems with it?" I asked.

I was surprised she was even using the alarm. Temp installed it for her shortly after Daddy died, but she'd resisted using it until I finally talked her into to it just last year. However, as luck would have it, the first time she got her nerve up to turn it on, she forgot to turn off the interior feature and she ended up setting it off when she got up to go to the bathroom.

"No, nary a one. I just mashed the numbers and turned it right off."

I loaded Mother and the girls in the car.

"Now, Mother, let's get this straight. We'll go to the bank, cash the check, then I'll drop you and the girls back off here while I go deliver the money."

She just smiled.

We drove to the bank in relative silence until Mother announced she intended to get the payoff money in a money order. It was all I could do to talk her out of it.

"That way we'll have a receipt," she insisted.

"Mother, trust me on this one. It's bad form to pay off a gangster with a money order. Besides, what do you need a receipt for? You can't write it off on your taxes. And what name would you put on it, Mr. Trey Dog Washington?"

"That shows how much you know. His name is not Trey Dog—I don't know where these kids get off, going around calling themselves dog and the like. His name is Lamar, Lamar Antoine Townsend."

"And how do you know all this?"

"I have my sources."

"Edna, huh?"

"Remember ole man Traxton? That's his uncle. And Catherine Bell is his first cousin on his mother's side."

"Catherine Bell the opera singer?"

"Uh-huh."

"So we have Noel Traxton, the folk artist, Catherine Bell, the opera singer, and Lamar Townsend, the petty drug dealer and murderer of old women. His family must be proud."

"You do the best you can. Sometimes kids just don't turn out the way you want them to."

"You make rearing children sound like taking Polaroid pictures or something."

"You know what I mean."

"Yeah, I guess I do."

Mother reluctantly agreed to get the money in cash. However, an incredibly tiny teller with big hair told her the bank would have to hold the Alston check for two business days until it cleared. Mother's ears got red, and she snorted with exasperation. She took the teller's pen and did some quick calculations on the back of a deposit slip. She stood there thinking for a moment, tapping the pen on the edge of the counter. Finally she withdrew $427 from her savings account refusing my offer to contribute. She sealed the money in a bank envelope and buried it in the inner recesses of her purse before she nervously left the bank clasping the purse tightly with both hands. Mother's uncomfortable carrying money unless it's tied in her safety sock, tucked in her bosom, and pinned to her bra. Her purse is strictly ornamental. Today it was thief bait, the way she was carrying it. And I was glad I was with her to run thief interference and marshal her and the girls back to the car.

"Okay, let's go," she said after she got buckled in.

"Let's go where?" I asked.

"To Lamar's house."

"Oh no, I'm not taking you and the girls there. I'm taking you back home, and then I'll go."

"I don't see why you're making such a big fuss."

"It could be dangerous. You could get hurt."

"And you couldn't?"

"I can handle myself," I said smugly. "Besides, if nothing else, I can move fast if I have to. Too many people would just slow me down."

"You don't know how to get there," she said coyly.

"That's all right. I'll just have to figure it out."

"I have the address," she announced.

"How'd you ... Your sources, right?"

She nodded. "He lives with his grandmother. That's bound to be pretty safe. I'll just stay in the car with the girls. That way you'll have somebody to watch your back."

I know when I'm beat. I agreed reluctantly.

"You have the gun?"

"Mother, am I going somewhere where I'll need a gun? 'Cause if I am, I'm definitely not taking you and the girls."

"No, no, I was just checking. You do have it, don't you?"

"Of course, I have it," I said with a hint of self-righteous indignation. I was hoping she didn't demand to see and find out it's all in pieces.

"Well, let's go," she said, settling back in her seat.

'Okay," I said. "But only as long as you stay in the car."

She smiled smugly and nodded.

"Where does he live?"

"You go straight down Twenty-fourth Street ..."

"Wait a minute, doesn't he have an address either?"

"This is better, I know exactly where he lives. Just go the way I'm telling you."

"Yeah, sure," I muttered under my breath.

"And don't mutter under your breath."

I sighed deeply.

"You'll hyperventilate, you keep that up."

Before I knew it, I was yelling, "Mother, please!"

She flinched and inched away from me. Her eyes filled with water.

"Mother, I'm sorry ..."

"No, just talk to me any way you want to. What does it matter. I'm just a nosy, annoying, pathetic, old, woman," she said, saying the word "old" with great reluctance.

"You left out bossy and overbearing," I reminded her.

She snuffled loudly.

"And manipulative," I added.

She refused to be baited. I put my head down on the steering wheel and pounded the dashboard with both fists.

"Okay, okay," I moaned. "Which way do I go."

Mother led me south on Twenty-fourth Street, west on Sutterville and back on to Twenty-fourth. When we finally ended up on Bonair Way in the Meadowview area, it was apparent that whoever gave her these very circuitous instructions was a veteran bus rider. What should have been a ten-minute trip had taken thirty-five minutes because we'd followed the 63 bus route.

Bonair Way was fighting a valiant battle to remain habitable, but it was too early to tell who was winning— the regular folk who went to work, paid taxes, mowed lawns, swept gutters, and scolded children, or the others. Signs posted at both ends of the street proclaimed it to be drug and firearm free. One of the signs was riddled with bullets.

"Which house is it?" I inquired of Mother.

"The one over there with the tomato plants in the yard."

I looked where she was pointing. The plants in the

yard were small. They appeared to have been recently set out. I couldn't see how she could tell they were tomatoes, but I took her word for it. I pulled over, and Mother slapped the envelope containing the money into my hand. I saluted, got out of the car, and went up to the house. It was a neat little bungalow, badly in need of painting, with a well-tended vegetable garden next to the front door.

The drone of a vacuum cleaner greeted me. I rang the bell. No answer. I rang again. Still no answer. I looked back over my shoulder. Mother and the girls had climbed out of the car and were standing, hand in hand, on the curb looking at me anxiously. I pounded on the door with my fist, calling to anyone inside. The vacuum stopped abruptly and the door was pulled open by a woman about Mother's age.

"Hello," I said. "I'm looking for Lamar Townsend." I had to make a conscious effort not to say Trey Dog.

"Oh, I'm sorry, baby, but he ain't in."

"Do you know when he might be back? I have something to deliver to him." Now I was making a conscious effort not to stare at the woman's head. She was wearing a faded cotton dress and fuzzy slippers, standard house-cleaning garb. But on her head she had what appeared to be a pair of men's boxer shorts. She noticed my furtive glances and reached up and snatched the boxers off her head and stuffed them in her pocket.

"I guess I must look like a fool," she laughed. "They keep the dust outta my hair when I'm working. They clean. See here, look."

She retrieved them and held them up for my inspection. I took a step back, nodding. She put them back in her pocket.

"Well, do you know when Lamar might be back?"

"He should be back soon. He just went to the store to get some milk. You want to come in and wait, honey?"

"No, that's all right," I said. "I guess I'll come back later."

I walked back to the car. "Let's go," I said to Mother. "He's not home."

"Wait a minute. Not so fast. Who was that?" she demanded.

"I don't know. I guess she's his grandmother or something."

"Maybe she can help us."

"I don't think so."

"You never can tell," said Mother as she headed for the door, dragging the twins behind her with me following in her wake.

The door opened after only one knock, and the lady stood there smiling, sans her boxer shorts.

"Excuse us for bothering you," said Mother. "But are you Lamar's mother?"

"Grandmother," corrected the lady, obviously flattered.

"I'm Lorraine Barkley," said Mother. This is my daughter Theresa, and this is Andrea and Cenne."

"Very pleased to meet you all," said the woman. "I'm Arthurine Tanny. Won't you come in?"

We stepped into the small living room. It was jam-packed with a sofa, a love seat, a coffee table, and a console TV. The living room opened directly into the kitchen and a minuscule dining area. The walls and window coverings were a fresh white, and this lent the room an air of spaciousness. The part of the house that could be seen was abjectly clean, as if it had been dusted and scrubbed and polished with such vengeance, it was terrified of being anything else.

When Mrs. Tanny had seated us, Mother asked, "Do you know your grandson goes around calling himself 'Trey Dog'?"

Mrs. Tanny laughed uncomfortably. "I've heard some of his friends call him that. But I told him to have them call him by his name. He ain't no dog."

"I hear tell, he's in a gang," said Mother.

"No, that ain't true. He got in a little bit of trouble here back drinking and acting a fool, but he ain't in no gang."

"I hear tell he's the leader of a gang," continued Mother. "Not just a member."

Mrs. Tanny looked more uncomfortable and a little

worried, as if she were wondering, "Who have I let into my home?"

"No, the boy's easily led, that's all. He was doing fine until he started running with those Scott boys. What exactly did you want with Lamar?"

"We came by to ask him not to kill these babies' mama," said Mother pointing to Andrea and Cenne.

Mrs. Tanny sucked in her breath sharply. "What do you mean, kill their mama?"

"I hear he's going to kill her. That's what he's promised. She owes him some money. Owes him fair and square, but she's so scared she's just about done lost her mind. You see somebody drove by her grandmother's house the other day and filled it full of bullets and her grandmother, too."

"Killed her?" asked Mrs. Tanny in a breathy whisper.

"Killed her dead," affirmed Mother. "Now, I don't want to see these babies' mama killed, too. That's just too much killing and dying in one family. So I stayed up all last night thinking and praying and calling on the Lord. And do you know what he told me?"

Mrs. Tanny looked dazed. She shook her head no.

"He told me to get up, stand up like a woman. So that's why I'm here. I've come to help you save your grandbaby."

"Save him?"

"Yes," said Mother. "Save him. You see, I got up this morning and I went to the bank and I took out just about all the money I had. And I had them put it in this envelope. Four hundred and twenty-seven dollars. Now, I could take this money and go out on just about any street corner and hire me somebody to kill your grandbaby. In fact, with this much money, I could probably hire three or four people to kill him and give a bonus to the one who got him first."

Mrs. Tanny was trembling. I couldn't tell if it was from rage or fear or both.

"But you see, there's been too much killing already. So I decided to bring this money here and give it to Lamar because, after all, these babies' mama owes him fair and square."

Mother pointed the envelope at Mrs. Tanny, but she refused it.

"Lamar ain't in no gang," she said weakly. "He didn't kill nobody."

"Take the money," demanded Mother.

Mrs. Tanny sprang from her seat. She stood clenching and unclenching her hands, working them into fists and releasing them. Mother sat calmly, unflinching. Taking my cue from her, I remained seated, but I scooted to the edge of my chair just in case I had to grab Mrs. Tanny. Andrea and Cenne buried their heads in Mother's lap.

"Get out of my house," Mrs. Tanny screeched.

"I'm going," said Mother calmly. "But I'm taking Lamar's life with me."

Mrs. Tanny dropped her head to her chest and wept.

"I don't have no control over him," she sobbed. "He don't do nothing I say."

Mother handed her the envelope.

"There's four one hundred dollar bills, a twenty, a five, and two ones in here. Count it. I want a receipt."

Mrs. Tanny opened the envelope and obediently counted the bills. Then she went to the kitchen and got a pad, wrote out a receipt, and handed it to Mother.

"If the word on the street doesn't change by tomorrow, I go back to the bank and take the rest of the money out," said Mother.

Mrs. Tanny nodded, still weeping. We gathered the girls up and left.

Chapter 14

"I wasn't playing and I wasn't fooling. I do what I have to do, that's all."

"You mean you'd take out a contract on Trey Dog?" I asked incredulously.

"If I had to, yes."

I shook my head, too dumbfounded to speak.

"But you don't know anything about that kind of stuff."

She cast me a long, steady, glance.

"Your sources?"

She nodded.

"Mother, I just can't believe this. I thought I knew you all these years, and now you come up with this— guns, contracts, your sources. Something's just not right. You can't get involved in stuff like this. You're . . . you're my mother, for pete's sake."

Mother patted my hand reassuringly, where it rested on the steering wheel. I snatched it away.

"Theresa . . ."

"I just don't want to talk about it, Mother" I said, cutting her off. "I'm the dope, I'm the pawn, I'm the gofer, while you and your friends sit around . . ."

"Theresa . . ."

"I said, I don't want to talk about it, Mother."

We drove in silence the next couple of blocks, the twins gurgling and chortling and singing little songs without words in the backseat.

"Did you and your geriatric home girls ever stop to think what would happen now? Or couldn't Mother Iola see that far? What if Trey Dog takes the money and still kills LaTreace? What if he takes the money, kills La-Treace, and comes looking for you because you dissed his grandmother? What if his grandmother takes the money and uses it to buy a lifetime supply of Lemon Fresh Pledge and doesn't even tell him, huh? What then? Did anybody think this through? Did anybody consider asking me what I thought? Huh? I'm thirty-eight years old and you guys still treat me like I'm supposed to be seen and not heard."

I was getting worked up and carried away and probably would have gone on to the outer boundaries of rationality—it's a family trait, on Mother's side—if not for the piercing blast of a whistle that cut through the car and ricocheted off the windows.

"Please don't do that, Mother. You know how I hate that."

"If you hate it so much, then learn to listen a little, miss. You passed my street about four blocks ago."

I stomped on the brake, and cars slammed to stops behind me, brakes squealing. A few people apparently died and fell over on their horns. I glanced in my rear-view mirror. We were on Fourteenth Avenue, a busy street, and a perfect place for a rear end. The driver behind me cut her wheels, preparing to pull out and pass me. But before she could, a gray four-by-four with tinted windows, three cars back, whipped out, and in a micro-second game of chicken, forced the woman to yield. The gray car pulled up alongside us, the window slowly rolled down, and the most beautiful child I had ever seen stared out at me with "malice aforethought" written all over his face.

"You fuckin' up the flow, muddear," he said in a quiet, conversational tone. The window rolled back up, and he drove off.

My heart skipped a beat, and it wasn't from love. I wouldn't describe it as fear either. It was something that came from somewhere further down than just plain old fear. It was a gut bucket, primal emotion that only those who have come face-to-face with a predator can ever understand. It didn't taste too good in my mouth either.

"That looked like the car," said Mother.

I nodded, knowing what she meant and wondering if it had been following us and if it had, for how long.

"Mother, I don't think you should go home. I don't like the idea of you being there alone."

"Well, I'm going," she said. "Regardless of what you or anybody else thinks. I've lived in that house for thirty years, and no one's going to run me off now. I'm too old to play those kind of games. Besides, if you can't go home, then where can you go?"

"It's not a matter of running off, Mother. It's a matter of your safety. You need to go somewhere else, at least until this thing blows over."

"And where do you suggest I go? I'm certainly not going to move in with you and Temp."

"Well, what about some of your friends?"

"Their houses are only big enough to hold one woman at a time."

"You're being unreasonable."

"I'm being very reasonable."

"I tell you what, let's not argue. I'll take you home, and then we'll decide."

I drove cautiously the rest of the way, keeping an eye on my rearview mirror. I didn't see the car again, but that was okay because every other car on the road looked menacing enough.

Mother's street had always seemed a haven to me. It had a pleasant, homey, inviting feel to it. But since the shooting, people were staying indoors more. Fewer children played in front of their houses, and the street took on a quiet, brooding look.

"Lord, have mercy," Mother cried as we approached her door. "Who would do something like that?"

Tucked back into a far corner of her porch, where it couldn't be seen from the street, was a floral funeral spray. It was the type called bleeding heart—white carnations over a heart-shaped frame with red gladiolus cascading down from the top. There was no card.

"Maybe one of your friends sent it."

"None of my friends would do a thing like that. They'd

know better. That should have been sent to the funeral home, not here."

"It's okay, Mother," I said. "I'll move it."

"No, don't touch it," she cautioned, grabbing the sleeve of my jacket.

Since Dad's death Mother has developed a deep aversion, more a superstition, about funeral wreaths, or any flowers, for that matter, that appear too funeral-like to her. She touched her fingers of her right hand to her forehead, chest, and shoulders, making the sign of the cross.

"Why are you doing that? You're not Catholic."

"It can't hurt," she replied.

I took my scarf out of my purse and used it to pick up the spray.

"Put it in the backyard," said Mother. "No, that's too close. Put it . . . Put it over in Sister Turner's house."

I took the key from her and went across the street lugging the spray while she and the girls went inside. The Turner house gave me the willies. I wasn't going in there if I could help it, not after my panic-fueled tour a couple of days ago and finding Mrs. Turner and everything. I swung around the side of the house and picked my way through the backyard, avoiding Tonton's deposits of processed dietary matter the best I could, and made my way to the shed in the corner of the yard. Tonton had roamed freely up until Mrs. Alston took him yesterday, and it looked like no one had been back there with a pooper-scooper in a while. His automatic feeder stood just outside the shed door. A clever contraption, a twenty-five pound storage canister suspended over an attached feeding dish. Measured amounts of dried food dropped into the feeding dish automatically. A water dish was set near the house under a dripping faucet. Tonton must have been in dog heaven.

I went over to the shed. Star jasmine marched up one side of it, and it listed in the opposite direction as if the delicate white blossoms were a heavy burden. The door was long since gone. I stuck my head in. The floor was littered with a tatty piece of carpeting and some old rags. On a shelf a little overhead, out of Tonton's reach, leaned another twenty-five pound bag of dog food. It had been ripped open carelessly, and dry nuggets spilled from its jagged opening onto the shelf. Mother had offered that food to Mrs. Alston. She really should have taken it. No need to let good food go to waste. Old cans of paint and a few canning jars shared the shelf space. A bicycle rim and a length of garden hose hung from the wall. A monument of newspapers, so old and moldy they had metamorphosed into papier-mâché, stood in one corner. I dragged the spray in and leaned it against the opposite corner, dusted my hands, checked my hair for spiders, and left.

It was just after one o'clock when I got downtown. Traffic usually dies down a bit after the lunch-hour rush, but the state's in the midst of a construction boomlet and several departments have new buildings going up. Construction activities had traffic tied up and slowed to a crawl, and tempers were stretched thin. I craned my neck as I passed the Parks and Rec building trying to see if the Greek was there. He wasn't, and for some strange reason I was disappointed.

I parked in the city lot at Seventh and H and went across the street to the County Administration Building. Checking my watch, I gave myself thirty minutes to find the county assessor's office, research property ownership records, and leave.

Unfortunately it seemed everyone else had a similar idea, and the county assessor was doing a brisk business. I finally snagged a vacant viewer after a ten-minute wait. At each viewer a plastic index-card-size box held microfiche cards containing the property records for the entire county. I thumbed through the cards showing property by name of owner. I pulled the "Tu - Sa" card and inserted it in the viewer. Microfiche is tricky. You have to put it into the viewer just right or you end up trying to read something that's upside down and backward. It took me a couple of times, but I finally got it. With a flick of the wrist, names, parcel numbers, addresses, and other data whizzed across the screen at a dizzying speed, and my eyes promptly began to water. I found "Tunny" and slowed down looking for "Turner, Louise." I found a Lawrence Turner and a Linton Turner but no Louise. My head started to pound. I finally gave up and went to the counter to ask for help and was advised to try looking up the property by address.

I returned to the viewer and found 2215 Capistrano Way almost immediately.

I stared at the information on the screen in disbelief. A buzz in my ears kicked up so loud it nearly drowned out the boom box pounding of my heart. Quickly glancing over my shoulder, I surveyed the room to make sure my internal organs' one-man band wasn't disturbing the people at the other viewers. They didn't appear to notice.

Wiping my eyes, I closed them tightly and kept them that way for a couple of seconds before I allowed them to open and refocus on the screen. It still read the same, the words hadn't reordered themselves, and I hadn't made a mistake or misread them. Right there on the screen, in video blue and electric white, the owner of 2215 Capistrano Way was listed as Penelope Troop.

I put my head down on the table and closed my eyes, trying to think. What did Penny have to do with all this? Mrs. Turner comes up dead, and her property ends up in Penny's name.

"Things don't look too good, girlfriend," I said out loud.

How long does a transfer like this take? I wondered. Mrs. Turner's been dead less than a week, so it had to have been done some time before she died, otherwise it probably wouldn't show up in the records yet. The whys were nagging me more than anything—Why would Mrs. Turner do something like this? What would make her sign her house over to anybody, particularly Penny— somebody she didn't even know? I'd heard of old people getting cheated out of their homes by unscrupulous contractors or repairmen, but this didn't seem to have been the case. What was their connection? Maybe Mother was right to be wary of Penny Troop. Mrs. Alston had better watch out, too, I thought.

I was deep into my thoughts when someone grabbed

me roughly by my shoulder and shook it. I bolted upright, bumping my head on the microfiche viewer.

"You can't sleep here, lady," came a man's voice over my shoulder.

I twisted around in my chair so I could see who this fool was. Nobody dresses in sand-washed silk to sleep in public places.

His lank blond hair was buzzed short on the sides, an unruly lock hung down over one eye. I could tell from his Metro-Goldwyn Mayer uniform he was a contract security officer, a rent-a-cop, but he had on a gun, so I waived my lecture on fashion and the homeless, grabbed my purse, and left.

I didn't bother getting my car from the parking lot, I didn't need it. I knew exactly where I was going and what I was going to do when I got there. I was going to find Penny Troop and get me some answers. I was going to extract the truth, if necessary. But either way the woman was going to talk to me. Today.

I headed east on H Street, cutting over at Eight to I and then to J. The Morrison Building, where the Alston campaign was headquartered, was not hard to find. It stood forlornly in the middle of the block, flanked on both sides by the soot blackened, boarded-up hulls of two elegant old buildings that had burned down within two weeks of each other last winter. A shopping cart outfitted with plastic bags for collecting and sorting recyclables stood in the doorway to one of them. I didn't see its owner.

The Morrison Building's gilt-edged doors opened quietly, and I stepped into a large, high-ceilinged room that seemed take up the entire ground floor. Arched floor-to-ceiling windows drenched the room in natural light that did strange, unnatural things when it struck surfaces. Eight-feet shadows danced around the room, whirling to stalk each other and merge amoeba-like only to break apart and dance again.

Off to one side, a woman was feeding envelopes through a stamp meter. It was the old-fashioned kind, and she had to feed the envelopes one at a time, but she had developed a sassy rhythm and kept up a steady flow. She seemed to be enjoying herself.

Two people sat at a table that held a bank of computers. Both were on the phone, talking, gesturing, emoting. When a call ended, their faces fell like somebody had turned off the juice that powered them, and then they quickly pressed their auto-dial buttons and began again.

A small knot of people that included Robert Alston stood huddled by the windows. They were involved in an intense discussion in which the word "fuck" seemed to dominate. A petite woman in a black leather miniskirt denounced someone bitterly.

"I say fuck 'em. Fuck 'em. Fuck 'em. Fuck every last one of 'em."

Toward the back, in an area that seemed to be higher than the rest of the room, sat Mrs. Alston like a majordomo. She had on a different Chanel suit this time, but her pillbox hat was there, firmly affixed to her champagne pink hair. The gloves, however, were missing.

I stalked over to where she sat.

She watched me approach with a set smile, her hands struggling with each other in her lap.

"Mrs. Alston," I said, "you and I need to talk."

"Of course, dear."

She made a tentative gesture toward the door a few feet in back of her.

"Perhaps we should step in here. Privacy, you know."

I followed her into a room that apparently was used for storage. Exposed pipes laced the ceiling, a single lightbulb dangled just above our heads. An old clunker of a bike with fat wheels leaned against the wall. Boxes stacked haphazardly at varying heights lined the walls. A door led outside to the alley and another led down a series of stairs. I couldn't see where they went.

"Now, what is it?" she asked anxiously. "You have something for me?"

"What do you know about Penny Troop?" I demanded.

"What?" she asked, obviously thrown by the question.

"What do you know about Penny Troop?" I repeated. "What was her connection to Mrs. Turner?"

"Louise?" she asked dully.

"Yes, Mrs. Turner."

"Why, I don't know. I don't believe they even knew each other," she replied hesitantly.

"Then, why is Mrs. Turner's house owned in Penny's name?"

The color drained from Mrs. Alston's face. She wandered over to a stack of boxes and sat down heavily. Dust rose up and circled her head like small wisps of smoke.

"That can't be true," she said weakly. "Louise loved that little house. She wouldn't just give it away. I feel very strongly about that."

"Well, I've just been over to the county assessor's office, and their records show Penny Troop as the owner of 2215 Capistrano Way."

"There's got to be some explanation for this."

"Where is Penny?"

"She went to do some banking for me."

"She handles your banking? Mrs. Alston, are you sure that's wise?"

"Oh yes, yes, of course. I've become quite dependent on Penny since she took over Bobby's campaign. She's kind of taken over some business matters for me, too. We mustn't speak ill of Penny. She's a jewel, an absolute jewel. I'm sure there's a perfectly good explanation for all this."

"Yeah, like what?" I demanded. I was getting tired of sorry old people and their sorry delusions. And I was especially tired of this one, who never had to struggle for anything. Everything had been handed to her on a silver platter. Never had to hit a lick at a snake, as Mother would say. Never had a child locked up and another cracked up. Never had to worry about keeping her great-grand babies off the county. Never had to worry about anything. And here she was practically throwing everything away, talking about "I'm sure there's a perfectly good explanation for all of this." Yes, there was. And when the Pennys of the world got through bumping her poor old sorry head with the cotton candy hair and pillbox hat still on it, she still wouldn't know it.

"There must be an explanation," she repeated.

"Well, if I were you," I warned her, "I'd check over any banking Penny did for me very carefully. And I'd check with the county right about now to see who owned my house."

I don't think my warning had much effect. She smiled and patted her hair. Not one strand had managed to escape from its petroleum-based confinement, and that seemed to please her. I noticed a bandage running across the palm of her hand, the fleshy part, near the base of the fingers. I was about to ask about it when a cloud passed over her eyes and her mood shifted.

"My papers," she whispered hoarsely. "Have you found them?"

"No, I don't think so."

"You don't think so? What does that mean?"

"We don't know what you're looking for, Mrs. Alston. We've found some things, old newspaper clippings, birth certificates. Stuff like that. But nothing, from what I can see, that would be of any value to anyone. You could make this thing a whole lot easier if you told us exactly what you're looking for."

Mrs. Alston looked stricken. "I can't. Oh, dear, I wish I could but I just can't."

"Okay, okay. We're still looking for her Bible. Mother believes she would have kept anything of importance in it."

Mrs. Alston got up wearily from the stack of boxes. "During the later years my husband, Dr. Alston, drank, you know. It is so very important that you find those papers, dear. And Bobby mustn't know about this. I must impress upon you, it's important to Bobby's future. You do understand, don't you?"

She grabbed me by both wrists. "Please, dear. You do understand, don't you? You simply must help me."

Her grip was so steady and strong, a panic swept over me. What if I had to hurt this crazy old woman to get her to let go of me? It was not a pleasant thought. Fortunately, it didn't come to that. The dust in the room and the White Shoulders she was wearing combined to send me through another sneezing fit. She let go of my wrist and leaped out of the way with surprising agility.

"Excuse me," I said politely.

I turned to go back into the main room and nearly collided with Robert.

"Theresa, there you are."

"Hello, Robert. Sorry I can't stay, but I was just leaving."

"Not so fast, not so fast. I take it Mother has been giving you the two-bit tour?"

Mrs. Alston looked at me imploringly, the batty old woman. I sighed and said, "Yes, she has."

"Well, today is your lucky day. As you are the 977th person to enter these hallowed walls, you have won the Grand Campaign Headquarters Tour to be conducted by none other than the Grand Campaign Candidate."

I sighed again. This man was probably destined to become the city's next mayor, and he was just as sorry now as he had been twenty years ago at Sac High.

"Okay," I said. "But I don't have much time."

Robert flashed me a toothy smile. "Since we are here, poised at the entrance to the catacombs, we shall commence our tour with a visit to their moldy depths."

Robert was keeping up a steady mock tour guide prattle, but he seemed to be straining. It just didn't ring true. For one thing, his eyes and mouth weren't working in concert. He vogued from a smile to a grin to a smirk, but his eyes were hard and unyielding and his grip on my elbow was tight enough to cause pain. Must be something that runs in the family, this tendency to grab people, I thought, twisting my arm loose.

He grabbed a flashlight from a hook by the stairway and gestured for me to follow him. We went down a steep flight of rickety stairs with open railings running along a brick wall.

At the bottom, Robert stood with his arms outstretched.

"Here it is," he said. "Hernando's Hideaway."

It was cold and dank, the kind of place that would produce prime, Grade-A river rats. I was disoriented. Maybe it was the tightness, the closeness of the space. Maybe the vague feeling that I had actually traveled farther than one flight of stairs, that I had moved, just a bit, beyond some important boundary that caused a wave of anxiety to wash over me. I don't know, but whatever it was, I fought it down.

The wall that ran parallel with J Street, if my bearings were right, seemed to be made of earth, earth that was so old and compacted, it was shiny in some places. Shadows danced and flickered each time Robert gestured with the hand holding the flashlight.

"Uh, this is really nice, Robert," I said. "Who was your decorator? I really like the nice cobblestone floors."

"Cobblestone streets," he corrected me. "We are now standing directly beneath J Street on the old J Street."

"Old J Street?"

"Yes. In the late eighteen hundreds downtown streets were raised a whole story to get them above floodwaters and to, I might add, give murderous pickpockets, robbers, and other river vermin places to dart into after doing their dirty deeds. Exciting stuff, huh?"

"I think I remember reading something about this. How far does this passageway go?"

"Over past the Traxton Building on this side and two buildings down on the other side," he said, pointing first east and then west. "Since the fire, we've been having problems with people getting down into here."

"The homeless?" I asked.

"Some, I guess. But we've had some break-ins. They get in through one of the burned-out buildings and walk along the underground until they get to one of the occupied buildings and force the door to the main floor."

I had to admit, after I got over my initial panic attack,

it was kind of fascinating, in a morbid sort of way. I stood in one spot, careful not to stray from the arc of light Robert's flashlight created, and pivoted completely around, surveying the chamber. Actually, it was more like a long hall.

I could hear the rumble of traffic overhead, on J Street, the dull thud of pedestrians' footsteps echoing through the chamber, and a soft hissing sound the air made.

The acoustics were the strangest thing about the chamber. Sounds seemed so distorted and muffled when they should have been loud, and loud when they should have been muffled. Sound waves seemed to ebb and flow, merge and diverge in weird ways, kind of like the shadows on the upper floor.

Just visible against what must have been the east wall was wooden framing, blocking off the passageway, that looked like it had been put up recently.

"What's that over there?" I asked, and pointed beyond the radius of light.

"We're having that part sealed off. That's where we think they've been getting in. We're also pouring a concrete floor so we can use this area for storage."

"Well, good luck and happy hunting," I said. "I think we'd better go up now. We wouldn't want your mother to worry."

"I thought you'd like it. It's history, you know. Besides, it's kinda sexy."

I looked at him from the corner of my eye. First his mother and now him. Lord, I prayed, let me get through this day without having to hurt one of these Alston fools. But if he does get funny, just give me the strength to cripple his sorry behind and leave him down here.

"You must have a very strange libido," I said.

"No, it's just that it's so dark, and close and tight down here and, not to mention, somewhat threatening. I have to admit, that's a real turn-on for me."

"Well, I tell you what. We can discuss it upstairs over cookies and milk."

Reluctantly he aimed his light up the stairs, and I

walked in it back to where we had come from with him following closely behind.

His mother greeted us as we stepped out of the stairwell with her hands on her hips and her shoulders hunched up like a bull ready to charge.

Chapter 15

They tell me the foothills are beautiful this time of the year, but I wouldn't know. If anybody asked me about my drive up Highway 80 to Forest Hill, I wouldn't be able to tell them a thing. In all honesty, except for my encounter with Mr. Gillian and my hasty retreat, I don't remember much about that trip.

My mind was just in too many places at once. It was in that back bedroom where we had found Mrs. Turner caked in her own filth, it was standing in her yard, looking at that shredded door and praying that Mother wasn't in there, it was back on Stockton at the motel, it was in Mother's kitchen with her friends, it was in the storage room with Mrs. Alston and it was underground with Bobby, it was at home in the bedroom with Temp and it was in the living room sitting between Aisha and Mr. Mark Wesley Talbot. But wherever it wandered, it kept coming back to the house and Penny.

Somehow, through what means I'll never know, I found Mr. Gillian's house in the older part of this picturesque little town. It was a stately, wood-frame house that sat a little farther back from the street than the other houses. It seemed to have been lovingly maintained. The paint was fresh and crisp, and the lawn was neatly mowed. A border of flowers followed the walkway from the street to the front door. The garage door was up, and I could see that its interior was just as neat and orderly. A shiny red truck sat in the driveway.

I parked and walked up to the door and rang the bell.

"Mr. Gillian?" I said to the man who opened the door.

"Yes."

He was a big man, at least six feet tall with an air of vibrancy about him. He must have been close to Mother's age, in his early seventies, maybe late sixties, but he could have passed for someone much younger had it not been for his bone-white hair and a slight sagging around the chin line. All in all, he was a very good-looking man.

He looked at me with hooded eyes as he chewed slowly and deliberately. It was as if he could not swallow until he had chewed one hundred times, and he didn't want my interruption to mess up his count.

"I'm sorry," I said. "I must be interrupting your dinner . . ."

He waved my apology aside.

"You don't know me, but my name is Theresa Galloway. I need to talk to you. It's about your sister."

He stepped back and beckoned me inside. I followed as he led me to a small sitting room to the right of the entry hall. Toward the back of the house, I could see the kitchen and a small table set with a vase of flowers and a service for one.

He offered me a seat on the sofa, and he sat across from me in a wing chair next to an octagonal table with a lamp on it.

He nodded at me and said, "Go ahead, speak your piece."

"I'm sorry to barge in on you like this. We've been trying to get in touch with you, but we haven't had any luck. Mr. Gillian, I'm sorry to have to tell you this, but your sister, Louise, is dead."

I don't like being the bearer of bad news. It was hard for me to sit in front of this old man and tell him his sister was dead. I didn't realize I was holding my breath until almost a minute had passed and Mr. Gillian hadn't said a word and I started to feel faint.

I let my breath out. Why doesn't he say something? Maybe he's still chewing, I thought as I studied his impassive face. Maybe he's chewing over what I just told him, and he hasn't reached one hundred yet.

"What do you want from me?" he asked.

His voice was calm and even. It had taken on the deliberate quality of his chewing.

"Why, uh, you're her brother," I stammered. "We thought you'd want to know. Arrangements have to be made and everything."

"Do whatever you see fit. Leave me out of it. I'm not interested."

"But she was your sister ... You can't just not be involved."

"Young lady, I can do whatever I damn well please."

"But the house ..."

"Burn it to the ground."

"What?"

"Burn it to the ground," he repeated. "And you'll probably still see the bloody footprints even in the ashes."

He already had me going and then he threw in the bloody footprint stuff. I wished I could call time-out, run to the phone, call Mother, and ask her what bloody footprints stood for in geriatric-speak? Was this some more of that "seeing" business?

"But the babies," I protested.

"What babies?"

"Mrs. Turner's. Her great-grandchildren. She was raising them."

"They are no concern of mine."

He sat back in the chair, his arms folded in a barricade across his chest.

"But if their people don't make some kind of arrangements, the county'll probably take them. They're really so sweet. You should see them. We'd hate to see little Andrea and Cenne ...

His head snapped back like he'd been shot.

"What did you say?"

There was a catch in his voice.

"The county ... ?"

He dismissed that with a wave of his hand.

"Uh, Andrea and Cenne ... ?"

He brought his fist down and crashed it onto the side table next to him with such force the lamp went flying, the wood splintered, and the table buckled and fell.

I had just about had my fill of crazy people for one day. I wished Mother or one of her friends had at least warned me that he was crazy, too. I measured the distance from where I sat to the door with my eyes.

"What right did she have to name them that?" he demanded, his chest heaving. "What right?"

I didn't know the answer, so I stood up clutching my purse, ready to duckwalk with fear out of there.

"Get out," he spat. "Get out of my house."

I left. He didn't bother to see me to the door.

I got in my car, and found my way back to the highway. I just wanted to go home, get in the tub, and soak for at least three days. That's all. But I got caught in traffic just outside of Auburn, and it looked like it might be three days before I even got home. A highway patrol car was in each lane ahead of me perversely going fifty-five miles an hour. No one dared to try to pass them, and traffic was backed up for miles.

Finally I couldn't take it anymore, and I pulled off at a truck stop in Newcastle. I had the radio on, just for background noise, when the news came on. I thought I heard a name I recognized and turned the volume up. The announcer was finishing up, ". . . and Lamar Townsend. The other man mortally wounded has not been identified, pending notification of next of kin."

From the snatch of the news I was able to catch, I was pretty certain Trey Dog had been killed. I know this is wrong, but for a moment I felt jubilant. I held my clenched fist up and shouted, "Yes!" Then I thought about his grandmother, Mrs. Tanny, washing and scrubbing and hiding the truth from herself. She loved Trey Dog, and tonight she would be hurting. I felt bad, but not for long.

I found a phone and called Mother. It rang about ten times before it was snatched up.

"I can't talk now. I'm in a hurry," blared Mother.

"Don't hang up, don't hang up," I said quickly. "It's me, Theresa."

"Theresa?" she said, her voice edged with annoyance. "Where are you?"

"Newcastle. I just got through talking to Mr. Gillian,

Mrs. Turner's brother. I just heard on the news, Trey
Dog's dead.''

"Yes," said Mother. "Most assuredly, every dog has
his day and a good one has two. LaTreace called right
after she heard it, too. But that dope's got her brain so
addled, she hardly knows whether she coming or going."

"Then, she's all right. Trey Dog's dead and she's safe."

"It hardly matters now, anyway. Sister Kaylene's been
hurt. Been hurt real bad. Some kid tried to snatch her
purse, knocked her down, and dragged her. I gotta go."

"Wait, Mother," I yelled. "What hospital is she in?"

"Stubborn old woman. She's not in the hospital.
Wouldn't let them take her. They helped her up, she got
in her car, and drove home. I got to go see about her."

"Is somebody taking you?"

"Look, child, I don't have time for all this chitchat. I
got to go."

"Mother, answer me. Is somebody taking you?"

There was silence on the other end of the line.

"Mother, listen to me. Don't take the car. You . . . It
is not safe. Mother . . . Mother?"

The phone slammed down in my ear. It was followed
by a loud disconnect tone so raucous it could have been
a raspberry.

I dialed home. Maybe if I could reach Temp, he could
intercept Mother and take her and the twins to see
Kaylene. I did not want to see Mother on the road, not
for any reason under any circumstances unless she was
preceded by a warning truck with a red flag. Her driving
was that bad. The line was busy. Aisha. I dialed Temp's
office number and got his voice mail. I left a message
asking him to call Mother.

I got back in the car. Temp, being into gadgets the
way he is, had installed a state-of-the-art cellular phone
in my car the week after I got it. But I had the service
discontinued. I found it disconcerting to get a phone call
while I was on the freeway looking for my exit or dodg-
ing big rigs, and downright dangerous, if the truth must
be told. I never used it and didn't anticipate ever needing
it. Now I needed it, and I regretted having it turned off.

The best thing to do, I decided, was to go to Mother's

and wait for her there. Her house was the most likely interception point. She had to return at some time or another and I could probably make contact with Temp there as I'd left a message for him to call her. I knew I wouldn't have any trouble getting in. Even after I had gone away to college and gotten married and everything. I'd never relinquished my key to the front door. And, come to think of it, Mother had never asked for it.

It was dark by the time I got to Mother's. Even though she had left in a hurry, she'd taken time to close the drapes and turn on the front light. The alarm system emitted a series of beeps when I opened the door. I punched in her code, disarming it and closed the door.

The house was back to normal. The aroma of fried onions and ginger cookies lingered in the air. Scattered toys, blankets, and overturned boxes decorated the room. The Bible lay open on the table next to Mother's chair.

I sat on the sofa but I was too restless to stay still, and before I knew it I was up pacing the floor. I wandered over to the window and pulled the drapes back just enough to peek out. Mrs. Turner's house seemed to stare back at me blankly with the unseeing eyes of the dead. I didn't see how Mother could continue living here after everything. How could she stand to get up every morning and look out that window, and see that house, and remember what happened there? The thought made me shiver.

I was getting ready to turn away from the window when a movement at the side of the Turner house caught my eye. I stared at the spot until my eyes burned. I was just about to give up, convinced that I was imagining things, when a car passed on the street behind the house and the light from its high beams hit the house from the back, illuminating it like a flash of lightning would. For a split second, a small figure with a long head was outlined in stark relief. I blinked and he was gone.

It was dark. I did not want to go into the charnel house again. But I was certain that the small figure I'd seen peering out from the side of the house was Sir—I'd know that head anywhere—and I couldn't rest until I checked.

I found Mother's flashlight, set the alarm, and left. I crossed the street and went directly to the side of the house where I had seen the figure. I turned the flashlight on, pushed the gate open, and stepped into the side yard.

"Sir," I called, playing the light over the yard.

"Sir. You here, baby? Sir. It's me, Theresa."

I trained the light on the house. None of the windows was open. The door looked closed. I picked my way around to the other side of the house and illuminated it with the flashlight. Nothing, just some stacked flowerpots and an old washing machine with the door torn off. I returned to the backyard and stood there. The light was getting weak, and I shook the flashlight. It flickered like a candle and went out. I shook it again, and it came back on.

Somewhere down the block a dog started to bark, but everything was still in Mrs. Turner's yard, as if it were crouched down, waiting, holding its breath. I fought down the urge to bolt out the way I came, to the safety of Mother's. I'd looked everywhere but the house, and there was no way I was going in there, not tonight.

I played the light over the yard one final time. Like the pointer on a Ouija board, it seemed pulled to the old shed in the corner. I sighed, knowing that I had to look, but dreading it nonetheless. I'd been in it earlier today, but that was in the daylight. Things take on whole new lives at night. The doorway was dark and foreboding with tendrils of star jasmine hanging down like grasping fingers.

I took a deep breath and trained the light on the doorway.

"Sir," I whispered.

Nothing but the sound of my own heart beating.

"Sir."

I pointed the light in one corner. Nothing but the old newspapers. The funeral spray leaned in the other corner. Just to the right of it, deep in the shadows, his eyes big as saucers, stood Sir.

"Sir," I almost shouted.

He put his finger to his mouth, reached out, and gently drew me into the shadows with him.

"Turn the light off," he said.

I did.

I squatted down and put my arms around him. I was so glad to see him. He didn't push me away as he had the last time. He crouched in the corner, staring at the house.

"Mama's in there," he said.

I looked toward the house.

"She talking to somebody. She say stay till she come get me."

"How long you been out here?"

"Long time. Since way before it got dark."

"Come on," I said, grabbing him by the arm.

He tensed. "Mama said stay out here," he said, bracing himself to struggle.

"LaTreace called us. She said we're supposed to keep you over at my mother's house until she comes and get you," I said, shading the truth just a little, but for a good cause.

He stared at me in the dark.

"Weren't you with her when she called?" I asked, embellishing my lie.

"Un-huh," he admitted.

"Come on, then. Let's go."

"They might see us."

"Who?"

"The one Mama's talking to."

"Sir, are you sure they're in there? I don't see any lights."

He started to cry in that quiet way of his. I wiped the tears away with the back of my hand, and he let me.

"Can we get out through the back around here somewhere?"

He nodded.

"Show me."

"Wait," he said. Climbing up to the overhead shelf with the agility of a cat, he grabbed the bag of dog food, tipped it to its side, and reached in the bag almost up to his elbow. Nuggets of dry dog food cascaded down on my head. I put my arms up to shield myself.

"Hey, what are you doing?"

"I got it," he said, pulling a bundle out of the bag. I

couldn't tell what it was in the dark. He handed it to me and climbed down.

"Grand told me to take care of it so mama couldn't get it. I had to come back the last time, 'cause I forgot to hide it good."

"That's when you got locked out of Mother's?"

He nodded.

"Come on," I said. "let's go."

I was anxious to see what secrets were locked in Mrs. Turner's Bible.

Chapter 16

I fed Sir and put him in the tub before turning my attention to Mrs. Turner's Bible. It was a large, old-fashioned, leather-bound volume, gilt-edged with gilt lettering on the cover. Tattletale corners of envelopes and dog-eared pieces of paper stuck out between the pages. I removed the two large rubber bands that held the covers clasped together and started at the front in Genesis. I worked my way toward the back, turning just a few pages at a time, trying to make sure I didn't overlook anything. The thought occurred to me that it might be quicker and easier to simply turn the book upside down, dump everything out, and then sort through it on the table. But somehow that just seemed too disrespectful.

The first thing I found of any interest was Sharon and LaTreace's birth certificates. I read through them, but I didn't know exactly what I was looking for, and I didn't find anything unusual. I put them back where I found them. I found old immunization records, an ancient bill of sale for a mule, and a curly lock of hair tied with a pink ribbon. I left them where they were. The Book of Ruth yielded the marriage certificate of Louise Esther Ewing and Samuel Turner and his death certificate clipped together. I put them with the birth certificates.

I continued turning page by page, looking for some scrap of paper, some morsel of information, anything that might make some sense of this mess. Some letters dating from as far back as 1945 were tucked in between the pages of the book of Psalms. Most of them were from Mrs. Turner's mother.

Close to the beginning of the New Testament, some-where near Malachi, I came across a single sheet of paper folded the long way several times and jammed in close to the spine of the book. I unfolded it, smoothed it out, and read through a list of eight names. There was no other information, just the names. They were not in any particular order as far as I could tell. They could have been anything—a guest list, the roster to a Sunday school class—anything. There were no dates, addresses, or phone numbers. Just the names: Darcella Mae Dupree, Lee Ann Mackey, Levinia Choy, Charlotte Spivey, Jua-nita Diane Brown, Clara Thomas, Mary Francis Ware, and Donetha Wells.

I was refolding the paper to put it back when I noticed something else. At the bottom of the page close to the edge someone had printed lightly in pencil: "I call heaven and earth to record this day against you." I stopped and smoothed the paper out again. For some reason that passage struck a chord with me. "I call heaven and earth to record this day against you." I knew that passage. What was the rest of it? I'd heard it before, but I just couldn't place it. I wish I had paid attention more in Sunday school; maybe I could identify the pas-sage now if I had. But it was no use. I'm not like some people, Edna in particular, who can quote the Bible book and verse. I read the names through again. The only thing I could come up with was the people on the list had done something that Mrs. Turner didn't think was too cool, and she wanted it noted. If only I knew the rest of that passage. I refolded the paper and set it aside. Maybe something would come to me later.

I found very little after that. Just a few church pro-grams, LaTreace's high school diploma (she'd graduated with honors), and some old sepia photos. I was on auto-matic pilot, thumbing through page after page. I nearly passed though Revelations without noticing the deed to 2215 Capistrano Way. It had been torn up, at one time, and carefully taped back together. The grantors were listed as Jonathan and Margaret Alston, the grantee Lou-ise Turner.

Why were the Alstons shown as the grantors? Did

Mrs. Turner buy the house from them? Maybe they helped her buy it? Or had it been some kind of gift? I discounted the gift idea right away. Why should they give her a valuable piece of property? But they could have helped her buy it. They even could have purchased it for her and allowed her to make the payments. That certainly wasn't unheard of, the none too credit-worthy Negro maid, the benevolent white employers. All the elements were there. I held the document up to the light. What was I looking for? Secret writing, a coded message. I didn't know, but something just didn't seem right.

So where did this leave me? I went down my balance sheet. Mrs. Turner's house had been once owned by the Alstons and then transferred over to her. The deed had been torn up into tiny pieces and then taped back together. Penny Troop ends up owning the Turner house, and Mrs. Turner ends up dead. Mrs. Alston gives Mother a thousand dollars and asks her to retrieve some papers belonging to her that were in Mrs. Turner's possession. It certainly seemed like something was rotten in Carmichael, but what? And this was all I had. Mighty slim pickings.

I'm not exactly a compulsive neurotic, but I do like neat and tidy conclusions. I want each negative balanced by a positive. In my way of thinking, there's an explanation, a reason, for everything. But I was coming up with a whole lot of blanks, and it was driving me crazy. The only thing I knew for sure was Penny didn't kill Mrs. Turner. If Trey Dog hadn't reared his ugly head, I wouldn't have been so sure about that either.

I thumbed through the rest of the pages but didn't find much except for some old, yellowed newspaper clippings on the Tuskeegee Airmen. I felt like a two-bit archaeologist but I read them anyway, just for the heck of it. They turned out to be pretty interesting. I didn't know we had a couple of the original airmen living right here in River City. I refolded the brittle clippings along the original creases and put them back where I found them.

Mrs. Turner's Bible had turned out to be somewhat less than the cornucopia of answers I'd expected. If anything, it posed more questions than it answered. I was tired and more than a little worried about Mother. She wasn't home yet. I put my elbows on the table and dropped my head in my hands.

I don't know how long I sat like that before the phone rang. I snatched it up expecting Mother. Instead I got a woman in the throes of panic.

"Theresa? Theresa? Please, Theresa, you got to help me."

"Who is this?" I demanded.

"It's me, girl. Penny . . ."

"You got a lot of nerve calling here asking me for help. First off, you got some explaining to do."

"I can explain everything, honest, I can. But you got to help me. They came here. They trying to frame me . . ."

"Look, calm down. You're blubbering in my ear. I want you to explain just one thing to me. That's it, just one thing. Okay?"

I heard her take a deep breath, and her blubbering quieted a little.

"Okay, Theresa," she said.

"What was your connection with Mrs. Turner? Why is her house in your name?"

"That's what I'm trying to tell you," she said, dropping her voice to a whisper. "They sent the police here. My fingerprints are in the house. They trying to frame me."

"Who's trying to frame you?"

"Old lady Alston."

"Oh, come on now . . ."

"No, listen. You see . . . LaTreace . . ."

"You're getting off the subject. I want to know about you and Mrs. Turner's real estate."

"Will you shut the fuck up and listen!" she screamed. "I'm trying to tell you."

I heard her gulp.

"Theresa? Theresa, I'm sorry. Okay? Okay, Theresa? Please, Theresa, I'm sorry."

I grunted. But there was something in her panic, her out-and-out terror that made me bite my tongue and listen.

"You have one minute," I said.

"Okay, okay, LaTreace stole a couple of Mrs. Turner's

pension checks and cashed them. She used a fake ID. Mrs. Turner didn't know, so she called old lady Alston to ask her where her money was. How come she hadn't got it yet. She said they better not be playing with her 'cause she had grandbabies to feed and they owed her that money.

"Alston didn't want to talk to her, so she had me handle it. Her pension comes out of a trust fund set up years ago by Dr. Alston. I had the bank trace the checks, and we found out they had been forged. We couldn't prove LaTreace did it, but I think Mrs. Turner knew.

"We got all of that settled, but pretty soon LaTreace started calling, asking for money, stuff like that. I made sure I took the calls. I knew she had cashed her grandmother's checks with a fake ID and a forged signature, so I asked her if she had any real estate she wanted to sell."

"LaTreace sold you Mrs. Turner's house," I said, my outrage rising.

Penny gulped. "Yes," she said softly.

"How could you . . ."

"Theresa, let me finish. This is important."

She was calmer now, but there was still a quaver in her voice.

"I had the transfer documents drawn up, and we went to a notary I know, and LaTreace signed the house over to me. I gave her a thousand dollars."

"You gave her a thousand dollars for a house that was worth at least a hundred times as much?"

I was screaming. There was silence on the other end of the line.

"Go ahead," I said finally.

"Well, after LaTreace messed over the money, she started calling trying to get more. I was able to catch most of the calls, but a couple got through to old lady Alston. She'd talk to LaTreace just as sweet as anything, but she'd fly in a rage when she hung up. Just like she would whenever Mrs. Turner's name was mentioned. I think she thought Mrs. Turner was putting LaTreace up to call her, trying to wring more money out of her. 'Long about then was when she started acting real strange, taking that old bike of hers out and staying gone for hours. Bobby was worried and asked me to kinda keep her under wraps. She started acting even more paranoid, accused me of being in cahoots with Mrs. Turner and La-Treace . . ."

"Wait a minute. Were Mrs. Turner and LaTreace in this together? Were they both trying to run a scam on Mrs. Alston?"

"No, I think it was just LaTreace. You see, Mrs. Turner was squeezing her out. LaTreace would steal anything that wasn't nailed down, and she told me her grandmother had locked everything up. She couldn't get her hands on anything to convert into quick cash. But somehow she came upon something else to sell. She bragged to me that she had something old lady Alston would pay good money for."

"What was it?"

"I don't know. I tried to get her to tell me, but she got real tight-lipped. I tried to intercept her calls, but she managed to get through anyway. After that, all hell broke loose and the next thing I knew, Mrs. Turner was dead."

"Are you saying Trey Dog had something to do with this thing between Mrs. Alston and LaTreace?"

"Trey Dog doesn't have anything the fuck to do with anything."

"He killed Mrs. Turner."

"That's what I'm trying to tell you. He didn't kill her. He may have shot up the house, but he didn't kill her."

She was shouting now.

"What are you talking about?"

"She was already dead."

"What?"

"Somebody took a razor to her. She was already dead."

"I don't believe you. You're lying."

"The police been here. They're trying to pin it on me. They'll find out about the house, and they'll pin it on me."

She was blubbering again. I was dazed. I couldn't see her face, couldn't read her body language. For all I knew she could have been reading from a script while she did her nails.

"You're lying, Penny."

"No, I'm not. Honest."

"Who killed her?"

"I don't know."

"Yes, you do. Who killed her?"

"No, really, this is the truth, I don't know. Honest."

"You killed her."

"No!"

She was screaming.

"How do you know what happened to her if you weren't there? You killed her yourself, didn't you?"

"No, no, I didn't. Wait, wait, do you think I'd call you and tell you this if I killed her?"

"I don't know, would you? And how do you know how she died if you didn't do it? The police wouldn't give out that kind of information."

"The police didn't tell me nothing. All they did was ask some funky questions. I called somebody. After the police left, I called somebody who could get the information and they told me. Somebody took a razor to her. Opened her up. Did some real freakish shit. None of that came out in the papers, but that's what happened. You gotta help me."

I was shaken. Thoughts were crashing about in my head like it was a blender and somebody had dropped rocks in and flipped the on switch. I didn't trust Penny. She'd jacked an old lady out of her house. She could have killed her to cover up the theft. And I wasn't about to forget that she tried to get next to my husband. For all I knew, this could be another of her scams.

"What do you want from me?"

"You gotta help me prove I didn't kill her."

"Penny, just for the sake of the argument, how do we prove you didn't kill Mrs. Turner?"

Her voice dropped to a conspiratorial whisper. "This is what we do. We go to old lady Alston, and we tell her we know about the deal with LaTreace and we're going to the police."

"You can do that yourself. You don't need me."

"I gotta have somebody else. I need somebody to watch my back, somebody I can trust."

"You have friends, political cronies."

"Theresa, I need somebody I can trust. Besides, they know about ... some other things I was off into."

"You mean, you have a little credibility problem. Okay, we go tell them that. Then what?"

"Either they deny everything and throw us out and call the police themselves, or they try to talk business."

"This is sounding more and more like a shakedown to me."

"No, just listen. The minute old Lady Alston pulls out her checkbook, we know I'm right."

"Then what?"

"Then what, what?"

"After we do our sorry little imitations of 'Rear Window,' I know what you did, and all that, then what do we do?"

"I don't know."

"You don't know? I thought you had a plan."

"I just know I got to do something before the police get too comfortable focusing on me."

The trill of panic returned to her voice.

I didn't know whether I believed Penny or not. I certainly didn't trust her. But I had to admit, there was a gleam of plausibility in what she was saying. Besides, I was curious about what she was really after.

"Penny, one more question. How'd your fingerprints get in Mrs. Turner's house?"

"I guess when I was searching it," she said sheepishly. "I wasn't too careful."

I was no longer surprised by anything she said.

"And when was this?"

"Right after the police left."

"The night of the ... shooting?"

"Yes."

"Why?"

"I was trying to find whatever it was LaTreace had that old lady Alston was so anxious to get her hands on."

"But why?"

"Security. I needed the security just in case."

"You try to take over LaTreace's little extortion scheme, you're going to need more than security. You going to need a new job."

"I already do. Bobby dumped me this afternoon."

"Okay Penny, I'll help you. But under one condition. You've got to turn Mrs. Turner's property over to her family."

"Okay, sure, Theresa. I'll do that. We'd better get busy. Meet me at the campaign headquarters in half an hour."

"Wait a minute. I can't just jump up and go running around town like that. How do you know they'll even be there?"

"They will. I'll see to that."

"I tell you what, set up the meeting and then call me."

"Okay, Theresa, thank you."

"Yeah, sure."

"Theresa . . ."

"What?"

"I want you to know, I didn't fuck Temp."

Chapter 17

Sir stood just inside the kitchen door with his bath towel dangling loosely at his side and his bathwater puddling at his feet.

"Was that my mother?" His eyes were pinched together with worry.

"Hey, what are you doing out of the tub?" I chided gently.

"What about my mother? Was that her?" he demanded, oblivious to the wet and his brown baby nakedness.

"No, but she's all right, honey."

"I gotta go see 'bout her," he said, moving toward the door.

I scrambled to block his path. "Wait a minute. You can't go out like that."

Suddenly noticing his state of undress, Sir whipped the towel around to cover himself with the aplomb of a burlesque dancer. But he didn't retreat.

"Go on, now. Put some clothes on."

He stood with his head down, refusing to answer.

"Your mom's okay, Sir. Honest she is. She'll call us when she's ready to get you, or she'll come pick you up."

I reached down and lifted his chin with my finger. "Go on, now. Put some clothes on."

"I'm going to see 'bout her."

"No, you aren't."

He planted his feet and held my gaze with tender green belligerence, unblinking and resolute. Then his shoulders sagged a little, not like he was backing down, more like he was giving up a heavy load, letting it rest for a while. He turned and marched back to the bedroom.

I sat at the table and put my head down on my arms. I must have dozed off because the next thing I knew I'd bolted upright with my heart racing. It took me a few seconds to get my bearings and figure out what I was doing sitting at the dining table in Mother's house. I didn't know what had caused my fright. Maybe it had been a noise or something. I listened. The house was still. Much too still.

"Sir?"

I stood up quickly, tipping the chair over behind me.

"Sir? Answer me, damn it!" I shouted, my fear getting a little ahead of me.

I went down the hallway to the bedroom, my fear way out front now, and pushed the door open to the darkened room. I switched on the light. The clean clothes I laid out for Sir lay spread-eagle on the bed just as I'd left them. Everything was in order. Nothing was out of place except for the lace curtains with butterflies embroidered on them that fluttered in the breeze from the open window.

It was hiatal hernia time again. I'm sure I would have sounded like I'd been at the helium if I'd tried to speak. I sank to the bed. How could I have let this happen? I shouldn't have let him out of my sight. I dragged myself up, closed the window, and locked it. I went to each room and checked the windows, assuring myself that they were locked. Finally I checked the back door. It was locked, too. I got Mother's flashlight and the key to Mrs. Turner's house and punched in the code arming the alarm. Almost on cue, the phone started to ring, but I ignored it and headed out into the night.

A light breeze had kicked up, and the trees dancing in front of the streetlights cast frantic shadows that skittered off the pavement, dogging my steps the short distance across the street. Neighborhood dogs relay barked just as they had a few nights ago the first time this scene played.

I got to the door of the darkened house and hesitated. My sweat glands lodged a silent protest. I looked back at Mother's house. It looked so warm and inviting enveloped in its yellow halo of halogen light. I wanted to go back so bad I could taste it, and I would have gone back, too. But I had to find Sir before he hooked up with that sorry mother of his again, and I ended up going from the Rose Garden to worse looking for them.

I turned the flashlight on and used its weak, wavering beam to illuminate the keyhole. I inserted the key and turned the knob. The door gave a little, just an inch or two, but it wouldn't budge beyond that. I stuck the flashlight under one arm and pushed, using both hands. It was no use, something was wedged against it. LaTreace was probably trying to keep anyone from coming in unexpectedly while she "conducted" business with whoever had been in there when I found Sir. I looked over my shoulder at Mother's house. It seemed to stare back at me reprovingly. "Okay, okay," I muttered and trotted around to the side of the house.

The shed stood hunched in the corner of the yard. The shadows were just as skittery back here as in the front. The flashlight's beam began to waver. I shook it and it went out completely, only to come back on weaker.

I walked rapidly up the couple of steps to the back door. It stood slightly ajar, but I knocked anyway. No need to bust in, scaring people.

"LaTreace," I called. "It's me, Theresa."

I pushed the door open a little more and stuck my hand in, groping for the light switch. I found it and flicked it back and forth, but the light didn't come on. I strafed the room with the flashlight a good thirty seconds before I got up the nerve to enter. Finally I stepped in, crunching broken glass underfoot.

Fast-food trash littered the kitchen counter and the floor. The sight of the scattered wrappings and cartons was comforting somehow. Everything else seemed to be just as Mother and her friends had left it after tackling it early yesterday with a small armada of buckets and cleaning tools and enough disinfectants to sterilize six city blocks. I called LaTreace and Sir again, but got no answer.

I made my way from the kitchen to the living room.

The soft tread of my rubber-soled shoes on the hardwood floors was the only sound in the house. There was no clock ticking, no grumbling rumble of the refrigerator motor as it kicked on, no gurgle in the house's old pipes. Nothing.

When I turned the corner to the living room and saw LaTreace, my first thought was, "Couldn't the child find a better place to sleep?" She sat with her back against the front door, her legs splayed out in front of her, her head hanging to the side. I called her name. She didn't answer. My second thought was, "She must be loaded to the gills." I nudged her with my foot. She didn't stir. A funny contraption fashioned from a baby-food jar lay on its side near her left leg. I bent down and put my hand on her shoulder, and it came back wet and sticky. Then I saw the dark stain on her bosom like a cassock and the rest puddling in her lap, and I started to tremble. It was something involuntary, I couldn't help myself. Before the thoughts even formed in my mind, before I could say to myself, "She's dead," my body reacted and I started to tremble. The flashlight sputtered and went out, and it didn't seem to matter. But when her head flopped over to the other side, bobbing like an apple on a string, I jumped back, dropping the flashlight, turned to the side, and retched.

I backed up until I couldn't go any farther, knocking my head against the wall. I forced myself not to scream and not to hyperventilate either. In spite of the roar of blood rushing past my ears and my heart kicking at my chest trying to escape, I heard something. At the very edge of my consciousness, I heard the faintest of noises, the kind of noise wood makes when it gives, or a window makes when it's raised, or a door makes when the wood is swollen and it sticks a little.

I froze, pressed up against the wall, a hand clasped over my chest to quiet my heart. Breathing as quietly as I could, I listened for the noise again. Nothing. Stiff-necked, I tried to look around the room without moving my head, but my peripheral vision was gone and all I could see was LaTreace sprawled in front of the door, her head at a weird angle. Then I thought about Sir, and my mind started to mess with me. Where was he? Please, Lord, don't let him be somewhere in the house lying in his own blood and filth like LaTreace. Maybe that was Sir, the noise I heard? One part of me, the idealistic, somewhat naive part, embraced the idea. The other part thought it knew better. That wasn't the child. Killers make noises like that, not little boys. By now I was scared to stay yet too terrified to leave. But I made up my mind. I had to search the house.

I slid down the wall and crawled over to where I'd dropped the flashlight. I picked it up and hefted its weight in my hand. I had to have something to protect myself, and this would have to do. I stood up slowly. Every nerve in my body seemed to be working independently, firing warning messages to my brain helter-skelter. I felt a peculiar affinity to Stepin' Fetchit, but I couldn't stop to savor it. I took a deep breath and walked quickly down the hallway to the bedrooms. I was nearly dancing with anxiety. I passed the open door to the bathroom. Two days ago the floor lay under an inch of water from the shattered commode. Someone had shut off the valve leading to it and dried the floor, but it gave of the dank odor like a fish tank that needed cleaning. The doors to the bedrooms stood open. I pointed the weak light at each doorway in turn, starting with the one nearest me.

"Sir?" My voice was little more than a hoarse whisper. I took a deep breath and marched into the room. I held the flashlight at arm's length and painted the walls with light. I looked under the bed, in the closet, and in the corners, and marched back out again. And breathed again. One down and two to go. I used the same modus operandi to search the next bedroom, and found nothing. No Sir, but no dead body either, and no killer. That left one more room. There was no getting around it. I had to search the master bedroom, the room where I'd found Mrs. Turner, the last place in the world I wanted to be.

I marched into Mrs. Turner's bedroom with authority, like I owned it, like I belonged there, like I didn't give a damn 'bout no killer. Copping an attitude helps sometimes. At least it got me through the door, even though something deep inside me was scratching and clawing trying to escape. I stood just inside the doorway and studied the room in the failing light. Somebody had removed the sliding doors from the closet and stacked them against the wall next to it. The mattresses had been placed back on the bed. All the furniture, the bed, the dresser, the chest of drawers, the armchair, had been pushed back against one wall out of the way. Cardboard boxes were stacked against the opposite wall. The window was boarded. Dark splotches and stains shoulder high mottled the walls. I stared at the stains without comprehending. I nearly lost my breath when it hit me that they were bloodstains—Mrs. Turner's blood.

There was no place to hide in the room. It was obvious Sir wasn't there. I turned and left, stopping just outside the door to try to clear my head and think what to do. It seemed that every step I'd taken had turned out to be the wrong one. I was going from one mess to another. Bloody, murderous, disastrous messes. I'd lost Sir, La-Treace was dead. And I still had to face Mother. I shook myself trying to clear my head. Actually I shook myself several times. I was like a punch-drunk boxer trying to clear my head and pump up my courage to walk back down the hallway and out of the door. My efforts were cut short by the loud electronic wail of Mother's alarm.

Goaded on by the thought that it could be Sir trying to get back in, I quickly negotiated the hallway back toward the kitchen. I tried not to look as I passed the living room, but no matter which way I turned my head, my vision was full of LaTreace.

I made it through the kitchen and onto the service porch, grabbed the door, jerked it open, and bolted out into the night. The trip from inside the house to the front yard couldn't have taken more than a few seconds. Which was a good thing, too, because I didn't breathe the whole time.

Mother's house was still locked up tight. I used the key to get back in. The circuit had been broken somewhere, something had been opened, either a window or a door, otherwise, the alarm wouldn't have sounded. It had to have been Sir trying to get back in. And if it had, he was probably still in the backyard somewhere. If he'd been over to the Turner house and if he'd seen what I saw, he wasn't off somewhere looking for LaTreace, that's for sure. By now he was plenty scared and hurting bad. He'd need someone now more than ever.

Another thought hit me, and it made my skin crawl. Had Sir seen who did it? Did he come tumbling in looking for LaTreace and catch the murderer in the act? I couldn't tell how long LaTreace had been dead, but if she had been alive when I picked up Sir a couple of hours ago, whoever was in there with her was most likely her killer. Had Sir seen that person? If he had, did the killer know?

I went through the kitchen and onto the service porch, picking my way through the clutter of junk and family heirlooms. I grabbed the knob, turned it, and the door swung open smoothly and easily. It wasn't locked. I went outside. I didn't have time to think about who else had a key.

Mother's halogen lights had the backyard lit bright enough to land a plane. Her large, well-tended garden took up most of the yard. Tomatoes, squash, pepper plants, and who knows what else basked serenely in the artificial light. The door to the single car garage was closed, a large lock swung from the hasp. I stood on the porch and called Sir's name. No answer. I climbed down and walked around the house and checked the side yards. He wasn't there. I went back inside.

My brain was roiling now. Somehow, Aisha and Shawn bubbled up to the surface and I pushed them back down under. I couldn't deal with them now. I simply didn't have the strength. I felt bad about them. I knew I'd neglected them over the past few days. And if I thought really hard I could probably come up with a few promises I'd made and not kept. But I didn't want to think about them. I couldn't and keep going. Temp would just have to pull double duty. I'd make it up later. I promise. Right now I had to find Sir.

Chapter 18

My finger was still on the bell when the door popped open. A woman who looked to be in her late twenties stood there. She wore leggings—extremely well—and a crop top crocheted of something soft and downy. She had blond, frizzy curly hair—the white girl's jheri curl—and friendly gray eyes.

"Excuse me, I'm looking for ... Wanda."

She smiled. Her upper front teeth protruded a little, and this gave her a cheerful, mischievous look.

"This is she. May I help you?"

I was fighting against a rising tide of panic, but I couldn't let that get in my way. I needed to get information, and the only way I could was by obeying conventional rules of etiquette. I had to show some raising, introduce myself, chat a little bit.

"My name's Theresa Galloway. My mother lives over on Capistrano."

She nodded.

"Excuse me for barging in on you so late." I glanced at my watch. It was after nine. "But I'm looking for my nephew, Sir. And I know he sometimes plays with Jamal and Ndugu. I wondered if I could speak to them and ask them if they've seen him."

"Oh, sure, come on in. They're getting ready for bed, but they'll welcome any distraction. Your nephew run away or something?"

"Or something," I said.

She smiled knowingly. I stepped into a living room that was a lot like Mother's and Mrs. Turner's. Most of the houses in the neighborhood are built on similar floor plans. A kid-size table and four chairs stood in the place where the dining table would ordinarily have been. Books, toys, and educational materials were stacked neatly on the shelves that covered one whole wall. Someone had created a kid's oasis, a bright and cheerful classroom.

"You really are home-schooling them. I thought they were just pulling my leg."

"I originally got set up to run a small, in-home preschool. I planned to quit my job with the county and become self-employed."

She gave a short, self-deprecating, little chuckle, almost a snort but not quite.

"Then I hurt my back ... then my son needed help with the boys after their mother went off to 'find herself.' So now they're my only students. But my biggest job is trying to tame them enough to teach them something. I don't know what that mama of theirs was doing, but she certainly didn't teach them much of anything. Just let them run wild."

"I hope you'll excuse me for saying this, but you look kinda young to be their grandmother."

"Believe me, honey, I am. But the rest of the time I'm too old to be going through these kind of changes."

We both laughed.

"Nu-nu, Jay, come in here," she called to the back room.

They entered on cue, freshly scrubbed, wearing matching jammies with red sailboats on them. They walked to the little table and sat down, placing their folded hands on the table like they were in a boardroom.

"You want us, Wanda?" asked Jamal with smarmy innocence.

"Now, what did I tell you about calling me by my first name like you're grown? Grandmother, Nana, even Mama Wanda would be just fine."

They nodded solemnly.

Wanda sighed and said, "This lady, Mrs. Galloway, would like to ask you some questions."

I pulled out the small chair across from them and sat

down. I felt like I was two inches off the floor. My knees were almost up to my chin.

"Hi," I said.

They looked at each other like "hi" was a loaded word full of trickery and deceit. Ndugu started to fidget.

"We don't know where he is," he blurted.

Jamal tensed and bit his lower lip. Ndugu looked at him imploringly. Wanda and I looked at each other. She pulled out the other chair and sat down.

"Nu-Nu, Jay, I want you to tell the truth, now. You hear?"

They nodded.

"Sir may be scared, and he may even get hurt unless a grown-up sees about him soon. You understand?" I asked.

They nodded but said nothing. I tried another tack.

"Even though you don't know where Sir is, where do you think he might be?"

That wary look again.

"Do you think he's somewhere near?"

Nods.

"Somewhere real near? Somewhere warm? Where he can get food?"

More nods.

"If you should just happen to see Sir, would you tell him to call me? You still have my card?"

They agreed, and Wanda dismissed them both with a hug and a pat on the fanny.

"Can I get you some coffee?"

"Thank you, but I've got to go."

"This little boy, this Sir, he related to the lady?"

I knew what she was talking about and nodded.

"Poor baby. They ever catch who did it?"

I shook my head.

"I think the boys may know where Sir is," I said.

"I think so, too. Jay won't tell once he makes up his mind not to, it's too much like a game for him. And Nu-Nu won't tell either unless Jay gives him permission."

"Can you leave a little extra food out, just in case, and maybe a blanket, too."

She laughed, "I'll set up a little shrine on the service porch."

"Don't make it too obvious."

"I won't. I'll keep a look out for him, too. Why don't you give me one of those cards? Have you notified the police?"

Her question jolted me like a smack up side the head. It took just about all I had to keep from recoiling. The police. I didn't even want to think about the police. I'd been fighting with myself back and forth, back and forth, trying to avoid that subject. I should have called them when I found LaTreace, but I wanted to find Sir first. I wanted to temper the shock of his mother's death as much as I could. If he's hiding somewhere around here, I didn't want him to see them hauling his mother's body out like they had Mrs. Turner's. The only problem was the longer I delayed calling the police, the harder it got.

Maybe it's the middle child in me, I don't know, but I felt compelled to do a little more searching for Sir, even though I was pretty sure he was hiding somewhere near and Jamal and Ndugu knew where. I had driven to Wanda's, so I got back in my car and slowly drove through the neighborhood, up one block and down another. Every few blocks I'd loop back around to Mother's street and cruise it slowly with my high beams on. I marveled at the difference a few blocks made. Mother's block was an oasis of quiet and order, even with the events of the last few days. But two blocks over, oblivious to the hour, children played in the street. I slowed to keep from hitting them and crept past, peering into their little overstimulated, stressed-out faces. I stopped to talk to them, asked if they knew Sir, but they scampered into their yards with nervous giggles and hid in the shadows.

I kept going. I thought about going door-to-door, but that didn't seem to make much sense. Instead I settled for peering into each yard as I passed. I studied each doorway and subjected each hedge to close scrutiny. On the third swing down Mother's block, I briefly considered checking parked cars, but gave up on that idea. That's a good way to get yourself shot. There were only a few cars parked on the street besides Mr. Aragon's semi, anyway—a '68 Maverick, a silver Metro with the left front fender bashed in, and a red truck. They all looked empty.

I settled into a rhythm of drifting from street to street, barely paying attention to where I was. I stopped when the lights turned red and went when they turned green. I was looking for a little boy with a long head like Yoruba sculpture and pinched, worried eyes. I had to find him. There was too much killing going on, and I didn't know who would be next or even who was doing it, for that matter. My pat answers had failed me. Trey Dog was dead, and LaTreace should be safe. But she wasn't. She should be alive, but she wasn't. LaTreace and Mrs. Turner were both dead. Who was next?

I had to find the baby.

At some point I looked up and found myself passing the nefarious "Safeway on Alhambra Boulevard," the former site of the Alhambra Cinema. A beautiful, old, rococo Sacramento landmark, the Alhambra had been knocked down and bulldozed into rubble to make way for this modern, squat concrete monument to the power of money. I swung right on H Street traveling east for about a mile. I made another left and that put me on Primrose Lane, a small street, barely two lanes and probably not a block long. It deadened into a pocket of six white stucco cottages with red tile roofs and flower gardens in front. One of these cottages, the Chantilly, was where Edna lived.

Her car was parked in the trellised carport next to her cottage. I pulled up behind it and got out. Edna had been a little testy lately, and she isn't the milk and cookies type—she'd just as soon offer you a shot of scotch as a glass of milk—but I thought I could count on her for some salty advice if not comfort. It was late, but I knocked anyway. I got no response and knocked again. I had turned to leave when I heard Edna say, "Come on in." I lifted my hand and tentatively touched the doorknob. It turned. The door wasn't locked. I don't sit at night with my door unlocked, and I don't know any of Mother's friends who do so either. Edna couldn't have been expecting me, and here she was in the middle of the city with her door unlocked. I'd have to speak to her about that. I pushed the door open and went in.

The interior of Edna's house is like one of those fancy Russian Easter eggs, all ornate and scrolly. It's furnished in French Provençal, the real thing upholstered in rich brocades, not some poorly rendered mass-produced copy. The sparkle of crystal, the muted glow of antique brass caught my eye. Despite its opulence, it was not overdone and cluttered like an "old lady's house." It was tasteful, if you can stand French Provençal, and very feminine.

The dining room was just to the left of the front door. Edna sat at the dining room table wearing a silk robe. She was barefoot. A folded towel lay across her lap. A small lamp shaped like a cherub holding a harp sat on the shoulder-height buffet behind her. The room would have been dark if not for the soft pool of light that spilled over the table.

"Well, look what the cat drug in," Edna said, eyeing me speculatively from beneath perfectly arched brows.

"Your mother know you here?"

We both laughed, acknowledging an old joke we'd shared many times.

"Come on in, baby. You look like you need to talk."

"So, you found the child then you lost him. LaTreace is dead, and you don't think the dog boy killed Louise, somebody else did, probably the same person who killed LaTreace."

I nodded.

"What makes you think that dog boy didn't do it?" she said, eyeing me through a veil of smoke.

"Don't you see, he was already dead before I even found Sir. I heard it on the news. He got shot."

"He could've had somebody do it, one of his friends or something. He could have set it up and got himself killed before it was carried out."

"I just don't think so. I think it was somebody La-Treace knew."

"Why?"

"Because she was expecting whoever it was. That's why she made Sir hide in the backyard. She didn't want him in there while she met with the person or conducted business, whatever. And her crack pipe was out. Whoever it was, she was comfortable enough she didn't have to hide her pipe."

"What do you know about pipes?"

"I read, I watch TV, I know what a pipe is. It was a baby-food jar with some kind of stem taped to it."

"Okay, so you know your pipes. Do you think maybe Sir saw who it was?"

"No, I don't think so. I believe he would have told me if he had."

"So where does this leave us?"

"I don't know."

"And Lorraine's got you running around like a fool trying to straighten this mess out. She ought to be ashamed of herself. Let it go, baby. Just let go of it. It's 'bout time we turned this mess over to somebody else. Take it to the police. Let them do their jobs. You call that young detective been trying to talk to you and tell him everything. You still have his number?"

I nodded and dug through my purse and found the card.

"I don't think this is the same one Mother talked to, but he's one of them working on the case."

I studied the card, reluctant to pick up the phone.

"What's the matter, baby?"

"It's just that I probably should have talked to the police before I got so involved. I mean, I went through the house and everything, and I knew about Trey Dog, for whatever good that did, and I did find the Bible."

"You have the Bible?"

"Didn't I tell you? Sir had it. He hid it in that old shed, in a bag of dog food, of all things."

"He thinks he's pretty clever, doesn't he? I hope he doesn't end up outsmarting himself."

"What do you mean?"

"These're grown folks he's messing with, not little kids. He can end up getting himself killed, that's all."

She took another drag on her cigarette and held the

smoke. Thin wisps curled out of her mouth as she spoke. "Well, what was in it? What did you find in the Bible?"

"Nothing much, as far as I could tell. There were some birth certificates, report cards, a marriage license, old newspaper clippings, stuff like that."

"That's all?"

"What do you mean 'that's all?' Isn't that the usual kind of stuff 'old' people keep in their Bibles?"

She slapped at me playfully. "Everybody's carrying on so about this Bible, it just seemed to me it had to have a map to a buried treasure hidden in it or letters from Thomas Jefferson to Sara Hennings. You know, something worth some money."

"I'm afraid not," I said, knowing as I spoke that wasn't exactly the whole truth. Why I didn't tell her what I found out about the deed and who really owned Mrs. Turner's house, I don't know. I guess I just didn't want to have to go into that whole Penny Troop thing right now. That really would have brought me down, what with Penny hitting on Temp and everything. I didn't need any more advice from old women without men on how to keep mine, so I didn't mention Penny.

Speaking of Mrs. Turner's Bible reminded me of the list of names I'd found. I didn't think it had anything to do with this whole mess, but I was intrigued by the partial Bible verse penciled in at the bottom of it. If anybody could identify it, besides Pastor Miller, it was Edna. She's a walking biblical concordance, although her interpretations often leave something to be desired.

"You know, I ran across a Bible verse the other day, and I've been trying to remember the rest of it. You think you might know it? It goes, 'I call heaven and earth to record this day against you.' "

Edna stared at me blankly.

"What's the rest of it?" I prodded.

"I don't know."

"Come on, Edna. I know you know. Just give me the book. I'll find it."

Edna ignored me. She bent her head and stamped out the cigarette she'd been smoking in a crystal ashtray. She had smoked it almost down to its filter, and I watched as she smashed the remainder of the butt repeatedly with escalating force until it disintegrated.

"Edna, it's dead."

She looked up at me slowly. Then she glanced down at the ashtray and withdrew her hand, hiding it in her lap.

"You ready to call the police now?" she said.

"I guess so."

"You still worried about implicating yourself?"

"Sort of."

"Give me the card."

She reached across the table and took it from my hand.

"I'll call. You've told me everything, I'll just report it like you told me, keeping you out of it as much as I can. You did tell me everything, didn't you? You didn't leave anything out, did you?"

"Like what?"

"I don't know. Did you notice anything or see anyone? You know, things like that."

"No, I don't think so."

"Good, don't worry about it. I'll take care of everything."

"Now that you've had a chance to go through Mrs. Turner's things, did you find anything? You know, anything that might be what ole lady Alston's looking for—something that might give us an idea of what's going on?"

"Just a lot of junk. But there's no telling what Louise was messed up in."

Until now I had viewed Mrs. Turner through Mother's see-no-evil eyes. Edna's remark had a vicious edge to it, and that made me a little uneasy. I felt disloyal somehow to both Mother and Mrs. Turner, but I was also curious.

"What do you mean by that? Do you think she was messed up in something?"

"Ain't no telling."

"Come on, Edna, Mrs. Turner was a nice old lady trying to help raise her great-grandchildren. You're the first one to try to bring up any dirt on her. You know what they say about trying to sling mud on people."

Edna bristled.

"I knew Louise a lot longer than you did and, suffice

it to say, I knew a few things about her I don't think she'd have wanted to get out. How do you think she lived all these years? She didn't draw Social Security, she wasn't on welfare. She had to be doing something. You ever give that any thought? She hasn't worked in I don't know how long. She owned her house free and clear. Forget that shit about a pension. Ain't nowhere on the Lord's green earth that a domestic draws a pension. I don't care if she worked in the White House."

"That doesn't mean anything. Just because you didn't know all her business doesn't mean she was doing something wrong, that she had something to hide."

"Everybody does, baby."

"No, not everybody."

"Live on child, you'll learn. Everybody has something to hide, and you're a fool if you believe otherwise. There's things about me I sure in hell wouldn't want out, and I bet you there's some things you'd just as soon keep to yourself, too. Even Lorraine has her own nasty, little secrets."

Mother? Secrets? I thought about the gun and Mother sighting on the lamp in the corner. Surprises maybe, messes—for sure. But secrets? Nasty little ones? I doubted that.

I shrugged and looked at my watch. "I guess I'd better go home. By the way, why were you sitting here with your door unlocked? Don't you know it's dangerous?"

Edna was lighting another cigarette. She looked up at me with one eye. The other was squeezed shut.

"I was waiting for the mailman."

I shrugged. She could be as sarcastic as she wanted. It didn't bother me. I was used to her.

"Well, I'm going now. You know, you really ought to get rid of those cigarettes."

Edna waved me away, and I left locking the door behind me as she sat smoking in a tight circle of light.

Chapter 19

I walked in the door and all hell broke loose. Temp got up in my face talking trash with Mother standing behind him clucking and nodding in agreement.

"Now, the boy's got a point, Theresa. You could've called. That's the very least you could have done. And your children sitting up here hungry. You know what you oughta do? You oughta fix up some stuff and freeze it. That's what you oughta do. Then, when you're out, your babies don't have to go hungry. They can just warm something up. When we got here they were just about hungry enough to pass out. Why, if I hadn't cooked ... By the way, baby, you really need to clean that stove of yours."

"Mother."

"What?"

"Shut up."

Her mouth snapped shut like it was spring-operated. I didn't care. Turning to Temp, I said, "I called ..."

"Four hours ago," he shouted. "Four motherfucking hours ago."

The street runs close to the surface in Temp in the best of times; he was angry now and regressing rapidly. At the sound of the "mother" word, Mother recoiled like he'd spit at her. With her lower lip tucked grimly between her teeth, she gathered Andrea and Cenne, grabbed their sweaters where they had been tossed across the railing, and began forcing their arms into the sleeves. One of them started to whine, and Mother comforted her, muttering almost under her breath about "respect" and "impudence" and what she would and would not take from anyone.

I interrupted her monologue.

"Excuse me, Mother, I need to speak to Temp in private."

She looked at me and sniffed. I touched Temp's shoulder, but he jerked away, tossing his arms like a fighter, nearly elbowing Mother in the eye. Shawn glanced up from his video game, sighed, and returned to it, manipulating the controls without looking, his fingers moving frantically, the game making cartoon noises when he scored a point.

Aisha, in the breakfast nook practicing her cheering routine, stopped and glared at us. Sighing deeply with a great show of weariness, she marched down the three steps leading to the family room, went to the entertainment center, and turned the stereo up so loud I could feel it in my teeth.

I didn't need this. After what I'd been through today, dead bodies, lost kids, frantic phones calls, crazy people, I didn't need any of this. If I hadn't been so tired, I would have turned around and walked right back out the front door.

I shouted over the hip-hop racket. "Turn it down, Aisha."

Rolling her hips to the music in a childish caricature of a fertility dance, she pointedly ignored me.

Temp stomped into the family room and grabbed the remote, firing first at the TV and then at the stereo. They both went mute. Shawn jumped up, throwing both hands above his head in frustration.

"Hey, I didn't get a chance to save it," he complained, dancing in place.

Temp whirled around, breathing heavily, pointing the remote like a gun.

"To your room. Out!"

"You could've let me save it." Consternation and despair twisted itself into a whine.

"Don't mess with me, man. Out."

Shawn slapped both hands against his thighs and ran out of the room, tears glistening in his eyes. Temp turned to Aisha, but she'd gathered her things and was already stomping up the stairs muttering under her breath about "sorry, incompetent, dysfunctional . . ." I couldn't catch the end, it sounded something like "assholes" but I let it go. I had other things to deal with.

Mother's eyes were as big as saucers. She talks a good game but she hates confrontations. She hustled Andrea and Cenne to the front door and stood there nervously fishing in her purse. Temp looked at me as if to say something but changed his mind. Sighing, he turned to Mother.

"Mom, I'll take you home, if you're ready to go."

"No, that's all right, baby. You can just call me a cab. I know you and Theresa have some things you want to work out."

"I said, I'll take you home," he snapped.

Temp grabbed a jacket from the closet by the door and stalked out. Mother was hustling the girls out after him when I stopped her.

She whirled around. Anger and frustration manipulated her face like it was made of putty.

"I . . . will . . . never . . . ever . . . set . . . foot . . . in . . . this house . . . again!" she said, drawing herself up higher with each word. She was so angry, she appeared to be levitating.

"Mother, I think you'd better sit back down. There's a couple of things I need to tell you before you go."

I told her about Penny owning Mrs. Turner's house and about Penny's call. I also told her about my trip to Forest Hill and my introduction to Mrs. Turner's brother. Then, when I couldn't avoid it any longer, I told her about finding Sir and the Bible, and losing him and finding LaTreace and my visit with Edna. Mother sat silently for a long time, and I could tell she was praying.

Temp opened the door and stepped in. He looked at me and Mother sitting next to each other on the sofa, and he wheeled around and left. A minute or so later, I heard him start his car and drive away.

Mother glanced around the room with a glazed look. "I'd better go home," she said.

I didn't want her to go. I'd been through so much

today, I needed the comfort of knowing she was nearby. Besides there was a killer loose out there somewhere.

"Stay here tonight, Mother. There's plenty of room."

"No, baby, I have to go home. I couldn't rest here; there's just too much turmoil in the air here."

An hour went by and Temp still hadn't returned. Mother finally agreed to spend the night. I put her on the sofa bed in the family room, and Andrea and Cenne bunked upstairs on the trundle in Aisha's room. Temp still wasn't home when I finally got to bed around one, and I was worried almost to the point of panic. I made no pretense of trying to sleep. By two-thirty I was up pacing the floor. Finally I broke down, threw my pride to the wind, and called Mother Alma's number. It rang a couple of times, and her answering machine came on. I hung up without leaving a message. I called a couple of his friends, but hung up before anyone could answer. I even thought about calling the hospitals, but I got a hold of myself before I could. Besides, I wasn't afraid he had been in an accident—not really. What I was afraid of was a whole lot worse.

Mother got up around six-thirty and found me sitting at the dining room table drinking coffee and biting my nails. She refused my offer of breakfast, electing instead to quiz me on Temp's whereabouts.

"Where's that husband of yours?"

"Uh, he had to leave early."

"I see," she said managing to sound accusatory and pitying at the same time.

After getting Aisha and Shawn off to school, I loaded the girls and Mother into the car and headed for Oak Park.

Mrs. Turner's house had weathered another assault, this time from city workers who had boarded up all the windows and doors and posted a condemnation notice on the front of the house proclaiming it unsafe for habitation. Mother averted her eyes as she climbed out of the car and helped the girls after her. I got them situated, helped clean up the mess I'd made the night before, and was on my way out of the door when Mother grabbed my arm.

"You know where my important papers are, don't you?"

I searched her face trying to see what she was getting at, trying to figure out why my stomach had suddenly knotted up.

"Yes, I think so, but why?"

She ignored my question.

"Most of them are in that cash box on the top shelf in my closet. Attorney Wilson has copies of all the important stuff like my will."

"Mother, I don't like this. You feeling okay? You expecting something to happen? You are taking your medicine, aren't you? Your pressure isn't high again, is it?"

She brushed my concerns aside with a wave of her hand.

"Why is it, once a person passes sixty-five she suddenly becomes a fool, can't take her own medicine or anything? Everybody running around, 'You take your medicine? You eat your vegetables? You move your bowels?' Yes, everything's okay. I just want to make sure you know where everything is, that's all.

"And one other thing, I want you to stay away from Edna."

"Stay away from Edna? Why?"

"Because I said so."

"Mother," I said, my exasperation mounting. "You've been hiding the truth and hoarding information while I ran around here like a fool. Now, tell me, is there something about Edna I need to know?"

"You know enough as it is. You and Carolyn thought you were so smart running to Edna, having her buy you cigarettes and who knows what else. Thought I didn't know, didn't you? I told you then and I'll tell you now, stay away from Edna."

"She's your friend . . ."

"That's just it, she's my friend, not yours. When you went to Edna's house last night, you said the door was unlocked, you just walked in."

I nodded.

"How was she acting?"

"What do you mean?"

"You know, what was she doing?"

"We just sat and talked."

"Where?"

"At the dining room table."

"What did she have on?"

"She was barefoot."

Mother nodded. She seemed to be waiting for some particular detail.

"And she had on a robe," I added.

"Anything else?"

"No, that's it. Oh, she was carrying a towel, too."

"Carrying a towel? How? How was she carrying it?"

"Well, she wasn't exactly carrying it. She had it laying across her lap."

"The whole time you were there?"

"Uh-huh."

"Did she get up, move around any at all?"

"No, she just sat at the table the whole time I was there."

Mother turned away from me so I couldn't see her face.

"So, she's up to her old tricks again."

She spoke so softly she could have been talking to herself. She turned back to me.

"Edna's life has been rough. I understand that. She's had to scrape and scratch just to get by. I understand that, too. She's been mixed up in more than her share of devilment. That's all right. But when she feels the need to point a gun at my child, the understanding stops right then and there."

"A gun?"

"What do you think she had under that towel, baby, soap on a rope? A gun. It's an old trick. Edna doesn't like getting caught in tight spots. You see her somewhere with a coat folded across her lap, a jacket, even a newspaper, you better watch out. You can bet she's feeling nervous about something, and she has her gun out."

"A gun, Mother, a gun?

"Guns don't mean all that much when you grow up in

the country hunting squirrels with your brothers. More often than not, it's these city folk who act a fool with guns."

"But, we're talking about Edna. Edna's who's seventy-five, seventy-seven . . . How old is she?"

"It doesn't matter how old she is. Like I told you, she hasn't always been old."

Mother had my attention now. And while the pieces weren't exactly falling into place, I was beginning to see a pattern, and I didn't think the completed picture would be very pretty.

"Who do you think she was waiting for?" asked Mother.

"I don't know. But now that you mention it, she had to be waiting for someone. I know it wasn't me. She had no reason to be waiting for me. There was no way she could have even known I was coming by. I didn't even know that myself. So she was waiting for someone else, someone she felt threatened by. But why would she undress? She was barefoot, had her robe on. That doesn't make sense."

"It may not make sense to you."

The puzzle pieces rearranged themselves on their own, and a terrible thought began to form in my mind. I tried to think of a delicate way to ask what I was thinking, but I ended up just blurting it out. There's nothing delicate about murder.

"You don't think Edna had anything to do with Mrs. Turner's death, do you?"

Mother's response showed she had given the possibility some thought, too.

"It depends on what you mean by that. If you're asking me if I think Edna killed Sister Turner, then the answer is no. But maybe Edna knows something. She may have gotten herself messed up in something a little too rough even for her. I don't know. And by the way, I don't know if I give much credence to what your friend, this Miss Penny, says about Sister Turner being stabbed and all. I just don't see how all that could've happened in the little time between when I spoke to Sister Turner and the shooting and everything."

"Remember, I saw what somebody did to LaTreace and this was after Trey Dog got killed. If it hadn't been for that, I would probably agree with you. But somebody killed LaTreace, and it wasn't Trey Dog, and whoever it was . . ."

I didn't finish that thought, at least not out loud, but inside I was shouting it—"Whoever it is may not be finished yet!"

Mother looked at me like she knew what I was thinking.

"What about ole lady Alston?" she asked with just a hint of too much zeal.

"What reason would she have to be mixed up in this?"

"She may have been after the house. Stranger things have happened."

"I doubt it. The Alstons probably own property all over the city. Besides, Penny had more reason to kill Mrs. Turner than anyone. Maybe Mrs. Turner found out she'd stolen her home right from under her, and threatened to go to the police or something?"

"I just can't believe anybody would be so brazen. You know one thing, I didn't like that Penny Troop the first time she set foot in my house, sashaying around like she owned it."

"Mother, we're overlooking one other person who might have had a reason for killing Mrs. Turner."

"Nobody had a reason to kill her, baby."

"You know what I mean. We have to consider her brother."

"He wouldn't do a thing like that. Kill his sister and his niece, too. No."

"You didn't see him yesterday, I did. He looked pretty crazy to me. And they say there was bad blood between him and Mrs. Turner. He could have hopped in that truck of his and been down here and back in a couple of hours. No one would even miss him, especially if he works out in the field part of the day."

"No, you might as well cross him off your list. I just don't believe her very own brother would do something like that."

But I didn't cross him off. I didn't cross him or Penny

off, although it was pretty unlikely the two of them would have any connection. As far as I was concerned, Penny had a proven motive, but there was something about Mrs. Turner's brother that bothered me. I just couldn't quite put my finger on it. It had something to do with . . .

I stood stock-still trying to think, trying to reel in the image that was hovering just on the outer edges of my consciousness. I squeezed my eyes shut trying to get a fix on it. My body must have given a slight tremor, I was thinking so hard.

"Theresa, I'd know that look anywhere. Here, let me get you some Pepto . . ."

The image I was conjuring up fluttered away like a startled bird.

"No, Mother, that's all right. I've lost it now."

She placed her hand on my shoulder. "You sure?"

"I'm sure. Why don't you show me this cash box you're talking about, and then I've got to go."

The box was sturdy enough with an intimidating lock swinging on the front. Mother turned it upside down and worked the bottom panel loose.

"It's kinda old," she explained. "You don't have to worry about the lock, I lost the key years ago. Every-thing's right here."

She patted the papers.

"Everything you'll need if anything happens is right here."

"I suppose, we'd better check your deed out while we're at it," I suggested.

We checked. Everything seemed to be in order. It looked like Mother still owned her home. But then again, you never can tell.

Temp still wasn't home when I got back. I checked the family's answering machine. There were four mes-sages, one from Aisha's orthodontist, two from Allen, and one from Miyako, but none from Temp. He'd never done anything like this before, stayed out this long with-out getting in touch. Sure, there'd been times when he'd gotten angry and stormed out. Once he even slept in his car right in the garage. But he'd always been there at the door, the first thing in the morning, ready to forgive me if I'd forgive him, ready to say he was wrong if I'd say I was, too.

I went to his office to check the messages on his answering machine. Even though he works from home, Temp tries to maintain as much professionalism as possible. We have a tacit understanding that his office is off-limits to the children and me. We don't answer his phone, take his messages, or screw around with his fax machine, which is just fine with me. But these were desperate times, and desperate times call for desperate measures. I punched the playback button—bid information, Black Chamber meeting, soccer stuff, and three hangups. Nothing of any help. All that guilt-induced adrenaline wasted.

I pulled out his chair and sat down. I was in this far, I might as well make a couple of calls to set my mind at ease. I thumbed through his card file and found Penny's card. It said Penny Troop, Robert Alston for Mayor, Campaign Manager. It had a street address, post office box, a phone number, and a fax number. She had written her address and home phone number on the back. I dialed that first. It rang twenty times, no answering machine, no voice mail, nothing. I hung up and called the Alston campaign. The phone rang only once. I asked to speak to Penny and was told she wasn't there. I asked to speak to Mrs. Alston, and she came on the phone.

"I'm sorry, dear, but I do believe Penny had some business to attend to out of town."

"When did you talk to her last?"

"Yesterday, yesterday evening. She called to say she was going out of town for a few days."

"Did she say anything else?"

"No, not that I recall. It was a very short conversation. Not much to it at all, really."

"Mrs. Alston, did she happen to mention that the police had been to her home?"

"The police? Gracious, no. What cause would the police have to visit her?"

"That's what I'm trying to find out."

"It wouldn't have anything to do with this dreadful business concerning Louise, would it?"

"I don't know. What do you think?"

"Mrs. Galloway . . ."

"Yes, Mrs. Alston."

"I'm sure you will appreciate that I am a very busy woman. We had a major fund-raiser last night, and I've neglected some important matters that must be dealt with immediately. I have neither the time nor am I in the mood for guessing games. If you would be so good as to answer one question, we could terminate this discussion and I could return my attention to more pressing matters."

"All right," I answered, somewhat taken aback by her sudden mood swing.

"Have you found the items I asked you to locate?"

"Yes, I believe so."

Don't ask me why I lied. I'd found the Bible, but it didn't contain anything even remotely connected to Mrs. Alston. Maybe it was her tone of voice. Maybe I got tired of listening to her call Mrs. Turner "Louise" while I very politely addressed her as "Mrs. Alston." I don't know, it just seemed right somehow. I had a feeling, a hunch, call it what you will, that I should say yes, that an answer in the affirmative would get me closer to the truth than a negative one. Maybe I have some powers I need to check out with Mother Simms and Cleotis. Anyway, I said yes, and that seemed to surprise and please her.

"Very good, wonderful," she crooned. "When may I have them?"

"Why don't I bring them to you? How about sometime this evening?"

"No, don't do that. I'll be busy tonight. I'm just about buried in work. I'll call you and make arrangements to take possession. Oh, and Mrs. Galloway, you can be assured, you will not regret the assistance you've provided."

Sometimes when you're putting a puzzle together, you have to try pieces that seem unlikely, just to see what will happen. And sometimes, not too often but frequently enough to keep you hopeful, you get a surprised fit. I decided to try an unlikely puzzle piece.

"Mrs. Alston, when was the last time you talked to Mrs. Thompson?"

"Mrs. Thompson? Oh, you mean Louise's friend, Edna."

"Yes, Mrs. Alston, Mrs. Thompson. When did you last speak to her?"

"Well, I don't know, really. When did she say we last spoke?"

"That's all right, Mrs. Alston. I've got to go now."

I hung up with the certainty that had we stayed on the phone all day, she still wouldn't have answered my question. She was too ... I searched for a word that would fit, but all I could come up with was "slick." "Slick Little Old Lady," an oxymoron if there ever was one. But if you forgot about the vintage Chanels, the cotton candy hair, and the white gloves, that's what you ended up with. The thought scared me. I realized that with her pulling the strings, poor, pathetic Bobby had a good chance of becoming mayor.

Also, somebody was lying. It was either her or Penny, maybe even both of them for different reasons. Penny swore the Alstons had sent the police to her home, yet ole lady Alston professed to know nothing about it. Somehow I leaned toward believing Penny on this one. Besides, if I got half the chance, I'd send the cops, animal control folks, and a couple of security guards from K-mart to her house, too, just for the hell of it.

Penny had been scared when I talked to her last night, but she had also been in a confrontational mood, ready to face down the Alstons as long as she had me to back her up. It seemed unlikely that after talking to me—ranting and raving and blubbering all over the phone—she'd calmly call ole lady Alston and announce she was going out of town for a few days. And what about the meeting she was supposed to have arranged with the Alstons? Dread, a clawed and tenacled monster, stirred in the pit of my stomach. If Mrs. Alston was lying, then what was she trying to hide? More important, where was Penny?

The phone rang. I snatched it up.

"Theresa, this is Dorothy."

"Dorothy?"

I'd heard the voice somewhere before, but I couldn't quite place it.

"You know, LaTreace's cousin. I heard what happened to her, and I got some of her stuff I want you to come get."

"I'm very sorry about LaTreace—"

"Uh-huh, yeah. When you going to come get the stuff?"

"We've been trying to get in touch with the rest of the family. Couldn't you hold it until we can make some arrangements?"

"No, I want you to come get this shit. I don't want nothing to do with it, you understand?"

"Wait a minute. What is it?"

"Some papers an' stuff."

"Okay, okay, I'll come get it. Where are you? You at home?"

"No, I'm at work. They put me back on the day shift. But I have it with me. I was scared to leave it at home. I'm at DMV headquarters. You know, on twenty-fourth right off Broadway. I go to lunch in fifteen minutes. Can you meet me out front?"

Dorothy was pacing the walk in front of the building with a cigarette in one hand and a large manilla envelope tucked under one arm. I pulled over to the curb and she came to the car, leaned over, and tossed the envelope through the open window on the passenger side.

"Here, take this shit." I took it and drove away. On the way home, I had to fight hard to resist the urge to pull over to the curb and go through the envelope right there. I didn't bother to check for messages from Temp when I got home this time. Instead I went straight to the dining room table, where the light was good. I upended the envelope, and the sum of LaTreace's worldly possessions tumbled out—three drivers licenses each in a different name, JC Penney, Wards, and MasterCard credit cards in Louise Turner's name, food stamp and medical identification cards, and an old *Ebony* magazine from September 1990. That was it. Talk about let down.

"Surely you didn't expect a signed confession," I reprimanded myself. But, as is often the case, I spoke too soon. Because I found something just as good.

Chapter 20

Denzel Washington was on the cover. Other than that there was nothing remarkable about the magazine. September 1990—it wasn't old enough to be a collector's item or anything. But Denzel—anything imprinted with his likeness ought to be worth something. I picked it up and thumbed through the pages, and I struck pay dirt right away.

It was a piece of binder paper, folded in half. Copied neatly in elegant lettering were eight names: Darcella Mae Dupree, Lee Ann Mackey, Levinia Choy, Charlotte Spivey, Juanita Diane Brown, Clara Thomas, Mary Francis Ware, and Donetha Wells. I knew I was on to something. These were the same names I'd found on the list in Mrs. Turner's Bible. The only thing missing was the Bible verse. Who were they? What did they have in common? And why was this list important enough for La-Treace to hide it with her most valued possessions—her money-making tools.

I got up from the table, went into the kitchen, and dialed Mother's number. I got a busy signal.

I picked up the phone again and dialed Brenda Delacore's office number. Her section clerk informed me that Brenda was out of the office. When I asked for how long, she said she didn't know for sure, but it could be for several days. This news did not please me. I hadn't approved vacation for Brenda the last time we'd talked, and besides, she was acting for me in my absence.

I dialed the phone again. I got a connect. Loud jazz, recorded from a scratchy, old stereo record, drowned out the recorded message. When the message ended and the tone sounded for me to leave my message, I shouted into the phone: "Pick up the phone, Brenda."

"Theresa? So, they finally caught up with you, huh?"

"Who caught up with me?"

"Allen 'n 'em. You can tell them I don't give a fuck 'bout how long they put me on administrative leave. I don't give a fuck 'bout no disciplinary action neither."

"What are you talking about?"

"You don't know?"

"Un-uh."

"I'll let them tell you."

"Never mind about all that, Brenda. I need some help on something. I got a list of names here. I'm going to read them off. Tell me if they mean anything to you. You know, from your work with the historical society or something."

I read the names to her.

"The Spiveys—they some of the box people and you know the Choys, there's a big family of them. Chances are this Levinia is related. I don't recognize the rest."

"Box people?"

"Yeah. They came to Sacramento in the forties during World War II, recruited from down South to work at McClellan building war planes and shit. Back then Black folk had a hard time finding places to live, so some of them got some of those big ass crates they ship planes or something in and set up housekeeping in them over there in the Heights. The Spiveys are still there."

"Living in boxes?"

"For your information, honey, Rev. Spivey of the Camellia City Christian Institute probably owns more land in Del Paso Heights than anybody. He's one of the 'Box Spiveys' all right, but he doesn't live in no box no more. None of the Spiveys do."

"You think Charlotte Spivey could be related?"

"Chances are, she probably is. I haven't met a Spivey yet who wasn't."

"Brenda, get a pencil and write these names down."

I read them again.

"Since you have a little time on your hands," I said,

leaning heavily on sarcasm, "I want you to do something for me. Find out about these names. Who are these people?"

"Why? What's going on?"

"I don't know, really. I found this list in the Bible of one of Mother's friends who got killed. It probably doesn't mean much, but I don't think she would have kept it in the Bible unless it was important—to her, at least. Some of these people could be relatives or in-laws or something, and we should be notifying them of her death."

"I doubt that's true of the Choys."

"Can you do it for me? Can you check on these names?"

"Yeah, I'll do it. But, Theresa, about that confidential report Allen has ..."

"Look, Brenda, I can't talk about that now. Just do this for me, and I promise I'll take care of everything when I get back to work."

"Promise?"

"Promise, promise. Now, how long will it take? Can you get back to me this afternoon?"

"I don't know. I'll try. Anything else I need to know?"

"Not that I can think of."

"Okay, I'll call you."

I hung up. Then I picked the phone up and dialed information for the city of Stockton and asked for the number for the Northern California Women's Correctional Facility. I dialed the number, and when it was answered, I explained why I was calling. I was transferred to several different people and finally ended up speaking to the chaplain, a Reverend Dobson. I told him I needed to get in touch with one of his "residents," "clients," "prisoners"—I really didn't know what word to use— Sharon Yvonne Turner. I explained that Sharon's mother had died. He asked me some detailed questions about the death—time, place, cause, things like that. I assumed he needed the information for verification purposes. He also asked about me, my relationship to Sharon, etc. I told him I was a close friend of the family and I was assisting with funeral arrangements. I asked if I could speak to Sharon. He said he would have to go through channels—Sharon would be told, in a sensitive manner, of her mother's death, and then she would be given the opportunity to call me or some other family member. In other words, I would have to wait. I gave him my phone number and hung up the phone.

I was sitting at the table waiting for the phone to ring, which has all the entertainment value of watching grass grow, when Aisha and Shawn came home.

"Hi, Mom."

Aisha grudgingly kissed me on the cheek, probably still mad from last night. She had on one of those granny dresses we used to wear in the sixties and a pair of platform shoes.

"How's it going, baby?"

"All right." Her listless answer gave ennui a new meaning.

"How's Mark Wesley Talbot?"

"Oh, Mom, don't start on that again," she said, turning on her heels and stalking out of the room.

Okay, I struck out that time. I was just too distracted with this LaTreace stuff and everything. But, I promised myself, as soon as I get this mess cleared up, I'm going to sit down and have a nice long talk with that child.

"Where's Dad?" demanded Shawn.

He was wearing the same clothes he left home in this time, shorts—well, not exactly shorts, these came to his knees and were so loose they created a breeze when he walked—and a flannel shirt. His legs were ashy, his knees scabby, and there were grass clippings in his hair.

"He had to go check on a job."

I don't lie well.

Shawn studied me for a minute. Then, sighing like Temp, he stepped over his backpack lying where he'd dropped it and went into the family room and turned on the TV.

I let him go. An hour or so of TV wouldn't kill him, and he could pick the backpack up later—after I took care of this LaTreace business.

The phone rang again, and I snatched it up.

"Baby?"

"Temp, honey, where've you been? I been worried sick about you."

"I'm at Mama's. I spent the night there. Listen, baby, I'm sorry about last night. I'll get home as soon as I can—"

"As soon as you can? How 'bout right now?"

"Can't. I got to finish up something."

"Finish up something? What?"

"Well, right now I'm painting the garage," he admitted sheepishly.

I laughed out loud. In fact, I guffawed in his ear. Served him right—stomping out like that last night— fronting me off in front of Mother. If I knew Mother Alma, he was going to have to sneak out of her house just to come back home. Served him right.

The house was in an uproar. Shawn was playing video games as he had for the last three hours. Aisha had the music blasting, and she was in Temp's office talking on his business line. I directed her there—I wanted to keep the family line open. The dinner hour had come and gone, but Temp never showed. Finally I broke down and ordered a pizza for Aisha and Shawn. I wasn't hungry. I was too anxious to eat.

Sharon called around eight.

"I called about Mama. They just told me . . ."

She sounded calm, unemotional.

"Sharon, I'm so sorry."

"Yeah, thanks. They didn't tell me much. What happened?"

"She was shot."

"Shot? Mama?" Her voice cracked.

"Drive-by. We think it had something to do with LaTreace."

Sharon swore softly.

"LaTreace, I should have known. The babies?"

"They're fine. Mother's taking care of them."

"Look, I can't stay on here long. Can you tell me what happened and who's taking care of everything."

I told her as much as I knew, which was probably

more than anyone else knew at this point. I could tell she was crying and struggling to hide it.

I told her about my trip to Forest Hill to visit Mrs. Turner's brother, and she was surprised.

"Oh, shit. He didn't like Mama, too tough. He slam the door in your face?"

"Not at first. But he went ballistic when I mentioned the twins."

"Theresa, I don't think you should have done that."

"Done what?"

"Told him their names. He didn't know."

"Sharon, what the hell is going on?"

"It's just that he never got over when she died."

"Who died?"

"His daughter, Andrea Cenne. That was her name. He blames Mama."

Background noises grew louder and then muffled out as a hand was placed over the phone at Sharon's end. She came back on the line.

"Look, I gotta go. Is everything arranged? When is the funeral?"

"It hasn't been scheduled yet. Mother's been trying to get in touch with family members. I'll let you know. Will they let you out to go to the funeral?"

"I don't know. Supposed to go through channels. I may need some help from the outside."

"Sharon, real quick, tell me about Andrea Cenne. What happened to her?"

She spoke rapidly.

"She was Uncle Walter's only child, his heart. Theresa, she was so smart and pretty—no, no, she was beautiful. She was absolutely beautiful. She was about eight years older than me, and I thought she was *it*.

"Uncle Walter sent her to live with us so she could go to City and get a nursing degree. He didn't want to let her go, but he knew there wasn't nothing for her in Forest Hill, and he didn't want her looking toward the bright lights at Reno. He kept telling Mama over and over, I know I can trust you to take care of Andy. That's what he called her, Andy.

"She wore straight skirts and had her hair bobbed and

polished her toenails. And me, I tried to do everything she did.

"Sometimes Mama would take her to work with her, but not often. Mama wanted to make sure she spent most of her time studying.

"Then, one day she died."

"How?"

"The obituary said appendicitis. It took me a long time to figure it out; I was almost grown. Mama wouldn't talk about it. And after Uncle Walter came down here with his shotgun, I didn't have the nerve to ask her."

"She bled to death. She was in her room real quiet. Mama came home and I remember hearing her scream, and I ran out my room and there were bloody footprints on the floor. And Mama had her in her arms. She was as tall as Mama and nearly as big, but Mama picked her up like a baby and carried her to the car and drove away, and I never saw her again. I gotta go."

"Sharon, wait. What happened?"

Sharon sighed. I could almost feel her weariness. Her rapid delivery gave way to a slow, dirge like recitation.

"Mama took her to Dr. Alston. Took her right up to his house. Begged and pleaded, but old lady Alston wouldn't let her see him, said he wasn't there. Told them to go to the hospital. Said Dr. Alston could lose his license.

"By the time Mama got her to the hospital, she was almost gone. They couldn't stop the bleeding. They never found out who did it."

"Who did what?"

"The abortion."

"I don't understand."

"They were illegal then. I gotta go."

She hung up. Two minutes later, the doorbell rang. I rushed to the door thinking it was Temp, but Brenda Delacore stood there. She was dressed in kente cloth from head to toe. She had on a kente cloth hat, blouse, and pants. Even her canvas shoes were trimmed in it. She marched in waving a piece of paper in my face.

"I got what you wanted, and I'm telling you, girl, it's good. I had to bring it to you personally."

She held the paper in front of her and cleared her throat. "They're all dead," she announced.

I took the paper from her. It had the eight names I'd given her. By one name she'd written "dead," by another "au revoir." Notations next to the others read "*muerta, adiós, hasta la vista,* RIP, kicked," and finally "swing low sweet chariot."

"That's it?" I asked. "They're dead."

"Wait a minute," she said snatching the paper from me. "This was a brilliant piece of research, if I must say so myself. First off I checked death records. Why? It's easier that way. Process of elimination. Some of them are bound to have kicked anyway. Second, they had old names—no Chauntays, Aisha's, Batishas, and Kanishas. Also no Brittanys, no Ashleys—see. If these were old people, there was a good chance a few more would have kicked. But never in my wildest dreams did I expect them all to be dead.

"Next I checked causes of death, all that. Here's where it gets freaky—most of them died of pneumonia, even the ones died in the summer. Pneumonia. Must a been an epidemic or something. Check this out, none of them were even old when they kicked. The oldest was forty-two, the Choy girl was the youngest. She died in 1962. She was sixteen. And the Spivey woman was one of the Box Spiveys, all right. Reverend Spivey's sister, to be exact. Pretty good work, huh?"

I turned from her without answering. I was shaken. Then, unbidden, the rest of the Bible verse that had been penciled in on the bottom of the list popped into my mind. I ushered Brenda out without thanking her, without even saying good-bye. I went to Temp's office, found the number I was looking for, and dialed it. No answer. I dialed two other numbers also without success. I was just about in my car before I remembered to run back in and tell Aisha I was leaving and she was in charge until her dad got home, and Shawn was second in command—politics. I kissed Shawn on the back of the head.

"I got to go. Daddy will be home soon."

He nodded absently.

The video game went "boop, boop, boop."

Chapter 21

I parked on the street and wandered around the grounds of the Shore Beach apartment complex looking for Penny's apartment. Shore Beach meanders along the western shore of Emerald Lake, a man-made lake that's the centerpiece of an upscale development bearing the same name in the Pocket area. After I'd passed the same abstract sculpture—resembling a large seal swatting a baby with a tennis racket—for the third time, I realized I was lost and sought out the manager's office.

Shore Beach staff wore nautical uniforms adorned with sparkling brass buttons. They were all young, good-looking, disgustingly fit, and so infused with enthusiasm and bonhomie they seemed to emit a kind of glow. The manager looked to be about Aisha's age.

"I can direct you to 11B, it's in the Surf building, but I don't believe she's in," she said, flashing a smile that only thousands of dollars of braces could have produced.

"Oh, I must have just missed her."

"She hasn't been in all day. She's having some alterations made to her quarters, and I had to let the workers in this morning."

"They came after she'd left for work?"

"That's possible, but she doesn't usually leave before six in the morning. That's when the tile men got here. Would you like to leave a message? I can take a message for her."

I declined and left.

I was surprised to find Mother wasn't home. Sunset is batten down the hatches time for her, and she seldom goes out after dark. But her door was locked and the interior was dark. I had the key and I could have let myself in, but I was in a hurry so I didn't bother.

A Delta breeze kicked up and started taking liberties with the shadows. I got back in my car and drove around the block to Wanda's house. I needed to check on Sir. I didn't want to lose track of him in all of the excitement. He was the type of child who could very easily fall through the cracks. And now that I had a pretty good idea about what was going on and who was doing who, I was more worried about him than ever.

I got out of the car and carefully locked it. A couple of blocks away a dog barked insistently. In the distance a siren sounded, and not too far away, maybe a couple of doors down, and a baby started to cry in the hoarse "wah wah" of newborns. I was nearly at the front door when I heard the other sound. It was one of those phantom noises. The wind shifts direction, and you think you hear something; it shifts back, and you're not so sure anymore. I stopped, straining to hear it again. Nothing, just the breeze murmuring in the leaves of a large tree, growing high enough from the backyard to nearly dwarf the house. I stood there, tensed, willing myself to hear it again. Then it came, a soft, rhythmic, repetitive sound. I turned from the front door and bolted to the side of the house and into the backyard. The tree was there to greet me. The same tree Jamal and Ndugu had spoken of so proudly when I first met them. A long time ago, someone had planted it too close to the house, and now the tree and the house leaned into each other almost touching.

I heard the noise again, this time as clear as a gong.

Dropping my purse at my feet, I reached up and grabbed a branch that seemed strong enough to support me, and through a series of maneuvers my dignity prevents me from recounting, I hoisted myself up into the foliage. I straddled the branch and sat there for a while. I was a little scratched, a little scraped, and I was breathing so hard it felt like I'd inhaled a chunk of dry ice, but I'd made it and I was kind of proud.

I heard the sound again, and I looked up. The tree

house was firmly anchored between the fork of two massive branches a little more than arm's length away and about four feet up. It was a whimsical structure of old weather-beaten boards, bent nails, cardboard, and plastic. A soft glow showed through the many and varied cracks in its walls. The sound beckoned. I worked myself into a kneeling position. Then I grabbed the trunk of the tree and walked it, hand over hand, until I was standing upright on the branch.

I could just see through the doorway of the little house. Sir was wearing two jackets and a hat to protect him from the evening chill. An army blanket was spread across his legs. He reminded me of the Greek a little in this getup. A toy, battery-operated lantern glowed at his side. He sat hunched over, his fingers moving frantically, almost on their own. The handheld video game went "boop" when he scored a point. Boop, boop, boop.

I reached in and grabbed his ankle. He gave a strangled yelp, dropped the game, and fell over backward with his hands over his eyes.

"Sir, it's me. It's me, Theresa."

He uncovered his eyes and looked at me. Then he arched his back and started kicking vigorously, trying to loosen my grip.

"Stop it!" I hissed. "You hear me, stop it!"

He was bucking like a young colt, and I was having trouble holding onto him and maintaining my balance on the limb at the same time.

"Boy, you better stop now. Don't make me come in there."

Wolf tickets. I was selling wolf tickets and selling them cheap. There was no way that I would be able to climb up into the little house, much less fit inside. Sir gave a particularly vicious kick, and I lost my balance. For a split second I was suspended there clinging to Sir, dancing wildly, trying to regain my footing. Then the tree seemed to shimmy, and I heard the grating sound of wood scraping wood. The little house tilted toward me, and Sir slid out like a gum ball from a candy machine. I fell backward, clutching leaves, straining against the pull of gravity, and somehow landed straddling the limb

again. A pain so exquisite it defies description shot from
my pelvic girdle all the way to my breastbone. But I
managed to hold onto Sir, and somehow we managed to
climb down out of the tree. I went first. When he got to
the ground, I grabbed him so he couldn't run away. He
struggled against me. I held him closer.

"Sir, I'm not letting you go. You hear me? No matter
what you do, I'm not going to lose you again."

He strained against me, but I held on tightly.

"I'm sorry about your mother, and I'm sorry about
your grandmother, too. But I think I know who did it,
at least I know how to find out who did it, but I can't
do that if I'm running 'round town chasing you. You
understand?"

He stopped struggling and stood listening, trembling
slightly.

"You understand, baby?"

He nodded. I stood up and took his hand. The lights
had come on in back of Wanda's house. I could make
out the silhouette of two heads backlit against the lighted
room. I led Sir around to the front of the house. By the
time I got there, Wanda was standing on the porch.
Jamal and Ndugu squeezed out from behind her and
stood one on each side. I waved at them.

"I'll call you. Thanks for everything."

Jamal and Ndugu waved back like tired battle com-
manders acknowledging defeat.

From the outside, the Alston campaign headquarters
looked deserted. Lights from passing cars pierced the
interior darkness and danced off the tall, arched windows. From what I could see, the postage machine was
still, the computer monitors were blank, and the young
politicos had adjourned, probably to one of the local watering holes.

I circled the block looking for Penny's car. I didn't
know what she drove and I didn't expect it to still be
there, but I checked anyway. I'd bet good money Penny
drove a flashy, status car. I didn't see a Lexus, large
Mercedes, or Jag parked near the building. In fact, very
few cars were parked on the street at all. Downtown

proper pretty well clears out after five when all the government workers and other businesspeople head for Elk Grove, Citrus Heights, Roseville, or wherever they call home.

I circled the block slowly a second time. Sir sat quietly in the passenger seat staring out the front window. Light struck his face, and I could see it was shiny and wet from tears.

"Sir, you all right?"

He nodded.

The central city streets are bisected by alleys running east to west. As I passed the alley entrance on the west side of the block, I thought I saw a flash of something. It was so quick, I couldn't tell what it was or if I really saw anything at all. It could have been the tail of a coat, light reflecting off metal, I didn't know. I stepped on the brake and slowed to a crawl, straining to see in the shadows.

It was probably just my mind playing tricks on me, but I had to be sure. I stopped completely, backed up, and flipped on my high beams. Something small scurried into a doorway. A large piece of paper, propelled by the wind, rolled by like a clump of tumbleweed.

On an impulse I pulled off the street and slowly drove the alley. It was hard to miss the Morrison Building. Even from the alley it stood out, the two fire-ravaged buildings on either side, bracketing it like quotation marks. I pulled up close to the building and got out of the car, leaving the engine running, and scanned the alley.

"Somebody left the light on."

Sir was pointing at the sliver of light that fanned out from the bottom of the door. I reached into the car, turned the engine off, got my purse and the flashlight, and asked Sir to get out and lock his door. He obeyed quickly and quietly. Now I was faced with the question of what to do with him. Although I was pretty certain nobody was in there, I didn't want him with me when I checked. You never can tell about things like this. For a moment I considered leaving him in the locked car with instructions to stay in it and not open the door for anyone, but I didn't feel comfortable with that. I'd already lost him once before, and I didn't intend to do so again. Even if I could have been certain he wouldn't leave, it wouldn't have been right to leave him outside, at night, downtown, in an alley, by himself.

I moved quickly with Sir close at my side. Downtown alleys after dark are not the types of places I like to loiter in, even in the best of times. And these were not good times. The picture of LaTreace sitting splay-legged against the door flashed through my mind, and I shuddered. Sir, thinking I was cold, put his thin arm around me. I looked down at him and smiled. He turned away.

The massive alley-side door was scarred and pitted, but it was strongly built and it looked like it could withstand a full-fledged attack from the local SWAT team and still remain standing. I grabbed the doorknob, but it wouldn't turn. I pounded on the door with my fist, calling first Penny and then Mrs. Alston. The sounds reverberated through the alley. I couldn't tell how close it was, but I heard what I thought was a shuffling noise and I whirled around, but nothing was there.

I turned back to the door and pounded again. It made a creaking noise and popped open. It apparently had been locked, the knob wouldn't turn, but somebody, whoever last used this door, probably had forgotten to check and make sure the latch had caught. This was either my lucky day or I should have been crossing myself like Mother.

I looked over my shoulder to make sure we hadn't attracted any unwanted company. We hadn't, we were still alone. I took Sir by the hand and stepped into the building, pushing the door closed after us and making sure it caught. Even though we were engaged in a common act of trespassing, I didn't want anyone creeping in behind us.

A few more storage boxes had been added to the jumble in the back room, and the old clunker of a bike was still there, in the corner where I had seen it earlier in the day. Sir was quiet, but I could hear him breathing. When he saw the bike, he froze like a small animal caught in the headlights of an oncoming car.

"What is it, honey?"

"The witch bike," he whispered.

"It's just an old bike."

"No," he insisted. "The witch lady ride the witch bike. And the witch lady take the dog, and she say she gon' kill him."

I had no idea what he was talking about. I wished I had Jamal here to interpret for me. Sir seemed to be speaking a variation of "Jamal speak."

Then I understood.

"Honey, that's just a movie. You don't have to worry. It's just an old bike. There's no witch here. That was just a movie, pretend, make-believe."

I could tell he didn't believe me. I looked over where the bike stood in the corner like something from a Stephen King novel, and I could understand why he didn't believe me. But I was allowing myself to be sidetracked, losing focus. I was here to make sure Penny wasn't and then to get out as quickly as possible.

"Penny? Mrs. Alston?"

The door to the underground storage area stood open.

"Shit," I muttered under my breath.

Until now this trip had been more precautionary than anything, something I had to do for peace of mind—the wages of guilt are self-flagellation. I was supposed to have met Penny here last night. Now I felt compelled to verify that she wasn't here, then I could leave, my duty done. The last thing I wanted was to actually find somebody. This self-flagellation thing is sort of like masturbation, it's a solitary endeavor. Add another player, and you're off into a different game altogether, and I wasn't ready for that.

There was no way of getting around it, I had to go down there and eliminate the possibility that Penny was there. I hadn't seen a car parked near the building, but that didn't matter. As slick as she tries to be, she'd probably parked a block over and walked. Her kind of slick could get her killed.

I was still worried about Sir. I needed to go down there, take a quick look around, and get out just as quickly, and I couldn't take him with me. Pivoting slowly,

I look for a suitable place to deposit him, out of the way, hidden from sight, just in case. The boxes were stacked four high in the corner nearest the door leading to the alley. I pulled them out from the wall, just enough to slide another box behind them, making a kind of fort with a box for a seat.

"Keep a look out for me. Stay back here and be very quiet. Okay?"

Wide-eyed, Sir nodded solemnly. All I could see of his eyes were pupils. The overhead light cast long feathery eyelash shadows on his cheeks. Impulsively I leaned over and kissed him on his forehead, and he didn't turn away. I pushed the boxes back, sealing him in but leaving a few cracks for him to see out.

"I'll be right back."

"Okay," he answered softly.

I took Mother's flashlight and pressed the switch into the on position, but nothing happened. I shook it, and it responded with a beam so weak, it barely mattered.

The uneven stairs creaked softly as I descended into the darkness, the flashlight giving off about as much light as a child's night-light.

I came to the cobbled floor and stood still, trying to get my bearings. I remembered the rumbling noise the overhead traffic made and the strange hissing sound of the air as it was sucked and pulled through. But the dull, rhythmic, scraping noise was new. I hadn't heard it earlier today when Bobby had taken me on the tour. I stood still, trying to make it out. I was concentrating so hard, I must have shut everything else out, because when I felt something tug at my elbow, I choked out a scream and dropped the flashlight.

"Theresa."

It was Sir, but my heart was beating so loud, I could hardly hear what he was saying.

"Theresa," he whispered insistently.

"What are you doing . . ." I gasped between, quick shallow breaths.

"Somebody's coming."

"What . . .?"

"They trying to get the door open. You told me to watch ..."

"Okay, okay," I whispered, turning back and forth in a half circle, trying to think what to do. "Somebody's coming," I repeated dully.

Sir retrieved the flashlight and gave to me. My chest felt like it was wrapped in barbed wire, and my head felt light enough to float off my shoulders. I knew the signs. Forcing myself to breath deeply and slowly, I studied the chamber more carefully.

"Come on," I said, and we retreated deeper into the darkness, heading west toward the river and away from the scraping sound. We had gone about thirty feet when the cobbled surface ended and the floor dropped away abruptly to compacted soil about a foot lower. I stumbled but managed to keep my footing.

A milk crate lay on its side against one wall, cans that had been opened without the aid of a can opener littered the floor, and a few rags were piled up against a pillar.

The path veered south sharply and then righted itself, forming a sort of alcove. I shoved Sir into it, and he crouched down instinctively. I put my finger to my mouth pantomiming silence; he nodded and just then the flashlight sputtered off. No amount of shaking it would make it come back on, so I discarded it with the old cans and dirty rags.

I stood still to give my eyes a chance to adjust to the darkness. It was dark but not pitch-black as I'd expected. In places, islands of diffused light glowed like pockets of fluorescence. If I felt my way along the walls, I had enough light to make it back to the stairs. Like a moth seeking out an open flame, I turned and headed in the direction of the scraping sound.

I had almost made it back to the stairs when my eyes went out, just like the flashlight. I lost my sight. At least that was what I thought, for a split second, when the powerful light hit me full force in the face.

"There you are, dear." The voice floated out of the darkness, directionless. I couldn't tell if it was coming from behind me or in the front.

"Mrs. ... Mrs. Alston?" I stammered.

"Yes, dear."

"The light ... it's in my eyes."

"I know, dear."

It's funny how three simple little words can take on meaning far beyond anything Webster ever dreamed of. With those three words, "I know, dear," the bottom dropped out of my stomach, my bra conspired against my breathing, and I nearly cried. Because suddenly I knew, too. And because I was too late.

"Where's Penny?"

"She's here, dear. We mustn't keep her waiting. Come now, give me your arm. I'll show you the way."

She lowered the light and extended her hand. I backed up. I wasn't going to let her get close enough to do to me what she did to LaTreace. I'd been through enough the last few days to know that I could handle an old woman, even one who looked like she had been pumping iron for a long time. I was ready to fight, and who knows, I probably would have won, too. After all, I was younger and quicker, and I had a lot at stake.

But I thought about Sir. I didn't want her to know he was here with me, and I needed time to figure out a way to get us both out safely. So, as they say in the westerns, I went along peaceably.

Chapter 22

Mrs. Alston hooked her arm through mine, clamped her hand over my wrist with surprising strength, and led me stumbling along as she chatted amicably about nonsense.

"Is there anybody else, dear?" she asked suddenly.

"What?"

"Is anybody else coming?"

"No," I answered dully.

"No? Well, what about your mother, or your husband? What is his name? Celsius? Either of them know you're here?"

I don't like people playing with my name or Temp's, for that matter, so I refused to answer. Besides, I saw no need to answer. As long as she kept prattling along, I had time to figure out something.

"Well, I take your silence to mean no. It does, doesn't it, dear?"

I didn't answer.

"Cat got your tongue, dear?" she asked, tightening her grip on my wrist and twisting it sharply, sending flashes of pain all the way up my arm to my shoulder.

"I expect you to answer when you're spoken to."

Her voice was rock hard and cold, all traces of the daffy, fluttery old lady having fled.

I jerked my arm loose from her. I had been through too much over the last few days to put up with this kind of mess. She didn't try to take it back. I stumbled along following her. She returned to her questions.

"Did you tell your mother or husband where you were going?"

"No," I answered, and I could have kicked myself for not lying. I should have said Mother knows, my husband knows, Boy Scout troop 72 knows, and the entire PTA at Martin Luther King, Jr., Elementary School knows. My answer seemed to please her. We went about forty feet more, and she announced, "Here we are," as she shoved me ahead of her into an enlarged area that formed a sort of chamber. I backed to the far side against the wall.

I recognized where we were. It was the area Bobby had shown me on the tour the other day. This was where they were going to block the passage off so people couldn't get in through the burned-out building and pour a concrete floor so the area could be used for storage. The area where the floor was to be poured had been staked off and framed, but someone had pulled the wooden stakes out and stacked them in a pile against the wall near me. A hole about two feet wide and six feet long had been dug in the bed where the concrete was to have been poured. The evacuated soil had been placed in a neat pile on top of a tarp next to the hole. A shovel leaned against the wall.

I took a step forward to see what was in the hole.

"Stay where you are," Mrs. Alston barked.

She put the lantern down on an overturned crate and shoved up the sleeves of her jogging suit. I was surprised she wasn't wearing her Chanel and her pillbox, but not nearly as surprised as I was when I saw the muscles in her arms. She moved with assurance. Was this the same dotty, old woman Mother and I had made light of? The champagne pink hesitancy was gone, and that vapid quality that had so infuriated Mother had evaporated into the night air.

"Where's Penny?" I demanded.

"Why, she's right over there, dear," she said, pointing into a corner the light barely penetrated.

I peered into the corner straining to see, but all I could make out was just a jumble of boxes and trash and something with a tarp stretched over it. Mrs. Alston strode over and snatched the tarp away. She came back to the lantern and turned it slightly and Penny sprang into full relief. She sat on the floor, splay-legged, her head bent at a weird angle, her blouse starched red with blood.

Seeing Penny like that after Mrs. Turner and LaTreace took everything out of me.

"You killed her," I whispered, struggling to regulate my breathing.

"No, dear. I aborted her ... retroactively." She snickered demurely behind her plowman's wrist.

"Why?"

"She was dishonest, deceitful, and greedy. And I will not tolerate blackmail. You see, she had the letters all the time."

"What letters?"

"Those infamous letters that my late husband so indiscreetly penned. The ones you claimed to have found, dear. But I got them back, every last one of them, including the one your other friend Edna had.

She'd been looking for letters all along, letters from her husband. My little ploy, lying that I'd found her papers when I didn't even know what they were, had backfired. Now everybody who knew about the letters was dead—Mrs. Turner, LaTreace, and Penny. How did Edna fit into this? I didn't know, but I was praying I didn't have to add her to the dead list. "Please, God. Not Edna."

Mrs. Alston interrupted my thoughts. "You know, I had to abort her, too," she said with a dreamy, faraway look and a slight smile.

"Who?"

"The girl, Louise's girl. I scraped it out and flushed it down the toilet. Ashes to ashes, dust to dust, effluent to effluent, and all that. I thought that quite fitting."

I knew who she was talking about, and I didn't want to hear any more. I just wanted to get out of here, find Sir and get out. But she kept on talking.

"And when Louise came scratching at my door, whimpering and whining, I sent them away."

"You sent her away to die!" I screamed, losing the control I'd been fighting to maintain.

"It was only fitting. Now, I'm ready for you," she said with a hard, one-sided smile.

I heard a snapping sound, and she held up both hands encased in rubber gloves.

"Andrea Cenne," I shouted. "Andrea Cenne, she had a name." I was fighting to hold back tears and fighting to hold myself back, too. I wanted to hurt that old woman so bad.

"Yes, I suppose so. You people do seem to be awfully fond of pidgin French, don't you dear?"

"Andrea. The letters were to her, weren't they?"

She smiled and nodded.

"It was Dr. Alston's baby. She was pregnant with your husband's child, and you killed her."

Her smile didn't waver.

"But why kill Mrs. Turner? She never did anything to you."

"Louise and I have been locked in a very elaborate little dance, a sort of minuet, for a long time—she pretending she didn't know who the baby's father was, and I pretending I didn't know who helped get rid of it. Everything was fine until she took the wrong step and I had to stop the music."

"Just like that, you killed her."

"It was LaTreace." She spat the name out. She turned her head. "They were in it together. Louise gave LaTreace the letters and had her make the calls. They were in it together."

"You don't know what you're talking about," I challenged, all the while edging close to the wood piled to the side of the hole. I had my eye on a piece that looked strong enough to use as a club. It was a two-by-four about six feet long. It had been tossed on top of the pile, and it was balanced there like the board on a teeter-totter.

"LaTreace called me demanding money, but when I demanded to speak to Louise, she wouldn't let me. She said she was in the hospital. Well, that didn't stop me; I knew exactly where she would go. I simply called, relying upon my late husband's good name and was put through to her.

"I told her I was going to her house and I was going to find those letters if I had to take it apart plank by plank. And I would have, too. But lucky for me, Louise panicked and got someone to bring her home. She walked in just as I was at the height of my frustration." She chuckled. "Lucky for me, unlucky for her."

"So you killed her."

"We had a nice little tête-à-tête first. I insisted she return the letters. After all those years, she turned out to be so deceitful. She insisted she didn't know where they were, that LaTreace had stolen them. Lies, lies, lies, all lies.

"I dragged her from room to room, made her show me all her secret little places. Oh, she was so deceitful."

"So you killed her." I was like a stuck record, unable to get beyond that one thought.

"She was just about dead anyway. She'd lost too much blood."

"Blood?"

"She was such a stubborn old woman. I had to do something to get her to cooperate."

She retrieved a black doctor's bag from the shadows and opened it, taking out an instrument. I didn't go to medical school, but I know a scalpel when I see one. I made an effort to keep her talking so I could do some fast figuring.

"So why the charade about Mrs. Turner's property? What was that all about?"

"Two things. One, I wanted you, or someone, to discover our largesse toward Louise. We, Dr. Alston and I, had treated her quite well. We'd given her the very house she lived in. Naturally it would have been poor taste to have said so myself. Somebody had to discover it. You did quite well, dear. Second, I suspected that Penny had found some way to convert the property to her own use, and I wanted that known so suspicion for poor Louise's death could be directed her way. We needed to provide her with a motive."

"You had it all planned out, didn't you?" I was within inches of my club. I could have stuck my foot out and touched it.

"Nothing is ever accomplished without a plan. That is something you people should learn."

"What are your plans now? What are you going to do when it hits the press that the late Dr. Alston was running an illegal abortion mill? That's what you're really afraid of, aren't you? You don't want that to become known because that would sink Bobby's campaign."

She threw back her head and laughed. "Dr. Alston didn't have a head for business. None of the Alstons do, including Bobby. Without me, my dear, my decidedly late husband would have been just another drunken, incompetent, slash hound, if you'll pardon the very crude but oh-so appropriate expression. I made him what he was. I made the money he left me. I molded him just as I've molded Bobby. Bobby has all the necessary ingredients for greatness. He is handsome and charismatic. He was a great city councilman, wasn't he? You people loved him, didn't you. He'll be an even greater mayor. From there it's only a short hop to the Senate. Then who knows."

"You forgot one thing. There's a list, a list of women, dead women. All the women you killed. Mrs. Turner had it, LaTreace stole it, now I have it. I took the precaution of giving a copy of it to a colleague of mine. So you see . . ."

She wasn't listening.

"Of what value is a list? Anybody can put together a list. The guy on TV does it all the time. Those were not our patients. We never did our own patients. So you see, Mrs. Galloway, I really don't give a fuck about your list."

She smiled sweetly and said, "Next." Then she reached for the scalpel.

I couldn't let her get her hands on it. I wouldn't stand a chance once she did. I was within grabbing distance of the club, but I'd leave the back of my head exposed if I reached down to grab it. The few seconds that would take would give her enough time to reach me and do the kind of damage she'd done to Mrs. Turner, LaTreace, and now Penny.

I sucked in my breath and stamped on the end of the board nearest me. The other end flipped up like a shot, heading straight for my head. I threw my hands up, in front of my face, my fingers opened wide and the wood slapped into my hands. Pivoting, I took one step and swung. I surprised her.

She threw up her arms a second before the club made contact with the side of her head, but I hit her a solid blow and she crumpled to the floor groaning, the scalpel skittering away into the shadows.

She was down, and I needed to keep her there. I raised the club over my head, but I couldn't bring myself to hit her again. I didn't want to kill her, I just needed to immobilize her long enough to grab Sir and get out of there.

It was at this point that I got stupid. I decided the thing to do was tie her up. That way I wouldn't have to hurt her anymore, and she wouldn't be able to hurt me. Never mind that I neglected to bring a rope with me, never mind that I've never tied up anyone in my life, never mind that she didn't intend to cooperate.

I looked around for something to hog-tie her with, carefully avoiding the area surrounding Penny. I found nothing and was beginning to rethink my idea when I noticed the doctor's bag lying on its side. I prodded it with my toe. Bending down, I picked it up and shook its contents out on the floor. A couple of hypodermic needles, a roll of gauze, and some little vials tumbled out—and finally what I was looking for, a roll of surgical tape.

I picked the tape up and went to find Mrs. Alston. She had stopped moaning and was lying where I left her in a pathetic little heap. I pulled out a length of tape and tore it off with my teeth. My plan was to tape her arms behind her back and hobble her at the knees, but when I grabbed the arm that had taken my blow earlier, she suddenly came to life, reared up, and smashed her other fist into the side of my head. I lurched backward but held onto her injured arm, nearly jerking it out of the socket. She let out a yelp of pain, and scuttling like a crab, managed to kick my legs out from under me. I went down, but not as hard as she had, and not all the way. I managed to break my fall with my hands and one knee, and swiftly regained my footing.

She growled and cursed and spit as she scuttled about on the floor, in the shadows and out, back and forth holding her injured arm close to her chest. I'd never seen anything like this before in my life, and I stared at her mesmerized until it was nearly too late. I didn't realize that she'd found what she was looking for until she came up swinging wildly. I dived for her, but I was too late. I rolled back, frantically trying to get out of her reach. She had a good grip on the scalpel, but she was an old woman and she was hurt. She was moving slowly. You really know you're getting old when you can't brawl the way you used to. I could almost hear her joints creak.

"Mrs. Alston, put the scalpel down," I pleaded. "I won't hurt you."

She only grunted and charged me in slow motion, hobbling and swinging the scalpel. I backed out of her reach. She was relentless. Every way I turned, she was there, hobbling and grunting and swinging the scalpel. I backed up to the open pit. This was my last stand. Either I stopped her here or it was all over.

"Mrs. Alston, I can't go any farther. Please put the knife down."

She only grinned a horrible little tick of a grin.

"Mrs. Alston, please."

My pleading seemed to invigorate her, and she came at me quickly, holding the scalpel tightly and swinging it expertly. I stood my ground until the very last moment before stepping aside and swinging the upper part of my body out of the way of her flailing arm. She was coming at me too fast to stop, and when she saw the open pit staring up at her, she knew she was in trouble. I laced my fingers together and slammed my fist down on the back of her neck, and she fell into the grave she had so carefully dug for Penny.

It wasn't very deep, maybe a couple of feet. But it was too deep for her to climb out of in her condition. I grabbed the lantern and went to find Sir. Mrs. Alston's muffled moans followed me, but I didn't look back.

"I'm coming, Sir," I muttered to myself. "I'm coming, baby."

"Who the hell's there?"

I froze but I couldn't hide, not holding the megawatt lantern.

"Theresa, what are you doing down here? What the fuck is going on? Where's Mother?"

"Bobby, your mother's been hurt."

He looked at me closely.

"Hurt? What happened? Where's Penny? She's supposed to look after her," he said, a whine creeping into his voice.

He wrenched the lantern from my hand.

"Where is she? Where's Mother?"

"She's back there," I said pointing.

He grabbed me by the neck of my jacket. "Come on. You're going with me. You're not leaving until I find out what's going on."

Without even thinking, I jerked free, loosening his grip on my jacket.

"Go see about your mama," I said. "I'm not going anywhere."

He took off in a trot, taking the light with him. I took off in the opposite direction, feeling my way without the aid of a light, moving as rapidly as I could. When I got to where I'd left Sir, he was gone. I sank to the floor calling his name. I wanted to cry, but I didn't have time. I had been banged up badly back there, and I wanted to lie down and hurt but I didn't have time for that either. In fact, time was running out for me and Sir. When I heard Bobby bellowing like a wounded bull, I knew it was just about too late.

"Theresa?"

"Sir. Baby, where have you been?"

"I found another way out."

"You did? Bless you. Where is it? Which way?"

"It's this way. Come on."

We half ran, half stumbled about another hundred feet. I could hear Bobby clamoring about up the stairs and bellowing, looking for me. He'd soon figure out I wasn't up there and come back down here to look. If we didn't get out of here, it was only a matter of time before he found us, and then all bets were off.

We came to another boarded-up area. Light filtered down from the top. About knee height, I could vaguely make out some sort of crawl space.

"Down here. You crawl through all the way to the outside."

"I can't fit in there."

"Yes, you can, Theresa. Just try. I know you can."

"No, baby, I can't. I know my hips. You go on and get some help. I'll stay here."

"No."

"Sir, listen to me. He'll be back soon. You've got go find some help."

"The po-leece?"

"The police, anybody. Go on quickly. Hurry up."

I kissed him on the forehead, and he turned and crawled through the hole.

I sat down in front of the hole. Bobby's mother had killed three people that I knew about, and he was probably capable of doing the same, especially if his mother was threatened. If I found my mother in the condition he found his, I'd be ready to hurt someone. But I couldn't just sit there waiting for him to come find me. I got up and crept back to the stairs. From what I could hear, Bobby was still up there tossing things about, breaking furniture, looking for me. I made it back to where I'd left his mother. He had helped her out of the grave and laid her carefully at its side with the doctors bag under her head for a pillow. He'd spread his jacket over her to keep her warm and left the lantern for light. Her eyes were closed. She looked like she was dead. I reached for my purse, and her eyes snapped open. She looked at me calmly.

"I told him you killed Penny and tried to kill me, too. Now he will kill you."

Chapter 23

I snagged the purse and started back. I thought about it, turned back, got the lantern, turned it off, and took it with me, too. Then I went back to the place where Sir had crawled through the hole. I almost knew the route in the dark by heart now.

I opened my purse and searched inside for the plastic baggie. Just as I was beginning to panic, I found it. I sat down in the dirt and put the bag in my lap. I wiped my sweaty hands on my jacket and opened the bag, dumping the contents into my lap.

I was huddled in the darkest corner I could find, which is good if you are hiding from someone. It is not so good if you are trying to reassemble a Sig Hauer P230.

I fumbled over the pieces trying to remember what Temp had called them and how they went together. I could distinguish the spring—that was easy. But what were all these other pieces? What was this long, straight piece? Maybe I should give up on trying to remember the names of the pieces and just concentrate on trying to fit them together.

My fingers were all thumbs and half of them sore. I picked up the main part, the handle thing. Temp had called it something else. The stock. That's right, the stock. I'd start with that. Now, what was next? Put the spring in, that was easy. Now, what was next? There was a little thingamajig with a lever. I fingered every piece in my lap but didn't find it. I tried again and still couldn't find it. My eyes teared up, and I wiped them on the shoulder of my jacket.

"Come on, girl. Don't fall apart now," I told myself.

I tried again and found a piece I thought might be it, but I wasn't sure. I tried to fit it onto the end of the stock thing. It wouldn't go. I turned it around and tried the other way, and it glided into place and blessed me with the sweet sound of a click as it locked in place. I was jubilant. I wanted to kick up my heels and shout, but I couldn't celebrate, not yet. I still had one more piece in my lap. I had to figure out what to do with it.

By now sweat was pouring down my face, and I was concentrating so hard, my ears were ringing. The ringing sound reminded me of other noises, and I realized I didn't hear any. I didn't hear Bobby's bellowing or his clamoring about upstairs. I heard the rumble of traffic overhead and the air hissing through the chamber, but nothing else.

Oh, Lord, where was he? He could be anywhere. He could be in the other side of the chamber, or he could be inches away.

I fumbled with the remaining piece of the gun. What was it? Where did it go? I ran my finger over the gun trying to find a groove or clamp, any kind of indentation that this piece might fit in. Nothing. I turned the gun upside down and repeated the search. The handle part was hollow. Eureka. Now I remembered. The piece in my lap was the bullet pack, the clip. I shoved it in, listening for the click that would tell me it was locked in place. I didn't hear the click. The faint, almost indistinguishable sound of something soft dragging against something hard and ungiving drowned it out.

"No need to panic, now," I told myself. "You have the gun. Get ready."

I moved the lantern in front of me on the ground and lay down on my stomach behind it. Grasping the gun in my right hand, I practiced holding it in a firing position supported by my left hand. "What am I doing?" I thought for a second. "I don't want to kill anybody. Please, God, don't let me have to kill anybody." But I heard the noise again and I saw a soft beam of light bouncing off the walls like a jittery sunrise, and I got ready.

He had found another flashlight somewhere, but that didn't matter. As soon as the light turned the corner and passed the jutted-out place where Sir had hid, I would turn the lantern on and blind him. Then I'd shoot him if I had to.

The light grew brighter, and the soft tread of his footsteps more distinct as he came closer.

"Get ready," I whispered. Then I started with the self-doubt: What if the gun doesn't work? What if you put it together wrong? What if it blows up when you try to shoot it like Dorothy's old man's gun did? I didn't have time to agonize too long, though.

He turned the corner, and I flipped on the lantern. He froze in his tracks.

"Don't move," I shouted. "I have a gun."

"Put down the gun, ma'am."

"Huh?" I asked dumbly.

"Police. Put down the gun. I want you to slowly and carefully place the gun on the ground in front of you. Then I want you to stand up and raise your hands above your head."

It didn't sound like Bobby, but I couldn't be sure. I'd been lied to, tricked, and misled so many times over the past few days, I was a bit leery, to say the least. We were at a sort of standoff. I had my gun and the megawatt light, and he had his and a not-so megawatt light. It would have gone on like that until one of us shot the other, or something, if his radio hadn't given off a cackle of static and I realized he really was the po-leece and I put the gun down.

Chapter 24

First off, let me say that I was never under arrest, not really. Sure, I was put in the back of a patrol car and driven to the county jail for questioning, but, so was Robert. Mrs. Alston was taken to the Medical Center—the very same place I'd taken Dorothy a few days ago—for treatment and questioning. Only her questioning never got far. They tell me she did everything but quack like a duck. The woman was stone cold, out of her mind—or at least that's what she wanted them to think.

I was allowed to make a call to arrange for someone to come get Sir. I called Temp. He answered the phone with so much anxiety in his voice it nearly broke my heart. I hadn't stopped to think about what he must've been going through. I'd dropped everything and left after Brenda's visit. No one knew where I was, not even Mother. Temp must have been wild with worry. After spending the night as a virtual captive at his mother's house, he'd come home to find me gone, the house in shambles, and the kids running wild through the ruins of pizza boxes.

He sputtered for a good five minutes when I told him, as delicately as I could, that I was being detained for questioning at the county jail. I could hear Aisha in the background, the screech of panic in her voice, demanding to know if something had happened to me. Shawn started to wail. I felt worse than I had in a long time. I finally got Temp to calm down. He calmed the children and agreed to call an attorney for me and come get Sir. Temp hasn't cultivated the type professional relationships that would be useful in situations involving criminal activities, so he sent Milton Leonard, his tax attorney and golfing buddy. But, I was happy to see him anyway.

The police kept me for four hours, systematically going over every detail of my story, asking me question after question, checking and rechecking my statements. Their collective shoulders seem to droop when I told them that Mrs. Alston had killed Mrs. Turner, Penny, and La-Treace as well as the eight people on the list. By then I had committed chapter thirty, verse nineteen of Deuteronomy to memory—*I call heaven and earth to record this day against you, that I have set before you life and death, blessing and cursing: therefore choose life, that both thou and thy seed may live.*—but I didn't bring it up. I don't think they would have made the connection, and it would only have complicated things too much. I also understood why Edna had refused to identify the verse for me. She was afraid I was getting too close to the truth, and once the truth is widely disseminated, its commercial value decreases.

The police fought the idea of Mrs. Alston as a murderer the way a small child fights sleep. In the end it overtook them. It would have been so much easier if Trey Dog had killed all those people, or if I had, or Mother, even. Anyone but the mother of a prominent political figure. I could see the weariness settling in on them.

I was finally released, and Milton walked me to the lobby where Temp was waiting. Temp had taken Sir to our house and left him in Aisha and Shawn's care and returned to wait for me. I greeted him tentatively and he pulled me to him, wrapping his arms around me and holding me close for a long time.

"Baby, you all right?" he finally asked.

I was tired, dirty, and bedraggled. All I could do was nod. "Come on, I'm taking you home," he said.

When we got home, Temp ran a bath, undressed me, and helped me into the tub. His tenderness reminded me of the early years of our marriage when he was so intent on making me happy. After my bath we talked well into the morning hours. I told him everything. I told him about Mrs. Turner's death and about LaTreace and Sir and Dorothy and the Rose Garden Motel. I told him about Mrs. Alston, Robert, Penny, even Mother and Edna. Temp's emotions played across his face as I talked. Mrs. Turner's death brought a shadowing of anger and outrage, LaTreace and the Alstons more outrage, and Penny, a profound sadness.

"I know you didn't like the sister, T, but she was all right. I hate to see her go like that."

I finally finished, and then it was Temp's turn. "Let me start by saying I'm glad you're okay. But woman have you lost your mind? I know you read the papers just like I do. Everyday there's something in them about somebody getting shot, getting killed—old people, young kids, babies. But it doesn't seem to register with you. Believe me, T, I've been out there. It's not where any woman of mine belongs. You shouldn't be getting messed up in this kind of stuff. Don't you know, there're people who wouldn't think twice about offing you and your mother. And you running the streets like a fool. You have responsibilities, T. You have children. Did you stop to think what it would do to them to have something happen to you? Don't you know you have a family to think about, and a job? I run a janitorial service and just look at this place. Look at it.

"And your mother. I love mom like she's my own. But everytime I turn around, you're at your mother's. You're doing this for her, you're doing that. And she just about got you killed this time. You've got to make up your mind which way it's going to be. Are you going to be your mother's little girl or my wife? You can't have it both ways. I've been patient. I've tried to be understanding, but I've reached my limit.

"All I can say is you've been lucky. You're hurt right now, you're sore, but it's a wonder you aren't dead or sitting up in jail with the hookers and whores and murderers. And what kinda man does this make me? My lady's out there banging while I'm at home trying make the buck—trying to make the note on her bimmer and keep her in bullets. If anybody should be in the streets, T, it should be me. And you don't see me out there, do you? That shit ain't worth a damn. No, T, things have got to change."

I had to admit, he was right. Right then and there, I made a promise to him and myself: no more of this fool- ishness for me. From now on, my family—Temp and the kids and my safety—comes first.

I slept until noon. Temp got the kids off to school and entertained Sir until I got up. He told me he had called Allen and explained what had happened, and Allen in- sisted I take the day off. He'd also called Mother and told her everything, too. He informed me that there was nothing in the *Bee* about last night, but it was on the local news of all three networks. I avoided the TV. I got dressed, and the three of us went to see Mother.

Andrea and Cenne squealed when we walked in the door and they saw Sir. He went to them with his arms outstretched, and they fell into them making cooing sounds and gurgling with joy.

Mother was Mother, only more so. She fussed over me, insisted I sit down and elevate my feet. She admon- ished Temp for letting me out so soon after what I'd been through. She also told us she knew all along that ole lady Alston was up to no good. All those girls dead, and now Sister Turner and the rest. She hoped she got what she deserved no matter how crazy she pretended to be. Mother was devastated about what all this had done to Robert Alston's campaign, and she said, "The sins of the mother are visited upon the son." We knew what she meant anyway.

I asked her about Edna.

Mother's mouth scrunched shut.

"Edna's gone," she said. "Left town," she added in response to the stricken look on my face. "After I fin- ished talking to her last night, she thought it best to leave."

Mother explained that Edna had been the only one to successfully negotiate a business transaction with Mrs. Alston. Edna had found one of the letters Mrs. Alston was so anxious to get a hold of when she and the women had cleaned Mrs. Turner's house. And she'd sold it to Mrs. Alston. That's who Edna had been waiting for the night I went by her home. Edna didn't trust Mrs. Alston, and with good cause as it turned out. That's why she'd been sitting there with the gun on her lap under the towel. That may be why she's still alive.

"What did you tell her?" I asked Mother. "What did you say to her to make her leave?"

"That's all right. Edna and I had a nice long talk. She's gone."

Andrea and Cenne were dressed in their finery—dotted swiss dresses, ruffled underpants, patent leather shoes, ribbons in their hair. Mother had given them a small handheld mirror, and they were preoccupied with admiring themselves.

I got up to go to the bathroom, and Temp leapt to his feet to assist me. Mother fluttered about shoving boxes out of the way.

"Hey, you guys, I'm okay," I assured them.

I went down the hall to the bathroom, and came back immediately. I was not okay, and they could see it.

"Mother," I said, "there's a man in your bed."

Temp leapt up again as if I'd said "somebody's breaking in."

"Child, I know that."

"What is he doing there?"

"What do you think he's doing there? Sleeping, of course."

Now Temp looked embarrassed.

"Mother."

"Don't mother me. Can't I have a man in my bed if want to? Correct me if I'm wrong, but I do believe I'm grown."

"Mother."

"That's the babies' great-great-uncle, Walter Gillian. He came down last night, but I wasn't home when he got here and he ended up sleeping in his truck.

"He's taking the children back with him. He's going to raise them. He could have retired years ago, but he just kept on working because he didn't have anything better to do."

Mother smiled when she said this, but it was a weak,

quivering smile. It was going to be hard for her to let the girls go.

"He said he's sorry about blowing up at you, but La-Treace had been calling him, too. She told him she knew who killed his daughter, and he could know, too, for a small fee. All that and she never even told him his sister was dead."

Temp and I left a little after one. We came home, went to bed, and made love to each other, tentatively at first, and then with a passion that rivaled that of the early years of our marriage when we both were so intent on pleasing the other. We were still in bed when the children came home from school. Temp was eating a snack, and I was dozing when they bounded in on us. Aisha stopped in her tracks and screamed, "Mother, cover yourself!" Shawn dissolved in a fit of nervous giggles at the foot of the bed. Aisha was telling us how disgusting we were—two old people—when the phone rang. I picked it up. It was Mother.

Don't miss the next entertaining novel
to feature Theresa Galloway,
due out from Onyx in 1996

The Cooked
and the Raw

"Don't nobody get nowhere 'round here 'less they kissin' somebody's ass."

The voice sounded like Brenda Delacore's, the number two person in the personnel office at the California State Department of Environmental Equity. But I couldn't be sure, the office acoustics are so weird.

I'm the Personnel Officer. I have a private office with a wall of windows—windows mean a lot when you work for the state. But my office is a jerry-built afterthought, and the walls on three sides don't even go all the way up to the ceiling. They wander to a stop about a foot away. Because of its peculiar construction, and the way the air flows, or maybe it's the ratio of negative to positive ions—I don't know—my office has some strange acoustical qualities. It's a kind of nose funnel. I'm always picking up ambient snatches of whispered conversations. The funny thing is, it's the whispered stuff that floats in from time to time, not the stuff spoken in a normal voice.

The voice I heard could have been Brenda's, but there was just enough distortion to keep me from being absolutely sure. However, there was no mistaking who she was talking to.

"That's just what I been telling you, girl," came the insistent reply. "Let a Nee-gro get some kind of position, any position—Chief Assistant Deputy to the Undersecretary Bathroom Monitor—it doesn't matter. The first thing she's going to do is turn around and mess over brothers and sisters. Am I lying? Am I lying?"

That could only have been spoken by Yvonne Pinkham, the second highest-ranking woman of color in the department. Poor child. I wanted to go out there, put my arm around her shoulders, and tell her to take those orange plastic braids out her hair and go back to her desk, sit down, and do some work.

The voices drifted off and I tried to go back to work, but I was angry now. Anger bit at me, distracting me, taking my mind off what I was doing. Whatever happened to unity? Whatever happened to gratitude, for that matter? Brenda had come *this close* to getting a permanent one-step demotion for a series of her shenanigans during a period when she'd acted for me. I'd fought hard for her, arguing that this was her first offense—actually, it was her first documented offense—and a permanent demotion was too severe. I'd prevailed, and she'd been demoted for two pay periods instead of permanently. This amounted to a $300 fine spread out over two months. I thought I'd done well. But Brenda apparently didn't. I hear she's been going around the department saying I sold her out. How sharper than a serpent's tooth.

The door to my office opened abruptly, and Miyako, my secretary, stuck her head in.

"He's on the line again. I didn't want to risk trying to transfer him. I might lose him like I did the last time."

"You sure it's him?"

"It's him. Come on."

I got up and hurried to the reception area to take the call. The receiver lay on its side. Miyako pointed to it with one hand and beckoned me with the other. I picked it up.

"Hello, this is Theresa."

The receiver sprang to life, pulsing with energy. I nearly dropped it.

"Hey, there, how you doing?"

"Clarence?"

"Yes, ma'am."

"I understand you're having some problems with your supervisor."

"No, ma'am, I got it all worked out."

I looked over at Miyako and flashed her the sign for okay.

"That's great, Clarence. You and he came to some kind of understanding?"

"Yes, ma'am. We did. I'm gonna shoot the som'bitch."

"Clarence, you're joking, aren't you?"

"No, ma'am."

I sat down in Miyako's chair and took a deep breath. None of the training I'd taken at the various management seminars the state had sent me to had prepared me for this. I knew I had to stay calm. Any show of emotion would only push him closer to the edge. I tried counting backward from ten, but I just got a bunch of random numbers. Miyako, sensing my struggle, stood tense and alert.

"Clarence, listen to me. Don't shoot him. Do you hear me, Clarence? Don't shoot him, please."

There was silence.

"Theresa."

"Yes, Clarence."

"I got to." He spoke in calm, measured tones, as if he'd given the matter a great deal of thought and had come up with the only logical solution.

"No, you don't."

"Yes, I do. I got to. He isn't a man, Theresa. He's just a small, nasty, little animal. A vermin. Something that needs to be smashed."

"Clarence, where are you?"

"I'm sitting right here in his office."

"Is he there with you?"

"No, ma'am. He's probably outside the building taking a smoke, or he's in a meeting somewhere trying to figure out how to ruin somebody's life."

"Clarence, we need to talk a little more, just you and me. I'm coming up there. Don't do anything, okay? Just wait for me. I want to talk to you. Okay, Clarence?"

I pressed the receiver to my chest and mouthed to Miyako, "Call the police."

She turned to go to another phone. I grabbed her arm. I snatched a pen from the mug on her desk and wrote in slashing capitals on her desk pad, "Find Arvin Gaines.

Don't let him go to his office." She nodded and left. I put the receiver back to my ear.

"Clarence, you still there?"

"Yes, ma'am. I'm here. I ain't going nowhere."

I crashed into Dot and her mail cart as I rounded the corner to the main corridor. I apologized over my shoulder, but I didn't stop to help her pick up the envelopes and small boxes that tumbled to the floor.

I got to the elevator and punched the Up button. I was on the first floor, and Clarence's unit was on the eighth. The elevators in the Resources Building are notorious for being slow and cranky. I looked at my watch. I couldn't afford to take the chance of waiting just one minute too long. The stakes were too high. I darted down the hallway to the stairwell. I wouldn't have taken the stairs a year ago, but I'd been thirty pounds heavier then.

My muscles started to protest around the fifth floor. They were loud and angry by the time I reached the eighth floor. But the thought of Arvin beating me to his office kept me going. I didn't exactly burst out of the stairwell when I got there, but I didn't crawl either. I allowed myself to pause for a moment to catch my breath and to get my bearings. The Internal Audits section, where Clarence worked, was at the far end of the hall on the northeast side of the building. I turned in that direction and faced down a long expanse of blinding beige. Beige walls, beige ceiling with fluorescent lights lit to a clinical degree of brightness, and discolored beige vinyl flooring. The unremitting beige was broken up by evenly spaced, numbered doors painted in a color derivative of camel dung. I took off running.

I passed Mr. Frazier, who had just finished cleaning the men's room and was removing the yellow barrier in front of the door. He looked up and tossed me a friendly wave, but I didn't have time for mid-morning niceties and I ran past him without responding.

Arvin's door was ajar an inch or two when I got there. I knocked and got no answer. I tried to peep through the small opening, but I couldn't see anything. The lights were out, the blinds were drawn, and the room was dark.

I thought about last year when my mother had talked me into searching for a missing little boy named Sir and all the doors I'd been afraid to enter then, and for good cause. Nasty surprises awaited me behind each and every one of them. Things I'd been trying to forget, put behind me. The blood, crazy jitterbugging fear, dry heaves. Things I never wanted to have to deal with again. But here I was.

I knocked again and called Clarence's name. Nothing. Finally I swallowed the bile burning my throat and pushed the door open. A gray metal desk dominated one half of the room. The desk top was neat and free of clutter. Two trays, one marked In and the other marked Out, were set side by side at the corner of the desk. Each tray held an equal amount of papers. A brown metal table with a fake wood vinyl top dominated the other half of the room. I didn't see any plants or family pictures. I didn't see Clarence either until he spoke.

"I guess you better come on in." He sounded sad, resigned.

Clarence stepped out of the shadows behind the door, and I saw the shotgun he was cradling in his arms. There was an odd look about him, as if he had shut himself away and cried for a long time. The bags under his eyes looked raw. The skein of lank wheat-colored hair that vanity compelled him to comb across his head from one ear to the other in a futile attempt to hide his baldness dangled just over his left shoulder. His bald head was as pink as an udder.

"Just leave it cracked. He always leaves the door cracked a little when he's out."

I did as he asked.

He stood there with the gun. I was as uncomfortable as I had been the time I'd shared an elevator with a naked man. Only this time I was more scared.

"I think you better move over here out of the way. 'Cause when he walks through that door"—he made a loud clicking sound—"I'm gonna blow his head off."

"Listen, Clarence, don't do this. You don't have to do this. You can work it out. I'll help you."

He stared at me impassively, not bothering to respond.

I thought of Arvin Gaines, the man he was waiting for. What could he have done to drive Clarence to this? I hoped someone had caught up with Arvin and warned him to stay away from his office. I was worried about Arvin, but the strangest thing was, I wasn't worried about dying. Sure, I was scared—Clarence had a gun and he was distraught enough to use it. But up until the very end I thought I could handle whatever came my way. I thought I could talk him through it, actively listen, whatever. I never even thought death was in the cards.

Using the barrel of the gun, Clarence moved me away from the door. I was fine as long as he didn't point the gun at me, but the thought that he would touch me with it had never entered my mind. The metal against my skin felt dirty, obscene. It was like being fondled by something strange and robotic.

I stopped myself from flinching, calmed myself, called on every resource I had, and started talking. I reminded Clarence how he and I had first met more than ten years ago when we both worked in the Department of Water Resources, he as an accounting clerk and I as a personnel analyst. We met at one of those mandatory workshops, "Working Together Effectively" or something like that. He wasn't so much an angry white man then as a confused, beleaguered one. The ground rules had been changed and nobody'd bothered to tell him. He didn't know what was safe to say and what wasn't. All those young college kids, colored people, women. AA this, EEO that. Most of them knew next to diddly. They all seemed to be on a fast track. Getting promoted, moving higher than they should. It wasn't so much what you knew now but who you knew or what color your skin was or whether you were a woman that counted now. And he was left standing in the dust, breathing their exhaust, doing the work they should have been doing. With all that baggage, somehow he and I still managed to become friends. Work friends. Not the kind of friend you'd invite to your kid's graduation, but the kind you're glad to see when you cross paths in the hallway or at a meeting. The kind you take a few minutes to chat with and maybe even have coffee with it you end up in the cafeteria at the same time.

Clarence didn't seem to be listening to me. He stood with his eyes fastened to the door, waiting for Arvin. I kept on talking, trying to get some sort of dialogue going, some give and take.

"Clarence, was it your time, the time you've been taking off? Is that what you and Arvin argued about?"

"No, ma'am."

He answered without looking at me, but I'd made contact. I tried again. "How's Linda Carol?"

I saw a flicker of something in his face. Then he turned to me with a movement so quick I didn't have a chance to react. Grabbing a handful of my blouse, he slammed me against the wall behind the door. Breathing raggedly, he held me there with my chin cocked awkwardly and my blouse bunching through his fist like a crepe paper flower, for what seemed like hours. Finally he looked at me like he was surprised to find us in such intimate proximity, and letting go of my blouse, he turned back to the door.

"Leave Linda Carol out of this."

I nodded.

I was shaken, and scared, and angry. Here I was trapped in a state office with gray metal desk and table with a fake vinyl wood top, and a man in emotional overload with a gun.

Clarence cocked his head. He seemed to be listening intensely. He'd picked up a sound somewhere. Then I heard it too, and I stared in horror as Clarence lifted the shotgun and placed it in the firing position.